GATES

OF

THREAD

AND

STONE

GATES
OF
THREAD
AND
STONE

Lori M. Lee

SKYSCAPE

SKYSCAPE

Text copyright © 2014 Lori M. Lee
All rights reserved.

Published by Skyscape, New York

www.apub.com

Amazon, the Amazon logo, and Skyscape are trademarks of Amazon.com, Inc., or its affiliates.

ISBN-13: 9781477847206 (HARDCOVER)
ISBN-10: 1477847200 (HARDCOVER)
ISBN-13: 9781477847640 (PAPERBACK)
ISBN-10: 1477847642 (PAPERBACK)

MAP BY MEGAN MCNINCH
EDITOR: ROBIN BENJAMIN

LIBRARY OF CONGRESS CONTROL NUMBER: 2014900603

PRINTED IN THE UNITED STATES OF AMERICA

To Kay and May, the best friends and sisters a girl could have

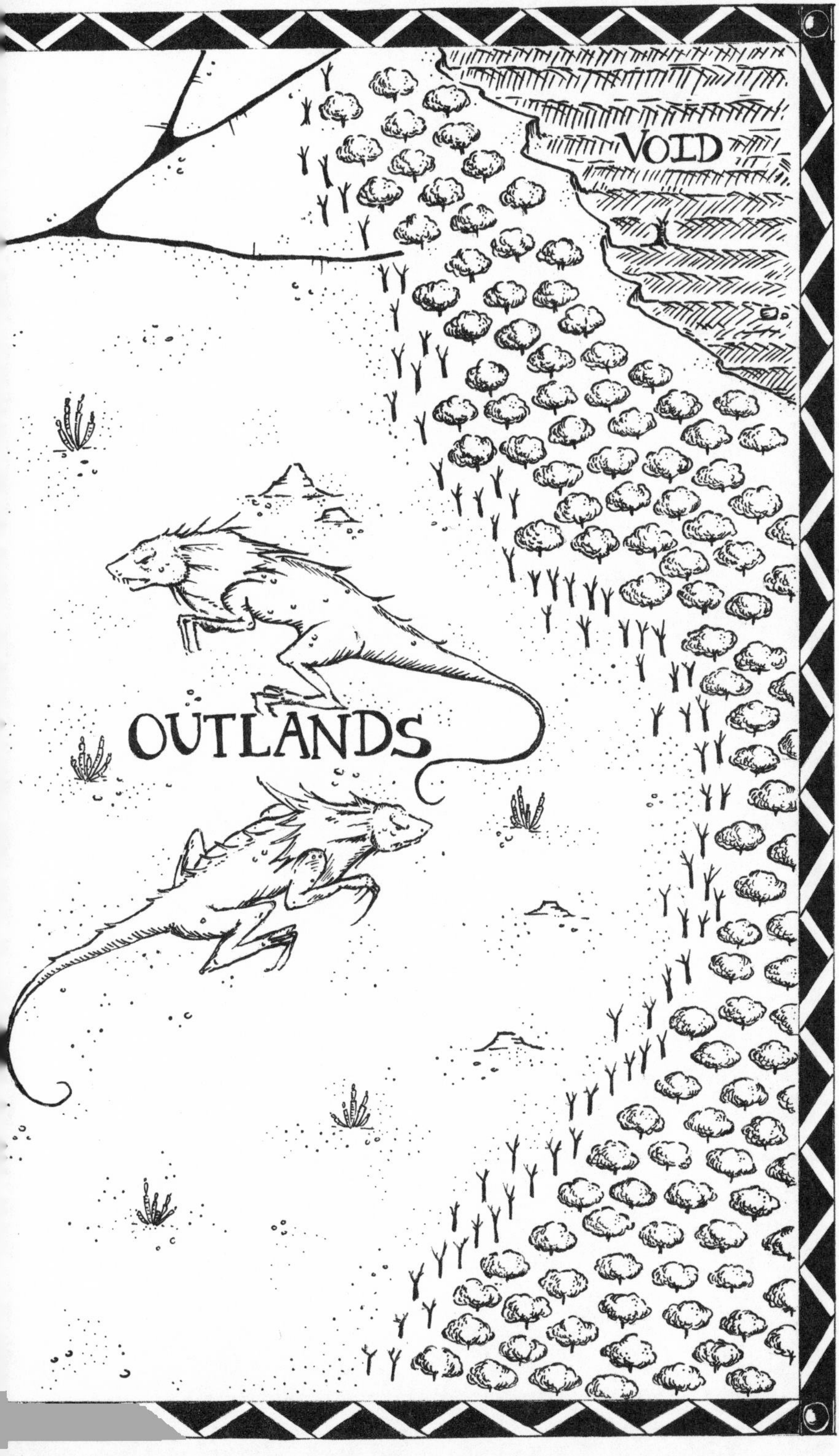
VOID
OUTLANDS

CHAPTER 1

DEATH LIVED IN A GLASS TOWER AT THE CENTER OF THE
White Court. I could see the tower from anywhere in the city.
It cut the skyline like a blade. Death—she probably had a real
name—was Kahl Ninu's right hand and his personal executioner.
Or, at least, that's what the rumors said. I didn't really care if they
were true so long as it wasn't my head on the chopping block.

The fact that the Kahl's executioner lived in the most impressive building in the city wasn't the only reason the White Court
unsettled me. I never went any farther than the barracks along
the inner wall, but I could see the Court's elaborate Grays dash-
ing through the cobblestone streets, some with monstrous forms,
their hulking bodies big enough to carry three riders at once.

The strap of my messenger bag dug into my shoulder, and I
hoisted it up as I turned right, toward the gate. Twenty-foot walls
separated the White Court from the rest of the city. Only people
with the right permissions could enter or leave.

"See you tomorrow, Kai." The Watchman on duty waved me
out. As a mail carrier, I had access during work hours.

Once through the gate, the tension left my body. The North District—fondly nicknamed the Alley by some and not so fondly called Purgatory by others—was nothing like the White Court. The buildings here were plain stone and brick, ugly and brown and comforting in their uniformity.

I stepped off the curb into the gutter to avoid a glittering patch of broken glass on the sidewalk. A shattered window sat in the crumbling wall of the building right above the mess, jagged shards still clinging to the frame. As I turned the corner, I glanced at a poster stuck to a dented lamppost. It was one of only a half-dozen posters in this particular neighborhood—no point advertising to people with no credits.

Today, the poster displayed a half-naked man and woman enticing people to visit them down at the docks. I snorted. Last week, it had featured some crap about the wondrous city of Ninurta. Really smart companion advertising there. Who were they trying to kid?

But, hey, as long as Kahl Ninu left me and my brother alone, he could do whatever the drek he wanted.

A shoulder smacked mine on the sidewalk. I didn't bother checking my pockets. They were already empty. But sometimes I left little notes in them I thought might amuse a pickpocket: "Try me again tomorrow. I forgot my diamonds at home" or "Might have better luck with that guy," alongside a scribbled arrow.

Well, they amused *me* anyway.

The sidewalk grew narrower here. Some boys from school loitered around the next corner, their loud voices carrying through the ruptured street. One of them finished off an apple and then lobbed the core at a passing Gray—the gleaming form of a stag with curved horns. Bound for the White Court. The Court Grays were easy to discern from the Alley Grays, which were dirty and rusted.

The stag threw back its head and the rider shouted, but the boys' laughter drowned out his words.

I avoided eye contact and gripped my messenger bag closer against my side. On my right was a row of shops. Striped awnings dangled from the wooden supports; and posters for the latest underground club, the kind my brother didn't approve of, plastered the windows.

I stepped over a lumpy brown stain on the ground and cut through an alley, taking the shortcut to the District Mail Center. Laundry hung on either side of the walls, while rusty pipes crawled up the bricks like veins. I kept to the middle of the alley; the walls looked slick with something green and possibly moving.

Up ahead, a young woman with a black-and-white Mohawk leaned against the rungs of a broken fire escape. The metal creaked on flaking hinges as she shifted against it. She stared down at her gray boots, her hands buried in the pockets of her sweater. I walked briskly.

As I passed, I gave her the barest of nods. Just to be polite. Reev always said to be polite even if no one else cared.

The girl lunged, shoving me up against the alley wall. I gasped as we hit the bricks, my bag cushioning the impact. I threw my arm up to deflect her, but she knocked it aside.

Strong fingers, gritty with dirt, clamped around my neck. A clammy palm pressed into my collarbone, and a sharp edge dug into my ribs.

If my tunic ripped, I would deck her. My tunic was drab gray, worn thin at the elbows and with partially unraveled loops stitched along the hems—nothing special, except that Reev had made it for me.

"Bit far from the White Court, aren't you?" The girl sneered, her lips stained bright red. "How much you think someone'll pay to get you back?"

I stopped struggling. *What?* Laughter bubbled up my throat. Okay, this was new.

The fingers around my neck loosened, and the girl jerked a bit. "What's so funny?"

"I live in the Labyrinth," I said flatly.

If the North District was Purgatory then the Labyrinth was Hell. The Labyrinth was what we called the East Quarter, specifically the maze of stacked freight containers–turned–homes, so closely packed together that it had transformed into a city within the city. Operating by its own unspoken rules, the Labyrinth sat about as low as you could on the social ladder—which, in Ninurta, was saying something.

"No one's going to pay a credit for me." Which was a lie, because Reev would pay every credit he'd saved for us to get away from the dripping metal walls and claustrophobia of the Labyrinth. He'd give up even more than that for me, and I could never let that happen.

"I saw you leave the White Court," the girl said, her sweaty hand sliding against my skin. Her nervousness didn't reassure me; it only made her more unpredictable.

"Look closer," I said, and glanced down at the messenger strap on my shoulder.

I brushed aside my long black hair, and the girl focused on the yellow bird sewn into the old canvas. It was the District Mail Center's logo—a quaint bit of symbolism about flying and freedom, which was deeply ironic and something I didn't think about for fear my eyes would roll clear to the Outlands.

The moment the girl realized what she was looking at, her body grew rigid and her already pale face went ashen.

"W-well," the girl began, "you—I—" She shouted a curse. The knife at my ribs dug harder; I sucked in my breath. The girl swore again.

"Are we done then?" I felt kind of bad for her. She couldn't have been much older than me. Maybe eighteen or nineteen, though most kids around here had broken into their first shop by the time they were five. Didn't know if that was true for me—I couldn't remember anything from before I turned eight.

I had to get going or I'd be late returning my bag to the DMC. My route was timed, and I couldn't afford to lose any credits.

The girl's hand tightened around my neck. "You're pretty," she said, her gaze flicking across my face. "And those eyes are something else."

I groaned. Here we go.

"Bet you'd get me a good price at the docks."

I had heard enough.

I reached out with my mind, feeling for the threads of time that flowed around us. They were everywhere, if you had the ability to see, intertwining the people, the weathered buildings, the stones beneath my feet. They moved everything forward in constant motion. Always forward. I imagined my fingers dragging the fibers, making them catch and slow.

Time never truly stopped. That, as far as I could tell, wasn't possible. But I could slow it down for a few seconds, just enough to get the advantage.

The girl's painted lips continued to move in minute degrees, her voice an indistinguishable thrum. I fought the threads that snared me as well, twisting out of the girl's grip and pushing at the knife against my gut. The weapon was crude, nothing but a scrap of broken metal with one end wrapped in rags for a handle.

I couldn't hold the threads for very long. Time slowed only in the space around me, and the mounting pressure to continue forward and catch up with the rest of the threads broke my grasp. Time snapped ahead, rebounding. I wrenched away, riding the momentum of speeded time, and hit the ground. Pain flashed up my arm.

Behind me, the girl gasped.

Dread rooted me in place. *She saw.*

I jumped to my feet, brushing off my palms as I spun to face her. She couldn't have seen. No one but Reev was aware of my manipulations. For everyone else, the perception of time remained unbroken, preserving the belief that no one but the Kahl possessed magic.

The girl wasn't looking at me. In fact, she wasn't even standing. She knelt beside the alley wall, her knife jutting from her belly where she'd fallen against it.

I watched as she slid sideways into a boneless heap. Her head hit the ground with a *crack*. I flinched, searching up and down the alley, but if anyone saw what happened, they had already moved on. Nothing I could do would help her now.

As I turned away, the girl moaned. I glanced over my shoulder. I couldn't see her face, but I could hear her mumbling.

I looked toward the exit to the open street. I should leave her. Her nervousness and the clumsy way she had attacked me made it obvious she wasn't a seasoned criminal. But she wanted to sell me at the docks—she deserved whatever she got. The city would be better off without another desperate mouth to feed, and with people disappearing every year, what was one more?

Besides, this wasn't a hidden alley. Someone would probably find her in time.

But what if she has someone waiting for her? A brother. A sister. A baby hungry for dinner. What would happen to her family if she didn't get up again?

Stupid conscience.

The nearest runner was around the corner. Alerting the runners was the only way to get ahold of the Watchmen—short of walking into their local post, which I sure as drek wasn't doing. But the runners charged a ridiculous tax for their services, credits Reev and I couldn't spare, and while I could lie about my name, they'd demand an ID to verify citizenship.

I glared down at the girl bleeding into the dirt. *Drek.*

CHAPTER 2

WHEN I WAS TEN, REEV HAD SPENT ONE OF HIS SUNDAYS OFF work with me by the river. We'd scavenged for bugs on the muddy bank and wondered what mutant abilities we might get from falling into the murky water. He pretended to throw me in, and I had been so stupidly scared he would actually do it that I twisted my ankle fighting him off.

Reev had felt terrible. He promised not to be so rough, and I told him to shove his promise in the river because nobody put restrictions on my brother, not even my brother. It made more sense in my head.

He had carried me all the way to our box in the Labyrinth. I remember the way his hair scratched my face, the heat of his shoulder against my cheek, and the smell of the river—sickly sweet like rotten fruit—on his clothes. His voice murmuring unnecessary apologies had been the only soft thing about him. Everything else had been—still was—hard, unyielding, strong.

Safe.

I hadn't wanted the weekend to end. I wanted another day. I

wanted it so badly that when I woke up the next morning to find Reev still home, I thought I'd gotten my wish.

The thing was—I had. It was Sunday again.

Reev had gone to work only to discover that no one else realized it was supposed to be Monday. After the confusion wore off, chilled anger had crept into his face—his mouth went flat, and his eyes hardened into gray stones. He'd never looked at me that way before.

"Promise me," he'd said, "you won't do that again. Ever."

I couldn't speak because the change in him scared me so much. We'd seen the Watchmen take people—drag them away on their Grays, through the gates of the White Court, never heard from again. In the Labyrinth, we had a saying: *Keep silent, keep still, keep safe.*

But only Reev had noticed. There were no Watchmen pounding down our door.

The threads moved around me, growing more tempting the more they came into focus. Rebirth had wiped out nearly all the *mahjo*, the magic users. The Kahl's line was supposed to be the last of them, and he used his magic to help the city. If I had a special ability, one that didn't hurt anyone, why shouldn't I use it, too?

"Kai," Reev had said. "Promise me."

We stared each other down, but the flicker of fear in his eyes finally made me nod.

I had broken that promise too many times to count. I couldn't help myself. That had been the first time I'd realized I was different.

Once I knew what the threads were and that I might be the only person who could see them, they fascinated me.

The next day, time had adjusted itself by continuing on with Tuesday. All around me, people muttered about how Monday had flown by, and they couldn't remember a thing they'd done that day. It didn't seem as if even Kahl Ninu had noticed. I'd never been able to repeat that level of manipulation, and I still didn't know how I'd done it.

Every source of energy in Ninurta came from the Kahl's magic, but nobody had ever seen him at work. New energy stones were available for purchase every month, and the Grays, constructed of magic and metal, continued to run the streets like shining beasts. Who were we to question it? I couldn't do anything half as useful, but whether my abilities were magic or a freak of nature, I couldn't say.

I didn't dare call myself *mahjo*, even in my head. That status felt too attached to the Kahl, and I had no delusions about being his equal.

And now, with a hefty tax headed my way, maybe I should practice some control.

After the stop at the runners—who were so slow that they should have been called crawlers—I hurried to the DMC to dump off my bag just in time. I should've been more worried about the woman who had almost died than the state of our credits. But I wasn't.

As I left the DMC, I stared straight ahead and walked quickly past the Watchman standing guard at the double glass doors. He followed me with his eyes.

A few days ago, that same Watchman had trailed me into the back room where I store my bag and offered me twice my weekly pay for "personal service." Fortunately, my boss popped in a second later to see what was keeping me, and I escaped.

Outside, a stream of human traffic blocked the sidewalk. Walking was the only way to get around the city without a Gray, and the streets were fairly crowded this time of day. I waded through the pushing bodies to reach the other side of the street. I kept close to the shop windows, most of them dark or boarded over. A row of pigeons fluttered away as my shoulder bumped a sagging awning. I looked up, but they only flew far enough to find a new perch across the street.

For 358 days a year, the birds didn't fly any higher than the buildings. As if they had forgotten how. But in five days, the clouds would part and release sunshine into the city. For one week a year, the river danced with lights. The trees dared to bud. And the birds took flight, becoming brown specks against a gray sky.

The Week of Sun was my favorite time of year. I couldn't wait.

Up ahead, a shop sat on the corner of what was once High Street and 6th Ave, but the street signs were so mangled they were no longer legible. As far as buildings went, it wasn't the worst. It had been painted green at some point in the last twenty years, but now the paint looked like flaking mold. Above the shuttered window front hung the shop name, "*Drivas,*" in peeling, yellowed letters.

Kahl Ninu had been promising renovations to the North District for years, but nothing had been done. All Ninurta's resources came from a closed-off district in the White Court, so there was little anyone could do but wait and hope for the best. And suffer ridiculous charges just to request help from the runners.

I sighed. I would need to budget carefully over the next weeks to make up for the tax. And I'd keep a close eye on the mail. A notice would be sent with three days' allowance to turn over the credits ourselves, or they would be taken automatically. I'd have to snag the notice before Reev found out. Good thing it was summer, which meant more hours and more credits to earn. During the school year, Reev let me work only on weekends.

Kids were required to attend school, but no one enforced it. I once tried talking Reev into letting me work full time so we could save more credits. He didn't even humor me with a response. Since most of my friends dropped out, going to school was a chore. An unpaid, monotonous, nine-month-long chore. The only real friend I had left was Avan Drivas, whose family owned the shop. But since he graduated last year, I didn't have much to look forward to once school started in a couple months.

I pushed into the shop. What I liked best about the place was that it was clean. While the stock wasn't the freshest, they at least had the decency to toss out the rotten produce. The counters were wiped down, the floors swept every night, and the windows washed once a week. I knew this because even though Avan claimed he was just helping out his dad, he practically ran the shop and liked to keep it looking tidy.

"Hey, Kai," Avan called from behind the counter. His cheek dimpled when he smiled.

I waved and ducked into an aisle, feeling like an idiot. He was a year older than me, tall and olive skinned, with dark hair. We'd been friends for long enough that he shouldn't have affected me anymore, but try telling that to my stomach. As if to mock me, it did a little flip.

I perused the shelves, picking out a package of dried pear slices and a cucumber sandwich. Meat was difficult to come by, but it would have been too expensive for me anyway. Then I told my stomach to settle down and brought my items to the counter.

"How was the illustrious White Court today?" Avan asked as he rang up my items.

He had nice hands, slender but strong, with long fingers. The muscles in his forearm shifted as he moved. I watched a few beats too long and hastily looked away.

"Blinding," I said. "I'll have to roll around outside to get rid of the clean feeling."

Avan smiled again, his dark eyes lingering on my face before he turned to place my purchases in a paper bag. A jagged black tattoo started under his jaw, crawled down the side of his neck, and disappeared beneath the collar of his shirt. He'd gotten the tattoo a few years ago, around the time I'd begun to think of him as a friend. I tried to imagine what the rest of it looked like.

He reached behind him and then tucked a couple other things inside the bag: a wrapped loaf of bread and a wedge of hard cheese.

"Came in this morning," he said. "Haven't put them out on the floor yet." His voice was deep. When he spoke softly like that, I could almost feel it rumbling inside my chest.

I nodded my thanks. Avan liked to slip me fresh products.

That was how it had started—our friendship. I'd always noticed him, of course. Impossible not to. But when I was twelve, he'd slipped me a few apples with a quiet smile. That was the first time *he* noticed *me*.

In the beginning, I objected. I wasn't used to random acts of kindness, and I demanded to know what he wanted. But he never asked for anything and never stopped trying to help. I eventually stopped arguing. Turning down free food would be pretty stupid.

"How's your brother?" he asked, placing my bag on the counter between us. I was grateful for the barrier, however small.

"Good. How—" I looked away, unable to help glancing at the door in the corner that led up to his parents' apartment. "How are . . . things?"

Avan saw where I was looking and tensed. He didn't really talk about his mom anymore, and asking about his dad wasn't an option, not since I'd kicked him in the groin when I was thirteen. I'd gotten tired of coming in to find Avan at the counter with purple bruises and bandaged hands. So the next time I'd seen Mr. Drivas, soaked in liquor and screaming at him, I'd come up from behind and aimed between the legs.

Avan had tried to shield me as his dad went red with rage. Mr. Drivas hadn't hit me, though. Even drunk, he knew that Reev would have put him in the hospital.

"My mom's fine," Avan said, interpreting my vague question. When he wasn't smiling, he looked kind of somber. Even sad. I wondered if he knew that. "So have you heard the news?"

"You know you're my best source." More like my *only* source. I didn't much care what was happening around the city if it didn't affect me or Reev, but Avan had connections and was usually well-informed.

And I liked the excuse to stick around and talk to him.

"There was another one," he said. "Upper Alley."

My fingers fiddled with the bag. Nobody talked much about the disappearances. They happened a few times a year at most—not enough to cause mass panic but certainly often enough to be noticed—and people either reacted with fear and paranoia, or they looked the other way.

With our own survival to worry about, we didn't have much concern to spare.

"The Black Rider strikes again?" I said with a hefty dose of sarcasm.

Neither of us believed Kahl Ninu's claim that a rebel named the Black Rider was kidnapping Ninurtans. What kind of self-respecting criminal would call himself the Black Rider? And aside from the propaganda insisting the Rider wanted to overthrow the Kahl, no one had ever seen or heard of him.

Frankly, it sounded like a half-baked cover-up. Probably because the Kahl had yet to catch whoever was actually kidnapping people. Although with magic at his disposal, I would've expected it to be an easy task.

"Someone you knew?" I asked.

"Not really. Met her a couple times, but . . ." He shrugged, and that was really all there was to do.

In a couple of weeks or months, once her family accepted she wasn't going to be found, they would go to the old *mahjo* temple at the center of the North District and hold a farewell ceremony. And then they would move on with their lives.

"Stay safe."

He told me those same two words every day, and I gave him the same answer: "Always do."

I thanked him again for the groceries and left. I turned down the hill toward the docks. The river separated the North District from the East Quarter, and while plenty of bridges connected them, only a few were safe to cross. The pimps ruled the river-front, and you had to be careful there any time of day.

A thick wooden post stood next to the dirt road leading to the docks. I traced my fingers along the post and smiled when I found a new notch cut into the moldy wood in the shape of a *K*. Whenever Reev or I passed this post, we made sure to leave a mark to let each other know that we'd been there and we were okay. I dug a fingernail into the wood below the *K* and carefully scratched in an *R*.

The city odors took a noticeable shift as I neared the river. The docks smelled like damp wood and mildew. Trees dotted the banks, but their branches remained stark even in summer. The bark looked scarred, rotted in areas, forming strange depressions: lumps and rivets like its organs bared.

Along the bridge, couples lingered. That would've been sweet except I knew most of them were prostitutes with their custom-ers. Some of them didn't even bother trying to shield what they were doing. I wondered if anyone had ever fallen into the river that way.

You'd think the smell would be a mood killer, but what did I know? I'd never even kissed a boy.

The Raging Bull was the fifth building down the long strip of businesses along the riverfront. All the windows were painted red. A large sign announced *"Half off during Week of Sun."*

I ignored the drunken calls of men on the boardwalk and opened the door. Reev stood near the entrance in his usual spot, arms crossed and doing his best "Don't mess with me" impression. He made it look natural. More than six feet and built like a stone slab, Reev could be pretty intimidating when he wanted to be. That was how he'd gotten this job. Not my top choice for him, but admittedly, there weren't many.

When he saw me, he frowned. I waved and held up the bag from Drivas's.

"How many times do I have to tell you to stop coming here? It's not safe," he said, pulling me into the lobby. His hand warmed my elbow.

I scanned the lobby. Two women chatted behind the front desk, the only people besides us in the small area.

I shoved the bag against his chest. "You never eat unless I bring you something, so quit complaining."

One of the women waved. I waved back halfheartedly. Angee liked to introduce herself as Reev's girlfriend, and I had never heard Reev confirm or deny it. She was nice enough, but I wished she'd stop trying to befriend me. The woman next to her had tight brown curls, heavy makeup, and nothing to cover her smooth, dark skin but a transparent slip. She nodded at something Angee said, while her eyes stayed on Reev.

I didn't like the way she—and the other prostitutes, men and women—looked at him. The way their gazes lingered, the way their half-naked bodies pivoted toward him whenever he entered the room. I wanted to step between them and Reev, and tell those people that he wasn't like the clients who paid for them.

But I suspected they knew that. And it was why they wanted him.

"Is this your sister?" the woman next to Angee asked. She looked at us and pursed her lips into a pretty pout. "She doesn't look a thing like you."

I scowled. Reev had wavy, dark-brown hair and gray eyes. His nose had a slight hook, and he had thin lips and an angular jaw. I, on the other hand, had straight black hair and almond-shaped eyes that weren't quite blue—more like a watered-down version. Reev once said they were like the icicles that formed on the tree branches in winter. My lips were fuller, and I used to press my fingertip against my pointy chin as if I could imprint a cleft there like Reev's. The rest of me was skinny enough to look malnourished, and the top of my head reached just shy of Reev's shoulder.

We didn't share a single physical trait, because Reev wasn't actually my brother.

He'd found me when I was eight. He'd been younger than I was now—sixteen and barely able to feed himself—but he rescued me off the riverbank and raised me as his sister.

"How much did it cost?" Reev asked, taking the grocery bag from me. "Should I transfer some credits?"

I shook my head. "Avan gave us fresh bread. As fresh as it can be, I mean. I'm pretty sure that's fresher than usual."

He frowned again. He didn't approve of Avan because of his reputation, but the free food required his grudging acceptance of our friendship. "You should get home now. There's an energy drive down the street, and they'll be here for the next couple days."

I understood what that meant. The Alley had several energy clinics, but the drives held near the river were geared toward the people in the Labyrinth—and those afraid to wander too far from the safety of its narrow walls. Energy drives meant free credits to anyone who didn't mind needles, and it brought out even the most desperate of folks. Reev didn't want me running into any of them.

"Where'd you hear that?" I hadn't seen it on my route this morning.

"One of the girls told me. She was just there."

I ignored the way my stomach knotted whenever he talked about the girls who worked with him. "If you even think about volunteering, I'll kick you. When you're asleep."

His shoulders relaxed. "Of course not. Same to you. Minus the kicking."

Donating blood for the energy stones always tempted me. Depending on how much I gave, I could cover the cost of the runners' tax, and Reev would never be the wiser. The problem was that the energy clinics were rarely clean, and a bunch of people died every year from infection. The energy drives, however, were sponsored by medics from the White Court, so they were probably safe.

But it was best not to test it. I wasn't keen on dying, and my abilities to manipulate time didn't include rewinding it—with the exception of that first experience, which had been a fluke.

I'd just have to work some extra hours and eat what Avan was willing to give me for a few days.

"Come for a job?" asked a voice like gravel.

I turned, backing up into Reev. Reev's hand came down on my shoulder. It felt like a shield.

The owner of the Raging Bull, Reev's boss, was a middle-aged man named Joss. He was thin, with orange hair that made his loose, pale skin look sallow. He smelled like cloves and something earthy and damp. I kept hoping he'd fall into the river and drown.

He snapped his yellow-stained fingers at the nearly naked woman, who then darted down the hall, but his eyes remained on me. When I refused to look away, his mouth twisted, and he gave my body a lazy inspection.

I leaned back against Reev, letting his warmth chase away the chill in Joss's eyes.

"She just brought me dinner," Reev said. "Go on, Kai. Get home." He nudged me toward the door.

"Let me know when you change your mind," Joss said, winking at me. He had fleshy lips that drooped at the corners and flapped when he talked. "I could get you double Reev's salary for your first time." He cocked his head and took another look at me. "Oh, yeah. Definitely a virgin."

"Joss," Reev said. I was probably the only person who could hear the anger in his voice.

"Come on, Reev, everyone's hurting for credits. Use what you got. Or rather, what *she's* got."

To be honest, I'd thought about it. There weren't a lot of other places I could get that many credits. It would be enough to get us out of the Labyrinth like Reev wanted.

But it would hurt Reev, and his approval meant more to me than anything. Not to mention the fact that Joss creeped me out.

I took half the bread for my own dinner and munched on it as I left the docks. In front of the bridge, a woman pulled her bawling kid along the dirt path. Out of habit, I studied her face, even though I knew I wouldn't see anything familiar. Nine years in Ninurta, and I'd yet to find anyone who looked enough like me to make me wonder.

"Quit that," the woman said with a sharp tug on her son's arm. "Get on home or I'll let the gargoyles eat you."

I snorted. Reev had never given me the gargoyles story, but I had heard it whispered at school. Parents told their kids that if they misbehaved, the gargoyles that lived in the Outlands would climb Ninurta's wall and slip into their rooms in search of easy prey. The more superstitious people believed the gargoyles were demons who'd sprung from the bowels of the earth, cracked open after the events of Rebirth.

Sounded silly to me, but considering what I was capable of, I couldn't completely scoff at the idea.

Not that I wanted to compare myself to gargoyles.

Reev had reassured me that the stories were all nonsense and the gargoyles had never breached the outer wall. But just in case, I had made him promise. Unlike me, Reev kept his promises.

CHAPTER 3

THE NEXT MORNING, A SANDWICH WAITED FOR ME ON THE counter. Reev had written *"Eat only with a smile"* on the paper wrapper. I unwrapped it and then poured myself the last bit of water from the pitcher. I'd get some more from the pump later. Reev didn't trust the pump water, but it tasted good enough. A little metallic, but I didn't see the harm in that.

I sat on a wobbly stool and ate at the counter. On his cot against the wall, Reev turned in his sleep. He came in from work around dawn, and he always made sure to leave me breakfast before getting into bed.

He lay on his side, arm thrown over his face so I could see only his rumpled head above his bicep. The only time he looked fully relaxed was when he was sleeping.

At the back of his neck, beneath the mess of his hair, was an elaborate red tattoo in the general shape of a rectangle, tapered at each end. It wasn't visible right now, but I knew the design by heart. The lines were raised like a scar. Around the edge, the skin was shiny and pulled tight, several shades paler than the rest of him.

I'd asked about the tattoo more than once, but Reev refused to talk about it. All I knew was that he hid it with high-collared shirts and his hair.

His large body fit awkwardly on the tiny cot. Everything past his calves hung off the end, and his broad shoulders didn't fit across the width. I had no idea how he could sleep like that. As amusing as the sight was, there was also something fascinating in the way he slept—the slight part of his mouth, the slack muscles, the inelegant sprawl of long limbs.

Some mornings, I lay in my cot against the opposite wall and watched his chest rise and fall.

Our entire living space was one room—one freight container, to be exact. Trains, like most industrial technology, had been out of service since Rebirth, but there were still remnants in the junkyard from which the East Quarter had sprung. Rows and rows of towering freight containers formed a giant cube of metal decay. The Labyrinth had been built around and inside it; walls and roofs erected, and hallways and staircases shoved into the spaces to connect everything. The only people who knew how to navigate the Labyrinth were the residents, and we liked to keep our secrets.

It made the East Quarter the ideal place for anyone wanting to disappear.

The cucumber and lettuce sandwich was bland, but the corners of my mouth turned up anyway because of Reev's silly note. He used to leave me random messages all the time when I was younger. He did it less often now, but I privately wished he'd kept it up.

Reev rolled onto his back, rubbing his face. "Eating with a smile," he mumbled sleepily. "That's my girl."

I beamed, cherishing the warmth that infused my chest. "Go back to sleep. It's still early."

"Wanted to make sure I caught you before you left," he said, pillowing his head against his arm. The position made his bicep bulge. "I don't need you to bring me dinner tonight."

"Why's that?"

"Angee's packing me something."

I ducked my head. "Oh."

I took a long gulp of water to wash down a final bite of sandwich. Then I wrapped the other half inside the paper with Reev's message and put it in the cupboard beneath the counter.

Reev watched me through half-closed lids. His eyes were the shining gray of the sky during the Week of Sun. The rest of the year, an endless wall of tumultuous yellow and orange clouds dominated the sky. Sometimes, at dawn or dusk, the colors flared, and the sky looked like it had been set on fire.

"What's wrong?" he asked softly. He did that on purpose, adjusting his voice to that low, sedate tone that soothed me.

"Nothing," I said. "I better get to work. Sleep in. That's an order."

I ruffled his hair as I passed. I made a quick stop at the communal washroom down the hall and then headed for the exit. Our corner of the Labyrinth had two sets of stairs, rusted metal sheets hastily nailed together with equally rusty nails. I usually took them slowly, which earned me a few curses from the people behind me. I didn't care. Better slow than dead.

The narrow halls had enough room for one person to pass through comfortably. I tried not to touch the walls—they were perpetually damp from the dips and cracks overhead where rainwater caught and remained. Nothing dried inside the Labyrinth, and the pockets of trapped water overflowed whenever it rained.

On the ground level, the paths grew wide enough for two people. A couple of lanterns burned here and there to ward off the darkness. The Labyrinth's construction didn't allow for much daylight to get through. People outside the East Quarter likened it to being buried alive. The comparison wasn't so far off, but the leaders here—a bunch of grumpy old people who made decisions on behalf of everyone who lived in the Labyrinth—refused to invest in energy stones because they claimed it meant reliance on the Kahl. That, and they couldn't afford them.

The mail keeper was just outside, each mailbox stacked behind her in a similar style to the Labyrinth. The carrier who covered the East Quarter didn't like me, which meant I'd never be able to convince him to give me the tax directly.

"Nothing for you today," the mail keeper announced cheerfully. She slapped her dirty gray cap against her matching tunic. One good thing about being a carrier was that I didn't have to wear the hideous mail keeper uniforms.

I frowned. "Are you sure?" Tax charges never took more than a day or two to arrive. I chewed the corner of my lip. Maybe the carrier had lost it.

A shout came from behind me. "Get out of here!"

I looked up. Residents had gathered at the entrance to the Labyrinth. I waved my thanks at the mail keeper and wandered over, craning my neck to see what was going on. Couldn't be anything good. The people here weren't exactly neighborly.

A young man about Reev's age stood off the path, facing down the growing crowd that circled him, closing in. He looked worried. A little desperate. It wasn't an uncommon expression, but I could tell by the quality of his clothes and his clean face that he wasn't like the people who hid in the creases of the city. He wore a fitted black leather tunic, matching pants, and high boots—the boots alone cost six months of Reev's salary.

"Go on!" someone shouted. "Your kind isn't welcome here."

The young man drew a deep breath. "Can you tell her I want to see her? *Please*. Just tell—"

Something flew toward the back of his head. I opened my mouth to shout a warning but stopped myself.

The man's arm snapped up, easily snatching the rock from the air. He hadn't even looked.

The crowd went silent, its hostility heavy in the sudden quiet. And I realized exactly what he was.

CHAPTER 4

THE MAN WAS A SENTINEL, ONE OF THE KAHL'S ELITE PRIVATE guard. Everyone outside the White Court called them his dogs. This was my first time seeing a sentinel, and I'd wager the same for everyone else now gawking at him. As far as I knew, sentinels remained solely within the White Court. I'd never heard of one entering the East Quarter before.

Every cadet who joined the Watchmen Academy hoped to gain the rank of sentinel someday, but Kahl Ninu awarded the status only to those who won the Tournament—the final challenge for graduating cadets.

Becoming the Kahl's dog, especially if this man had lived originally in the East Quarter, was a betrayal of the unspoken code of the Labyrinth.

He dropped the rock. His other hand clutched a folded slip of paper.

"I just wanted to see her once," he said. He spoke quietly, but I had no trouble hearing him over the hushed crowd. "Can you let her know I came? Or give her this for me?"

"Just go away," said a man near the front. His voice trembled. Everyone around him nodded in agreement.

The man's eyes lowered, the slip of paper crumpling in his fist. Without another word, he turned. Those behind him leaped aside to let him through, and the crowd began to break up as he marched away.

I had no sympathy for the sentinel. He'd chosen to leave us for the decadence of the White Court.

He bent his head, his hand dragging through his shoulder-length hair.

There—at the base of his neck—was a red, oblong tattoo.

My feet charged forward. Without thinking, I shouted at his back, "Hey!"

He looked over his shoulder.

"Hey," I repeated stupidly. The tattoo was just visible, the scarred skin raised like welts beneath the red ink.

He flipped his hair back into place and yanked his collar up higher. My face grew hot. I hadn't meant to stare.

It wasn't any of my business, and he had a right to his secrets.

But it was still worth a shot. "What is that on your neck?"

The way his eyes narrowed was answer enough. He began to leave again.

"Wait," I said. I gestured to the letter. "I'll give it to her for you. What's her name?"

He just watched me. I shifted awkwardly and rubbed my palms against my sides.

"If you want," I added.

"Lila Sevins," he said curtly. He handed me the crumpled note.

"Your sister?"

"My mother. Thanks." He didn't sound convinced that I would really do it. I didn't blame him.

I smoothed out the note and then slid it into my pocket. For some reason, I wanted to reassure him. Reev would want me to.

"I promise I'll get it to her."

He went still. Then he nodded. "Thanks," he said again, and this time, it sounded like he meant it.

"I'm sorry," I said, "that you couldn't see her." But if he had loved his mother enough to come back, he shouldn't have left her in the first place.

"Won't matter after tonight anyway." He continued up the path toward the bridge.

I watched him go. Red flashed beneath his hair. My jaw tightened, and I looked away.

After work, I'd find Lila.

Reev was late.

I rolled onto my side and opened my eyes. I could make out the lines of the empty cot across from me in the dark. I strained my ears, listening for the telltale creak of footsteps out in the hall.

Reev was never late.

I drew a slow breath through my nose and released it through my mouth. And then again. It didn't help the fear stirring in my gut. Reev was big enough that most people left him alone, and he could defend himself if he ran into trouble. I still didn't feel any better.

Maybe he'd gone to Angee's. The thought made me grimace.

Reev was entitled to a personal life, even if it made me feel . . . I didn't know how I felt about it. Uncomfortable. Unsure. Left out. I groaned into my pillow. Could I be any more pathetic?

It wasn't the fact that she was a prostitute that bothered me. In Ninurta, you did what you needed to survive. To be honest, I didn't know if anyone would ever be good enough in my eyes for Reev.

For as far back as I could remember, it had been the two of us. I didn't like having to share him, no matter how childish that was.

Few people would've taken responsibility for a kid picked up off the riverbank, and Reev had still been a kid himself. When he turned eighteen, he looked into officially adopting me, but simply filing the request cost more than he could afford. He continued to bring up the idea over the years, but I told him that it didn't matter. Those were credits better spent on keeping us alive.

I buried my face in my pillow. Reev had taken care of me for long enough; he deserved his own time.

After work, I had kept my promise to the sentinel. It had taken me an hour, but I found Lila. She lived in the southernmost section of the Labyrinth in a freight container caving in on one side. When I told her who'd given me the letter, I thought she'd slam the door in my face. Instead she had taken it with a scowl and *then* slammed the door. But I had heard her muffled sobs through the metal walls.

That kind of pain—it was why I'd given up any real hope of finding a familiar face a long time ago. The citizen registry said I had no living relatives, and I had no reason to believe that wasn't true. In fact, I *wanted* it to be true. It would mean they hadn't chosen to leave me.

An hour later, I gave up trying to sleep and rose from my cot to light the lantern, which cast a warm glow across the metal walls. My internal clock told me it had to be about seven. The only breakfast waiting for me in the cupboard was the leftover sandwich, which I had no appetite for, so I threw off Reev's shirt that I liked to sleep in and pulled on a pair of worn pants and a belted tunic. Then I grabbed my toiletries and made a quick visit to the washroom. I hated it in there; the smell hit you like a roiling wall of fumes, and the staff only got around to cleaning it—not very well—once every couple of weeks.

When I finished and Reev had yet to appear, I began worrying in earnest.

The bridge creaked as I hurried across. The river sloshed green and brown beneath the boards. This early, the docks were quiet, the buildings twice as drab in the daylight. I headed straight for the post and ran my fingers along the wood.

There was nothing beneath the *R* I'd scratched in yesterday. There should have been a mark for when he'd left work last night.

Keeping in touch was Reev's rule. Even if we didn't see each other, we'd know we were safe.

Reev had never broken that rule before.

Caging my fear, I turned down the road to the docks, my pace quickening until I was running. I almost ran straight into the closed door of the Raging Bull but caught myself in time to tug it open. I prepared to yell at Reev for working late without telling me.

He wasn't there. My pulse jumped beneath my skin.

Angee's spot at the desk was empty. The door nearby opened. Joss paused when he saw me.

"Where's Reev?" I demanded.

Joss grunted. "He left same as always. What do you want? Ready for a real job?"

I fled, chased out onto the boardwalk by Joss's laughter.

This wasn't right. Reev would never go anywhere without making sure I knew where he was. He was Reev: consistent, reliable, unfailing.

I'd been afraid even to think it until now. . . .

People were disappearing. Had been for years. Like many others, I pretended not to notice. The Watchmen were supposedly still searching for them, but as long as it didn't affect me and Reev, it wasn't my business. Worse things happened in Ninurta.

I was safe with Reev. With his silent strength and the subtle tenderness he reserved just for me and the way his arm felt around my shoulders.

He was untouchable.

He was supposed to be untouchable.

CHAPTER 5

REEV WASN'T IN THE HABIT OF MAKING FRIENDS, SO I DIDN'T
know who to ask if they'd seen him. Besides Angee, that is; but
she hadn't been at the Raging Bull, either, and I didn't know
where she lived.

Reev's past was as much a mystery to me as my own. He
avoided talking about the time before he'd found me. Now I wish
I'd been bold enough to push him.

The idea of going back to ask Joss for information made me
shudder. He wasn't the type to give anything for free. Few people
in Ninurta gave information freely.

Since I had nothing to give, I'd have to rely on myself.

I started my search in the Labyrinth. I doubted I'd find Reev
hidden in some obscure corner, but I wanted to cover all my
bases. I'd spent months exploring the entirety of the Labyrinth
when I was younger, so I knew my way around the maze-like corridors. Checking the ground level and the common areas where
people liked to gather was easy enough, but poking around the
less stable floors was trickier. I didn't know how anyone could

stay in those sections and not feel as if they were living on a spinning top that could tip over at any moment.

With no sign of my brother in the nooks of the Labyrinth, I left for the North District. I started at the docks and headed up through the cracked streets. My mind tortured me with images of Reev lying bleeding in a hidden alley. Maybe he hadn't been kidnapped. Maybe he'd just been outnumbered by one of the street gangs.

I peered down alleys and searched through neighborhoods I hadn't dared enter before. The buildings slanted from poorly constructed foundations. Most of them bore holes where the elements had eroded through stone and wood, revealing the rotting frames beneath like skeletons.

By noon, I was tired and frustrated, and hours late for my shift. *Drek.*

When I walked through the doors of the DMC, my boss's nostrils flared. My shoulders drooped. I had to keep this job, but I really didn't want to beg.

"You're usually a reliable worker, Kai."

I winced, waiting for the catch.

Ellane planted her fists on her nonexistent hips and sucked in her hollow cheeks. "Tell you what," she said. "I got a package I need delivered. Do that for me, and I'll only cut half your credits next week."

It was a shoddy deal, and we both knew it. But we also knew I couldn't turn it down. The address on the package was in a neighborhood a little farther north than my usual route. Since I planned to search the area, it wouldn't be out of the way.

By the time I reached the neighborhood two hours later, my feet ached. I sank against the side of a building and tucked the package beside me. The uneven stone dug into my shoulder blades.

My plan wasn't working. People noticed when a new face wandered into their part of the district, and they weren't friendly to outsiders, especially outsiders with questions. A couple of guys even stalked me back to the main road, but I lost them on the crowded sidewalk.

How was I going to find Reev? I closed my eyes, keeping the panic at bay. When I opened them again, my gaze settled on the outer wall, the one that bordered the entire city, visible above the drab buildings.

The wall marked Ninurta's border and protected us from the gargoyles that all but ruled the Outlands. They ran in packs, but there was little else anyone knew about them. Despite what the bedtime stories said, they'd only ever been seen at a distance.

I didn't know how anything could survive out there. The Outlands could be glimpsed easily through the city gate—flat, barren earth as far as I could see. What if Reev was out there? What if he really had been kidnapped by some crazy rebel?

My fingers curled around the cloth of my shirt. *No.* The Black Rider was a cover-up, either because the Kahl didn't know where the missing people were or because he didn't care. Kahl Ninu never even tried to explain why some poorly named rebel would need to kidnap anyone.

The popular rumor in the Alley was that the Rider had tamed his own pack of gargoyles, and he kidnapped Ninurtans to feed them. Not sure what that had to do with overthrowing the Kahl, but maybe it was a psychological tactic. Demoralization or something.

Or it was just another ridiculous explanation to appease the questions. Those taken were never heard from again. Ninurta was a big city, but nothing a thorough guard unit wouldn't be able to sift through if it put in the effort. If the missing people were still here, the Watchmen would have found them by now.

I gritted my teeth and pushed away from the wall. I would worry about all that later, after I ran out of other options.

I shifted the package, gripping it against my stomach. Delivering the thing seemed so trivial compared to Reev's absence, but I couldn't lose my only source of credits.

I'd never been this far north before. I repeated my boss's directions in my head and turned left at a corner where a large poster boasted the freshest bread in the city. I doubted it.

The folks in the North District considered everything past the abandoned train tracks and the boarded-up station the Upper Alley. The streets here were still dirty, threaded with cracks and riddled with potholes, but they were better kept than those down by the docks.

I followed the road and ignored the pedestrians who stared at me. A couple of women strutted past in high-collared silver tunics and heels that would've made my sore feet sting in sympathy, except the added height only made it easier for them to look down on me. The people here liked to think of themselves as White Court residents living outside its walls, because they had more credits to spare than the rest of us.

If you asked me, though, Purgatory was Purgatory.

I found the house next to a shrine dedicated to a god I didn't know. Built before Rebirth, the carved facade was crumbling, but it was clear it had been sculpted by a talented hand. Not many people visited the shrines anymore, and the *mahjo* temple was used now only for farewell ceremonies. Faith and prayers could take a person only so far, especially without the *mahjo* to reinforce the old beliefs. But I understood why people would want to believe in those sorts of things—they made the world feel less lonely. And you never knew what a person could do fueled by hope.

When I was younger, I used to pretend my powers had been a gift from some higher being. Or that, maybe, these powers had a purpose. That *I* had a purpose. I had toyed with the idea that I was *mahjo* or, possibly, even a distant relative of the Kahl. But the history texts never spoke of *mahjo* with the ability to slow time, and once I got older, I came to accept that I was probably just a freak accident. I didn't know if or how that connected to my memory loss or why someone had left me on the riverbank, but these were questions I had stopped asking years ago. No point torturing myself.

Once, when Reev was at work, I had watched a farewell ceremony through the paneless stone windows of the temple. After the candles were blown out, the caretakers collected the body and transferred it onto a long, enclosed wagon pulled by a Gray. Led by Watchmen, they'd taken the body outside the walls to be released into the sea beyond the cliffs. The city that stood here before Ninurta had burned its dead and scattered their ashes to the sea, but the tradition had been somewhat streamlined.

I had wondered: Is this what happened to my parents? Had their bodies been sent down the final leg of the river, dumped over its edge into the depths below?

The man who answered the door gave me a quick once-over. His lip curled. He covered his hands with a cloth before accepting the package. In return, I rolled my eyes and dusted my clothes off on his doorstep.

Glad that was over, I searched the Upper Alley for another couple of hours until the soles of my feet screamed and every step felt like walking on thorns. The sky had grown dark, and the shadows between buildings stretched black fingers into the open street. I trudged back home, forcing my thoughts to center on the pain in my feet instead of the panic in my chest.

All the while, I held on to the hope that Reev had spent the day with Angee and forgotten to let me know. But when I pushed open our door, I found the place as empty as I'd left it.

The entire day had passed without a word or message from Reev. I had no more doubts that something was wrong.

Reev's shift at the Raging Bull had started hours ago, but I knew he wouldn't be there. He was late once to work—I had been helping Avan wash his shop windows while guessing what his soapy stick figure drawings were supposed to be, and Reev hadn't wanted to leave the apartment without knowing where I was. I got back to the Labyrinth in time to see two of Joss's men arguing with the residents and demanding to be let in. The only reason Joss hadn't fired him was because Reev agreed to work a month without pay.

But today, Joss's lackeys hadn't come around.

I didn't think about what I had to do. Thinking would lead to doubt, and doubt would lead to hesitation. I couldn't hesitate. Not on this. Not for Reev.

I packed the bare essentials, which was pretty much all I owned. Most of my shirts—loose, long-sleeved tunics mainly—had been hand-sewn by Reev. It cost less, and he could charm the textile workers in the Labyrinth to sell him fabric for cheap.

The only food in the cupboard was the leftover sandwich and a few packages of dried fruit. I gathered them up as well. Then I stopped by the bank and went to see Avan.

I found him sitting on the curb outside his shop with his friend. I was too worried about Reev to let Avan distract me—much. His long legs were clad in gray pants, and he held a cup of water in his hand. He looked like he belonged on a White Court poster, the ones with people too pretty to be real.

"Come on, Avan, we need you there," his friend was saying. I think his name was Wen. Aside from inviting me to a couple of parties—I always had to turn them down because of Reev—Avan's friends never had much to do with me. "Jag's got this new brew she wants us to try."

Avan rested his cup on the stone beside his hip. "You guys can go without me. I'm over it."

He waved when he saw me, his eyes lighting up. The sight made my breath catch.

Wen flung an arm around Avan's shoulder. "You're getting boring."

Avan shoved him off with a smirk. "And yet I'm still more interesting than you."

"Ass," Wen said, laughing. He jumped to his feet and brushed off the seat of his pants. "We'll look for you in case you change your mind." Before taking off, he acknowledged me with a playful salute. I returned the greeting by pretending to doff an invisible hat.

"Hey, Kai," Avan said in that voice that hinted at a smile even when he wasn't wearing one.

When he wasn't behind the counter serving customers, he was more subdued. I preferred him like this. It felt more real, even though I had no idea if it was. Avan had always been difficult to pin down.

"Working hard, I see."

"My dad's got it covered." He pushed a hand through his hair—an action I'd imagined myself doing too many times to count—and regarded my pack. "Moving?" He grinned, flashing his dimple at me in a way I knew was completely deliberate. Heat filled my face anyway. "There's space in the freight yard. I could show you around."

"I need a favor."

The teasing disappeared. I studied his features—I'd long since memorized them—before looking away.

"I'm giving you shared access to my credit balance," I said.

For a second, he didn't react. Then his eyes narrowed. I wasn't sure how he'd take this news, but I wanted him to understand that I trusted him.

The thing was—before knowing Avan, I'd known his reputation. According to the rumors, Avan used to refuse to go home, crashing with whoever would have him and paying with whatever they asked from him. Girls. Boys. He rarely objected, even though he was beautiful enough to be as selective as he wanted. It was why I'd been suspicious the first time he'd slipped some apples into my grocery bag.

I didn't think I'd ever stop feeling ashamed for having doubted him.

"Just go to the bank and tell them who you are," I continued. "I've already arranged for it to be approved once they verify your ID with the registry. I'll need you to pay our next month's rent, and if you don't hear from me after that, then . . . well, keep the credits. Consider it late payment for all the free food."

I had covered a lot of ground today, but the North District was large enough that it could take a couple of weeks to explore fully on my own. I didn't know how long it'd be until I found Reev. Days or weeks or . . . No. I refused to consider the possibility of not finding him at all. But if I couldn't find him in the North District, then I would have to leave it. Which meant leaving Ninurta.

Something turned unpleasantly in my stomach, but I ignored it. One thing at a time.

Avan stood. He wasn't quite Reev's height, but standing next to him still made me feel small. I avoided his eyes, dark and searching, and instead focused on his lips. They were great lips. Quick to smile, but just as quick to tighten into an unreadable line. Like now.

"What are you planning? Where's Reev?" He touched my arm. This was the closest we'd been in weeks.

"He's—" I choked on the word *gone*. He wasn't gone, just— "Not here. I have to do something important, and you're the only

41

person I trust not to blow the credits on something stupid."

He arched an eyebrow with a steel bar pierced through it. "I'm flattered, honestly, but I don't think you've considered—"

"It doesn't matter what you think," I said harshly, because I was letting him distract me. I shook off his hand and swallowed the guilt.

"You don't care about my opinion, but you want to give me access to all your credits," he said flatly. "Makes a lot of sense."

I forced myself to meet his eyes. Despite the cool disdain in his voice, I saw concern there. I didn't know if he'd ever shown me his real self. I wanted to believe he had.

"Look." I could try to reassure him, but there was no point. "If you don't want the credits, that's fine. Just keep your mouth shut about it, okay?"

"Kai—"

"Take care of yourself." I hurried away. I didn't look back, and he didn't call my name again.

The front desk was still empty. I hoped nothing bad had happened to Angee, but my concern was for Reev. I had no idea if Joss knew anything, and I doubted he would tell me if he did, but I had to try.

I didn't think the Raging Bull ever closed, but with no receptionist and no security guard, it felt unnervingly empty. I could tell it wasn't, though, by the smells. A mix of soured sweat and overly sweet perfumes.

Joss's door was closed. I dropped my bag and leaned it against the desk. I wiped my hands on my pants, then slapped my palm on the little bell at the corner of the desk.

Joss sauntered out of his office, brown liquor bottle in hand, followed by another of his security guards. Reev had introduced us once. I forgot his name, but I remembered the guard had an easy laugh.

When he spotted me, he immediately looked away. My hands curled into fists.

"Knew you'd come back," Joss said.

"Where's my brother?"

Joss scratched his forehead with the bottom of his bottle. "I told you. He left."

"Reev hasn't come home yet. Did anyone actually see him leave?"

Joss clucked his tongue. "Really should leave it alone."

There was a challenge in his eyes, daring me to push him despite his warning. He *did* know something.

"What did you do to him?" I asked, my voice shaking.

"What makes you think I did anything? I'm his boss, not his babysitter."

"You almost fired him the last time he was late. His shift started hours ago, he's not here, and you don't seem to mind."

"Maybe I gave him the day off."

"You're lying," I said, slamming my fist against the desk. Reev had never been given a day off in all the years he'd worked for Joss.

For a long moment, Joss stared at me.

"All right," he said, tilting his head and jutting out his chin. "If you want to know so badly, I sold him."

I repeated the word in my mind—*sold, sold, sold*—but I didn't understand its meaning. "What?"

"You know, exchanged for credits," he said slowly, as if I was an idiot. "Peddled. Bartered. Pitched."

"To *who*?" How was this possible?

"The Black Rider. Ever heard of him?"

The Black Rider wasn't real; he wasn't—

"Gave me a price I couldn't turn down. I'm a businessman, after all. I know how to spot a deal." His eyes trailed down my body.

I crossed the room in an instant. The guard grabbed me. I thrashed, fists aiming for whatever they could reach. I could see only Joss. The smug curve of his mouth. His eyes on me. Gloating.

Something dark and wild twisted inside me.

"Calm down, Kai," the guard said, his soft voice countered by his hands like steel binding me. "This won't end well for you."

"I'll kill you. I'll drekking kill you!"

The guard grabbed my flailing wrists and secured them both in one hand. He clamped his arm around my shoulders and chest, lifting me and pinning me against him. Joss watched me struggle, taking a languid sip from his bottle.

I immediately stopped. He enjoyed seeing me like this. My heart raced, pounding against the arm that held me immobile.

"You know, I was willing to give you time," Joss said, leaning close. "Time to realize that working for me was your best option now that big brother's gone. But I'm glad you came back. Expedited the process, so to speak. And let's not kid ourselves here. I know you want this." His breath was thick and cloying against my cheek. "I've seen it in your eyes. You've thought about it."

I spit in his face.

At first, he did nothing. Then pain burst in my jaw, my head knocking into the guard's shoulder. My vision blurred. I could hear a low buzzing laughter.

I groaned and blinked. My face throbbed. Only the arm around me kept me upright.

"Didn't know you had a temper," Joss said, leaning close again.

His fingers dug into my chin. I couldn't stop the tiny moan of pain that slipped past my mouth.

"Look at your pretty face. Now we'll have to wait for you to heal up. But we'll open the bidding in the meantime. Those eyes ought to intrigue a good number of clients—never seen blue that pale before. And you'll need some training."

It was taking way too long for the spinning to stop. I squeezed my eyes shut, senses extending around me. My mind skipped across the threads, waiting. Time vibrated against me, as if in anticipation. But the guard still had me pinned. I wasn't sure I could break his hold even with time slowed.

The front door opened. Maybe if I shouted for help—but if it was a customer, I doubted he'd care. If anything, he'd probably start the bidding.

CHAPTER 6

"KAI?"

Avan! I spun my head around, the sudden motion making my jaw ache. I craned my neck, twisting my body, but I couldn't see past the guard's burly shoulder. What was he doing here?

The guard turned. I saw a dark shape, then there was the crack of knuckles meeting cheekbone, and the arm around me slackened.

My mind jumped at the threads. Time crawled. I dropped to a crouch, wrenching my wrists free. Then I spun around and kicked out at Joss.

My grip on the threads slipped. Time flew forward. My foot smashed into Joss's knee, and he went down in a tumble of limbs. His head smacked the floor. I grabbed for time.

Everything slowed again. Behind me, Avan and the guard grappled. My fingers wrapped around the neck of Joss's fallen liquor bottle. I brought it up in an arc just as time rushed forward. The bottle shattered against the guard's head. Glass spewed through the air, so rapidly that the shards looked like an explosion of lights.

Pain sliced through my cheek. I whirled, diving for cover as a crash rang out behind me. I'd managed to knock out the guard.

I remained where I was, breathing hard. My body trembled. Warm hands gripped my arm. The touch was gentle, but I flinched anyway as Avan helped me to my feet. He peered down at me, his fingers sweeping along my bruised jaw and brushing glass out of my hair. I shuddered again, but for a different reason.

"Kai, did you—" He looked from me to the men sprawled on the floor.

The way he spoke my name, combined with the look in his eyes—intense, questioning, uncertain—made me realize. He'd seen it. He'd *felt* it.

I couldn't deal with that right now. I reached for my bag, ready to run. "Why did you follow me?"

A strangled gasp came from the hall. We both looked to find a woman gaping down at the mess on the floor, her hand pressed to her barely covered cleavage.

"Come on," Avan said, touching my waist.

"You're Reev's sister?" the woman whispered.

I gave her a closer look. She was young, with hair as smooth and white as milk. My skin was pale, but hers was ivory. Her only spots of color were a black streak through her hair and bright-red lips that shone wetly, as if she'd painted them with blood.

Her eyes were like polished metal, framed by snowy lashes. She looked familiar. Maybe I'd seen her here before. But I was pretty sure I'd remember.

I crossed the lobby, stepping over the glass. The woman shied away, her gauzy robe fluttering around her thighs. Her hands braced against the wall, and her long hair shielded her face.

"Did you see what happened to him? Or where they took him?" I asked.

She kept her face averted. I studied her delicate profile. She probably made Joss a lot of credits.

"Reev," she murmured.

I didn't like the way she said his name. Like a plea. Like a wish. Was every prostitute here in love with him?

"He didn't talk much, but he didn't treat me like spoiled meat."

My nails dug into my palms. I knew how much my brother was worth. "Did you see what happened to him or not?"

"Yes," she whispered to the wall. "There were people. . . . They moved like shadows. They drove something metal against the back of his neck and"—a shiver ran through her thin arms—"and he seized up. Passed out. They took him."

I couldn't breathe. I stepped back clumsily, glass skidding beneath my boots. My foot bumped Joss's leg, and I glared down at him. He was still knocked out. Fury blazed beneath my skin. I should throw him in the riv—

"Kai." Avan touched my side. His fingers curved against my ribs.

I jerked away. If this woman liked Reev so much, she should've done something to help him. "Do you know who they were? Did you see the Black Rider?" I asked her.

"I didn't see any faces, but I think I know someone who might know something." She bit her lip. "Wait for me."

She disappeared down the hall, her feet silent on the dingy wood.

I looked at Avan. He surveyed the bodies on the floor. Probably thinking the same thing I was: they wouldn't be out for much longer.

"Do you think they're telling the truth? That the Black Rider is real?" For the longest time, I had scorned that name. It had been nothing but a pathetic joke. Now, I didn't know what to think. People who moved like shadows?

"We could wake him up and ask," he said, nudging Joss with the toe of his boot. His eyes flicked over my shoulder.

"Here," the woman said from behind me. Apparently, she was used to creeping about the building. With Joss as her boss, I didn't blame her.

She held up a folded square. Her fingers passed with a dry hiss over the aged paper as she unfolded it to reveal a map.

"Where did you get that?" I asked, moving forward to get a better look. It was old enough that the ink had completely faded along the creases.

Ninurta was little more than a mess of sketchy lines beside the Outlands, but I recognized the city's general layout. The White Court occupied the lower left corner. A black line bordered the Court, with the southernmost portion of the wall protecting the city from the sharp cliffs beyond. The map didn't show what existed past them. Maybe the sea. Maybe nothing at all. Looking at it this way, the White Court resembled a prison more than a refuge.

The river snaked through the lower right corner, separating the much larger North District from the East Quarter, which was taken up almost entirely by freight containers. Beyond the square that represented the Labyrinth was another freight yard, one formed after the founding of Ninurta. Now that area, too, had become residential. Avan lived there.

Finally, the outer wall encased all of Ninurta, protecting the city from the Outlands. The Outlands stretched across most of the map, ending on the right with the forest. Beyond that, a dark swath marred the edges: the Void.

Maps were hard to come by. Ninurtans didn't leave the city, so there was no need for them. The maps from before Rebirth remained within the city records hall for research and history. It seemed unlikely that a prostitute would happen to have one.

"One of my regulars makes me keep things for him," she said. She looked down nervously at the map in her hands. "Things he wouldn't like to be found with. I would be thrown out if anyone knew. B-but I overheard him talking once on the docks, and he said something about meeting with the Black Rider. At the time, I thought he was joking. But he might know something." She pointed to the freight yard on the outskirts of the city. "This is where he lives. His name is DJ."

"DJ?" Avan said. "Dusty Jax?"

"You know him?" I asked.

"He lives a few places down from me."

The woman tipped her head to the side, her hair sliding against her skin. The movement was both sensual and innocent. "Then you won't have any trouble."

Avan gave her a cool, assessing look. I was skeptical, too, but if Avan knew this guy, then there was no harm in checking him out.

She folded the map on its well-worn creases and then withdrew something from her robe. A blade flashed. Avan's hand snapped out and caught her wrist before she could raise it.

She didn't struggle. She just looked at Avan's hand and said, "This is mine. I thought you might need it." Her eyes flicked up to his face. The smile she gave him made me want to shove them apart. "You have kind hands. Maybe too kind."

Avan released her. She offered the knife to me. The blade was chipped and scratched and in need of a whetstone. Engraved marks decorated the handle, but they were indistinct and dulled with age.

"Why are you helping us?" Not that I wasn't grateful.

"Because," she said, fingers clenched around the knife handle, "if you find the Black Rider and Reev, then that means you might also find my sister. E-even though Tera's been missing for years. Maybe . . ."

I accepted the knife. It was unexpectedly heavy, and I tightened my grip.

"Thanks." I took the map as well and shoved both items into my bag. "I'll ask about her, if I can."

The woman watched me with slender fingers wringing at her waist. "Please be careful with the knife. It means a lot to me. If . . . After you find the Rider, I'd like for you to return it."

It would depend on where my search took me. I couldn't guarantee whether I'd even see this woman again.

"I'll try."

CHAPTER 7

"WE SHOULD CLEAN YOUR CHEEK."

Avan's hand brushed my face. Heat shot down my neck, and I stumbled over the crooked boards of the bridge. Annoyed, I pushed at his fingers, and then blinked in confusion when they came away red. I touched my cheek, surprised to find it wet.

"It's nothing," I said quickly, and wiped at it. I didn't wince at the sting, but I clenched my teeth, which only made my jaw ache more. I ignored Avan's knowing look.

"And you're willing to trust that the bottle was clean?"

He had a point. Okay, after we cleaned my cheek, then we would talk to DJ. Knowing which direction to take, any sort of lead, helped to temper the fear. The suffocating uncertainty of where the Rider might have taken Reev. The thoughtless rage that made me want to go back and throw Joss off the bridge.

Once we reached the other side of the river, Avan gestured with his chin for me to follow him. We walked along the bank, the waning light dyeing the river with ink. We kept above the sinking mud, alongside the stripped trees that stood like corpses in the gloom. The Labyrinth loomed behind us, a black shroud across the sky as the river angled north, and we continued east toward the freight yard.

Unlike the Labyrinth, the freight containers here had been arranged into neat rows, one level only, and with enough space between to provide the illusion of personal property. It wasn't much, but the happiest I'd ever seen Avan was the day he moved out of the apartment above his dad's shop.

My feet still ached. I tried not to limp but didn't succeed. If Avan noticed, he didn't show it.

We made our way through streets carved out by the large rectangular metal boxes. Some of the residents had set potted plants out front, bits of green that fought to survive beneath a sea of yellow clouds.

I cast furtive glances at Avan as we walked. I could barely see him in the dark, but he didn't seem bothered by what had happened. Why didn't he ask about what he'd seen? Now that we were safe, wasn't he curious?

I wanted to know what he was thinking, but I didn't want to ask. His silence was both frustrating and a relief.

His place turned out to be the last in his row. It sported a fresh coat of green paint. He unlocked the door and held it open for me to enter first.

Avan shut the door behind us and switched on a lantern. The place was larger than mine, in length anyway. A distinct kitchen area took up one end, sectioned off with a built-in counter and a stool. A rumpled bed larger than a cot—but not by much—sat against the adjacent wall beside a standing closet with a couple of tunics spilling out the bottom. There was even a real wall separating a washroom in the corner.

"It's wonderful," I said. His shoulders loosened a little. "You must love the freedom."

"Bit of a downgrade from the shop, but it's my own."

He gestured to the stool and then disappeared into the washroom. I sat down as he came back with a jar and a clean rag. He dipped a corner of the rag into the jar and reached for my face.

I leaned away, catching his wrist. His arm tensed. The muscles in his forearm stood out. The inside of his wrist felt smooth against my thumb. My hand looked so pale next to his.

Was I seriously ogling his *wrist*?

"I can do it." I reached for the rag.

"It helps if you can see what you're doing, and I don't have a mirror," he said wryly. He brushed my hand aside. "Relax. It's not a big deal."

I held my breath as the rag drew closer, smelling sharp with disinfectant. The cut burned on contact.

He was so close. Beneath the disinfectant, I could smell the earthy, almost spicy scent of his soap—and his own scent underneath it, fresh like a cool wind. He hadn't trimmed his hair in months, and it had begun to grow past his ears. I almost gave in to the urge to skim my fingertips along the hair that fell across his brow. I focused instead on the black lines inked into his neck. The tattoo was completely different from Reev's. Graceful swoops alongside jagged arcs. Since I could see only a fraction of the design, I didn't know what it was supposed to be. Maybe something abstract.

"Good thing I don't have a mirror. It looks worse than it is." He spoke quietly. I wished he'd stop being so gentle.

I remained still and didn't respond.

"You fight well," he said.

Maybe I was mistaken. Maybe he hadn't seen after all.

"But you still suck at conversation."

I frowned, and he smirked at my reaction.

"Reev taught me," I said.

"No wonder. He sucks at conversation, too."

"I mean to fight," I said, and then batted his hand away when his thumb smoothed over the bruise that was probably darkening my jaw.

"I know." He capped the disinfectant and placed it on the counter. "Give me a second. There's some food in the cupboard if you're hungry."

I wasn't, so I stayed on the stool to rest my feet and watched Avan dig through his closet. I could see that he didn't own much beyond the bare essentials, either. He pulled out a linen bag from a drawer and shoved some clothes into it.

"What are you doing?" I stood, shaking my head even though he couldn't see with his back turned. "You're not coming with me."

"Looks like I am," he said with a nod at his bag.

"No," I said, louder. "This doesn't have anything to do with you."

"I saw what you did in there. When you were fighting, you . . ." He stopped.

I rubbed my palm against my stomach, but it didn't help ease the churning. I didn't know how to deal with this. I wasn't going to offer an explanation until he asked, but I hoped he wouldn't ask because I didn't know *how* to explain.

"I'm not walking away from this. Whether you like it or not, I'm involved now." Then he glanced up at me, gaze steady. "And I'm your friend. I can't let you do this alone."

It wasn't that I couldn't use the help. But Reev was *my* brother, and Avan had his own responsibilities. I didn't know exactly what was wrong with his mom because he'd never said, but everyone knew she wasn't getting better, not with the limited care available in the North District. She never even came down to sit with Avan behind the counter anymore. The sicker she got, the less sober his dad was. What would his parents do without him to help run the shop?

"I don't need your help."

Avan shrugged. "But if you do, then it's a good thing I'll be there."

I sighed. It sounded like a sob.

Drek. I clamped my lips shut. I covered my face and pushed past Avan. He looked away.

The washroom door slammed shut behind me, and I collapsed against it. I pressed my palms against my eyelids and forced myself to breathe. In and out. Steady.

A tear slipped out, dampening my palm. My shoulders shook. Another sob escaped my lips, and I clamped my mouth tighter.

I needed Reev. I'd never been alone before. Sure, I could take care of myself; but Reev had always, *always* been there. How was I supposed to do this without him?

I swallowed hard. *Stop.* I couldn't cry. Not now, and definitely not with Avan in the other room, completely aware of what was happening in here. Drek, I'd embarrassed myself in front of him. Now, on top of being a freak, he probably thought I was a stupid kid with no idea what I was doing.

It scared me that maybe he was right.

CHAPTER 8

AVAN DIDN'T SAY ANYTHING AFTER I LEFT THE WASHROOM. HE offered me some water and didn't try to comfort me or offer empty words of reassurance. He just told me to grab my bag so we could find DJ. I was grateful.

At DJ's house, the door was opened by a grizzled man with coppery skin and hair the color of the clouds. Not quite yellow, not quite orange, and just as unnatural.

"Avan," he said. His smile was broad and, for lack of a better word, dirty. He lifted an eyebrow at me. "This your girlfriend?"

I did *not* blush. "No," I said stiffly.

"This is Kai. Can we talk?"

DJ stepped aside and ushered us in. The place was laid out the same as Avan's, except the walls had been painted an obscene yellow. I felt as if I'd walked into an egg yolk, except egg yolks didn't have people making out on a bed in the corner. The couple on top of the sheets carried on, completely oblivious. I turned my back, my face hot—only to see Avan watching them. I jabbed him with my elbow. Staring was rude, even if the couple didn't appear to notice or care.

"What happened to your face?" DJ asked, his eyes on me.

People here usually knew to mind their own business. "I thought it needed a change," I said.

DJ snorted and moved into his kitchen.

Avan propped up his elbows on the counter. "We need information about the Black Rider."

DJ stopped shuffling through the cupboard. Then he straightened and flung the cupboard door shut so forcefully that the couple on the bed jumped, rumpled heads popping up.

They were both guys. The one on top glared at us, his messy hair all over his face. "Closed party."

"Get out," DJ said. At first, I thought he was talking to us, but he was looking at the bed. He flicked his head at the door.

The guy gave him an incredulous look. I would probably react that way, too, if I'd been in the middle of . . . Yeah. He tugged his partner up by the arm. They were slender but wiry, with black hair and buttery skin, their faces flushed. Even though I'd seen much more skin, especially down by the docks, their intimacy embarrassed me. They were more than a prostitute and his customer.

I tried not to stare but couldn't help noticing the way one of them looked at Avan. It was a full-body look.

Avan's lashes lowered, but not before his eyes met mine.

"You're welcome next time," the guy said to Avan before the door closed after them.

Avan tucked his hands into his pockets, his mouth tipped into a half smile. He looked uncomfortable, which was weird because Avan had always seemed unaffected by the attention. He glanced at me again and then looked away just as quickly.

"What makes you think I know anything about the Black Rider?" DJ asked, grinning.

I filled in DJ on what had happened at the Raging Bull. When I finished, he lifted his cup of water in a salute.

"Congratulations," he said, and took a large gulp.

I tensed. What did he mean? "I'm getting my brother back."

DJ groaned and set down his cup with a loud *clink*. "Oh, you're one of *those*."

"So he's real?" Avan asked. He leaned against the wall, arms crossed.

"Well, that depends," DJ said. There was that dirty smile again. It reminded me of Joss.

I opened my mouth to snap at him, but Avan interrupted me. Probably for the best.

"We don't have anything to give you," Avan said.

"Then I guess I got nothing to tell you," DJ replied.

I wasn't going to walk away with nothing.

"A thousand credits," I blurted. It was a good chunk of what Reev and I had saved to get out of the Labyrinth. A couple more months and we would've had enough for a decent place in the Alley. But that money meant nothing without Reev.

DJ looked at me. "Twelve hundred."

My lips tightened. "Deal."

"I'll go with her to complete the transfer as soon as we're

done here," Avan said. "You know I'm good for it."

DJ grinned. "I like that about you, Avan. You keep your word."

"So is the Rider real?" I asked impatiently. I wasn't giving him a credit if his information wasn't worth it.

"As real as you and me," DJ said.

I felt ill. "Is he inside Ninurta?"

"Of course not."

I curled my fists against my stomach. I'd been holding on to the hope that the Rider operated from within the city—underground, definitely, but at least within the walls. Within reach.

"But how was it possible to get Reev out?" Avan asked.

"Oh, easy. The exits are everywhere."

That didn't make any sense. The wall protecting Ninurta from the Outlands was higher than the one around the White Court. And the only way in or out was through three guarded gates. So unless the Black Rider could walk through walls, there was no way he would have gotten past the Watchmen.

"Let me ask you this," DJ said. He steepled his fingers in front of him, as if he was about to impart some great wisdom, which I seriously doubted. "Do you know what the sentinels are for?"

Of course I did. Everyone did. "They're Kahl Ninu's personal guards."

DJ nodded vigorously. "Yes, yes, but why would the Kahl need a personal guard?"

"He's Kahl. He could walk around in nothing but a pink wig, and no one would question it." For all I knew, maybe he did. Only those in the White Court ever saw the Kahl in person.

"*I'd* question it," Avan said.

"Okay, bad example," I mumbled, "but you know what I mean. Why *shouldn't* the Kahl have a personal guard?"

"But what are they protecting him from?" DJ pressed.

"You tell me," I snapped. Why did he keep answering my questions with more questions? I was giving him twelve hundred of our hard-earned credits for information, not riddles.

Before any of this happened, I would've said Ninu's dogs were for show. But if the Rider really was targeting him and the citizens, maybe the sentinels had a purpose after all. I recalled the sentinel outside the Labyrinth and saw again the way he'd reached back and caught that rock without even looking over his shoulder. The sentinels were certainly as well trained as they were reported to be.

"They're not just his guard," DJ said. "They're his personal *army*. If they were only guards, why would Kahl Ninu need more recruits? Why continue to build a guard unless . . . ?"

"Unless they're losing fighters," I finished. I looked to Avan, who seemed to have drawn the same conclusion.

"But even if the Rider does exist," Avan said, "we're not at war."

"What makes you think Kahl Ninu would tell us if we were at war?" DJ asked.

"Who would we be at war with?" I countered. "The gargoyles? There's no one but us, and the Black Rider is *one* person."

"Don't be stupid. He wouldn't be able to kidnap all those people by himself."

"But we would *know*," I insisted. "War isn't something you can hide."

"Being that naive is going to get you killed," DJ said. "Keep that up and you won't last a day outside the walls."

I was *not* naive. Everything this guy said impressed me less and less, and I wasn't very impressed to begin with. But I was desperate, and he was our only lead.

"So we're at war," Avan said simply.

DJ nodded at him and continued, this time without the patronizing tone. "The Black Rider has already slipped through the cracks of the wall—her brother and all the others who've gone missing are proof of that. He's amassing a force strong enough to overtake the city. For years now, Kahl Ninu's been sending out his sentinels to find the Rider's base, but they've never found it."

"The Black Rider has taken Reev to join his army?" So that was why DJ congratulated me. He thought my brother had been conscripted. It sounded ridiculous, though. How could that ever work?

I guess conscription was better than being taken as gargoyle food. Although, if the Rider was real, then who knew what other rumors might be true.

"Reev would never cooperate," I said.

I knew my brother, and if DJ's information was even partly right, then what worried me most was that Reev would never give in. He'd fight the Black Rider to the end.

"How would he convince a bunch of kidnapped people to fight for him?" Avan asked. I couldn't tell if he believed DJ or not. "With threats?"

DJ's eyes gleamed with a manic enthusiasm. "Consent isn't necessary. Those taken are turned into hollows: empty soldiers with no sense of self or will."

My guts twisted, but my mind rebelled. It couldn't be possible. The threads shimmered as if to mock me—what did I know about what was possible?

"How do you know all this?" Avan asked.

"I'm the Rider's gatekeeper into the city."

That got my attention. I jumped forward, fists clenched on top of the counter. "Then you saw him take my brother!"

"*Into* the city," he repeated, regarding me with an unimpressed purse of his mouth. I didn't intimidate him. "His hollows leave when and how they please, and never by the same route."

I didn't want to trust his information, but we didn't have any other choice. Reev was gone—*that* wasn't a lie, no matter how much I wanted it to be. And no one who disappeared had ever come back.

I would change that.

"Fine," I said, and then repeated it louder. "Fine. So how do we find the Rider?"

DJ spread his arms wide. "That's the question, isn't it? First, you'll need to get to the Void."

Dread swelled inside me. I held my breath. The last thing I wanted was to show DJ how his words affected me.

Beyond the outer wall lay the Outlands. Beyond the Outlands was the forest. And beyond that, the Void.

"And then?" I asked.

"And then you lose yourself."

CHAPTER 9

AVAN TOLD ME HE HAD A PLAN. SEEING AS HOW MY OWN PLAN involved stealing a Gray I didn't know how to ride and hoping we could outrun the gargoyles, I was open to it.

We headed for the river and the nearest bridge. When we passed the post marking the path down to the docks, I had to pause to run my fingers along the wood. Reev's numerous *K*s. My *R*s. And then the single mark Reev had left yesterday. It had been only a day, but already so much had happened. It felt like ages since I'd last seen my brother. My chest hurt with missing him.

Avan walked ahead, his shoulders relaxed and his stride casual, as if he knew exactly what he was doing. He was so good at pretending to be okay that I often let myself believe it because it was easier.

He was a much better friend to me than I had ever been to him.

I should leave now. Slip away and disappear into the Labyrinth until he gave up. A good friend would have done that.

I didn't. I didn't want to do this alone. How could I be so selfish?

Like we promised, Avan and I stopped first at the bank. Once they checked my ID with the registry, I arranged for twelve hundred credits to be transferred to Dusty Jax. I hated losing so much money, but I didn't regret it. And I didn't bother removing Avan's access to my funds.

We headed to Avan's shop next. He said he had something that would get us across the Outlands.

Light from the shop cast dim blocks on the sidewalk and outlined the pole of a broken lamppost. I headed for the front door, but Avan's hand on my arm stopped me.

"This way," he said, and we cut around the shop through the alley.

A shed was nestled in the back beside the trash bins. Avan undid the padlock and pulled open the door. The rusted hinges screeched so loudly that I expected Avan's dad to come rushing out the back door in search of burglars.

He didn't, of course. He was probably passed out and wouldn't wake even if a herd of Grays ripped through the shop.

Avan lit a lantern sitting on a crate against the wall. The light shone across a cramped space filled with barrels, boxes, and a cart connected to a Gray. The creature had been crafted in the form of a horse, the same shape as most of the North District's Grays. The glow from the lantern caught the curves of its body, burnishing the drab metal.

"I didn't know you had a Gray," I said. I'd never been this close to a resting one before. There were plenty of North District Grays, but no one would risk leaving theirs out in the open when it wasn't in use.

Avan's lay on the dusty floor, its legs curled beneath, looking unnervingly like it was sleeping.

Avan reached behind the Gray and unlatched the cart. "I bought this to deliver packages," he said. "It needed a lot of work, so I got it cheap. I don't use it much, but it's nice to have when I do need it."

He pushed the Gray onto its side before opening a panel in its chest. A red energy stone about the size of my fist was fitted into a metal bed. I didn't know much about how the Grays worked, only that no smithy could make the creature run without the magic of an energy stone.

"Won't your dad need this?"

"I'm the one who takes and fills orders. Dad won't even notice it's missing." Avan poked the stone, which flickered red briefly, highlighting the bridge of his nose and the curve of his lips. "This isn't going to last if we're going to the Void."

According to the map, the Outlands stretched a solid five hundred miles east to the forest. Depending on how fast the Gray was, it could take us a full day or longer to reach the Void.

"Is this going to outrun the gargoyles?" Considering our school texts claimed the gargoyles had either eaten the rest of the native wildlife or driven them into hiding in the forest, speed was a pressing concern.

"Won't matter if it doesn't even make it halfway across the Outlands."

"We should take the energy stone from the Raging Bull," I said. "I'm sure Joss could afford another one with the credits he got selling Reev." I wanted to do a lot worse than steal his energy stone, but those dark, violent urges scared me. And they would disappoint Reev.

"Would you really do that?" Avan asked without looking up. Shadows carved deep lines into his face where the light from the lantern didn't reach.

"No," I admitted. "There are a lot of workers in the building. Joss would make all of them pay for it."

Avan shut the panel. "Come on."

He dropped his bag into a compartment behind the saddle and pushed the controls along the Gray's neck. I flinched when the creature rose to its feet. Sheets of overlapping metal made up its body, and despite the rust and scratches, they rippled smoothly in eerie mimicry of muscles shifting under skin.

I stepped back as it trotted out of the shed and came to a stop in front of me. I glanced at Avan uncertainly.

After locking the shed, he gripped the saddle and pulled himself onto the Gray. He held out his hand to me.

"I've never ridden one before," I said. Reev didn't think they were safe. Before my job with the DMC, he never let me go too far from the Labyrinth on my own.

"You don't have to do anything except hold on," Avan said.

This didn't reassure me in the least. With a deep breath, I put my bag alongside his and took his hand. My other hand grabbed the saddle as he pulled me up, and I swung my leg over the creature. The angle of the seat forced me flush against Avan. My pulse fluttered wildly beneath my skin. Good thing the darkness hid my blushing. Avan leaned over to position my feet on notches built into the Gray's flanks. I could feel the strength in his fingers even through my flimsy boots.

Stop it. Telling my body to shut up worked until Avan reached back to snag my hands and wrap them around his waist. He was so warm, his stomach firm against my palms. I tried to remember to breathe.

He flicked something else along the creature's head, and the energy stone lit up. The Gray's chest glowed red, the light escaping through the vents to illuminate the ground in front of us. I clutched Avan as he gripped the handles on either side of the Gray's neck and leaned forward.

Every muscle in my body clenched tight as the Gray took off. Avan laughed. We were so close that I could feel the vibrations in his chest.

We weren't going very fast, really. A slow gallop at most. Scouts—military Grays reserved only for sentinels—were the fastest because they were built specifically to outrun a gargoyle. I wished we could steal one of those, but scouts were stored in the White Court.

Traffic was light in the North District because Grays were expensive to maintain. The few blacksmiths in the Alley with the expertise to repair them had fallen under city control and charged more than the average person could afford. As far as I knew, most of the riders went the illegal route and bought services from the street smithies.

On the Gray, it took us less than five minutes to reach Avan's place. He cut the power, and the energy stone went dark. The sky was almost pitch-black without the city's lampposts.

"Stay here," he said, hopping off the saddle. "I'll be right back."

I shivered in the cool night. Without Avan in front of me, I felt unsteady. I leaned forward, resting my hands on the seat. It was warm. I drew away, flustered.

Sometimes, with the shop counter between us, it was easy to look at Avan and admire him from the safe standpoint of a friend, to see him as just a boy from the Alley.

And sometimes, like now, with his body heat still clinging to the front of my shirt, the sight of his silhouette through the mottled windows left me unbalanced, and I didn't know if reaching out would steady me or knock me off my feet. And because it was Avan, I wasn't sure I would mind either way.

Beyond the freight containers, I could make out the lumpy mounds of the junkyard. My school friends and I used to explore its precarious hills on quiet mornings after Reev went to work. It was always exciting when we found pieces of things that hinted at the city's past.

The city's original name—illegible in the maps from the records' hall—had been discarded and forgotten, but some of the city's history and traditions remained archived. This had once been a bustling fishing town filled with seafaring people. They had worshiped *mahjo* who could manipulate wind and water. The cliffs hadn't existed before Rebirth, and the sea had risen right up to what was now the White Court.

You wouldn't think it, seeing the city as it was now, but we'd found evidence of its past there in the junkyard: the skeletal remnants of boats, rotted masts, stray anchors, and rusty hooks. After one girl got a hook caught in her palm, we had to stop exploring the yard because Reev found out from her parents.

His disappointment had always been so much worse than any punishment.

I looked away from the shapes in the distance and scooted up on the saddle to examine the gears along the Gray's neck. I should've watched more closely when he turned it on. I reached for a switch just as the light from Avan's house went dark. A moment later, I saw a tall shape moving through the night.

He carried a metal box in one hand and a sputtering lantern in the other. I slid off the saddle to give him room.

"What are you doing?" I asked.

"Replacing the energy stone." He opened the creature's chest again, tools in hand, and began unscrewing things.

I sat in front of his door, folding my hands on top of my knees. "Looks complicated."

"Not really," he said, his face lit by the yellow glow of the lantern. "But I'm just replacing the stone. I'd need a blacksmith for anything else."

After a few minutes, he withdrew the energy stone. It looked as if he was removing the Gray's heart. He placed it carefully inside his tool kit and then withdrew from the kit another energy stone. Even at rest, this one glowed dimly.

"Where'd you get that?" Most people could afford only one energy stone a month and didn't have spares lying around. But with Avan's connections, it didn't surprise me.

"Ripped it out of my energy box."

I jumped up. "What? Why? You'll need that in the winter."

Winter here lasted a month, but without the Sun, the temperature could plummet to a wicked cold overnight.

"I appreciate the indignation, but it's not a big deal. I have the room at the shop."

"You hate it there." He'd never said as much, but his every action had made it obvious.

He shrugged. Neither of us voiced what we both must've been thinking—that it wouldn't matter anyway. If we left Ninurta, it wasn't likely either of us would be coming back.

He reconnected screws and bits of metal, and closed the panel. "All set."

He put the tool kit inside his place and shut the door. He didn't lock it. I wanted to tell him he should. It was his home. Why would he give it up, for me of all people?

We were friends, but we weren't . . . I hardly knew anything about his personal life other than what I'd heard, and I didn't ask for the same reason I'd never asked Reev about his past—I was afraid to push too far and lose him.

"You should stay," I said. "Show me how to use the Gray."

He didn't even respond, just pulled himself into the saddle and tilted his head at me, waiting.

"Avan," I said. "Your mom needs you. Your dad . . ." Avan and his dad had a rough relationship, one I didn't pretend to know about. But, in spite of that, he still took care of his dad and the shop. "He needs you, too."

Everything warm and comforting about him drained from his face, leaving behind a cool blankness. "You don't know anything about what he needs."

If he had shown sadness, I might have been shamed into silence. Instead, I was angry. I knew talking about his family was taboo, but I wouldn't be intimidated into shutting up. This was about more than just him or me.

"I know that your family needs you. You should stay with them."

It was too dark to see his eyes clearly, but I felt their intensity. Now that I had given voice to my objection, I couldn't back down until he said something.

When the tension grew too thick for the space between us, he said, "I know."

"Show me how to use the Gray."

"You remember that time you kicked my dad?"

I frowned, caught off guard. Avan *never* talked about his dad by choice. "Um. Yeah. You wouldn't talk to me for weeks after."

His chin dipped, and he looked down at me. "I never got around to thanking you."

"I thought you were pissed at me."

"I was," he said, shifting uneasily in the saddle. He dragged a hand through his hair. "Because you did what I never could."

"Kick him?"

Avan released a quiet breath, half laugh and half sigh. "Stand up to him. You've always done the right thing. You and Reev. I can't let you go out there alone."

"You don't need to—"

"You're not going to change my mind. You can keep talking if you really want, but we're wasting time. We've got a long way." He touched the seat behind him.

I ground the heel of my boot slowly into the dirt. I considered arguing further, but I didn't know if it would be for my pride or his safety. Back straight and muscles taut, I took his hand and mounted the Gray.

This time when he started it, I watched more closely. The creature's chest lit up, much brighter than before, and I scooted closer to Avan. I thought I felt his breath catch, but it was hard to tell.

We rode through the freight yard. The heat from the energy stone warmed the metal, but it wasn't as hot as Avan pressed against the entire front half of my body. Any remaining frustration I felt toward him vanished as we continued through the city. We were really doing this.

The nearest gate was several miles north. We had to get to the main road, which would lead directly to the exit. I clenched my sweaty palms against Avan's stomach.

We cut through alleys, people darting out of the way and shouting curses as we squeezed through. Even though we were only going at a canter, the buildings passed in a colorless blur. At the main road, I pressed my cheek against Avan's back as we joined the busier traffic. On the other side, two sleek, single-rider scouts in the shape of large cats sped past. They were headed for the White Court.

Avan turned just enough for his voice to reach me over the beat of metal hooves. "Ready?"

No. "Yeah," I breathed.

The gate came into view, the familiar sight of the Ninurtan banner—a red sword crossed with a silver scythe—draped above the opening. The massive metal door remained closed between midnight and four in the morning, when all Grays were prohibited from entering or leaving except for city business. During operating hours, the gate was open. I couldn't think of anyone in recent history who'd forcibly tried to leave Ninurta. The security was mainly there to keep out the gargoyles, not to keep anyone contained. Only two bored-looking Watchmen were checking each waiting scout to ensure it was approved to leave.

All we had to do was catch them by surprise and push through. The Watchmen wouldn't pursue us into the Outlands.

It sounded so easy, but the physical act of leaving had never been the hard part. Accepting what it meant to pass through the gate and let everything here go—that knowledge stuck like a hook in my throat, dragging me back toward the city, my job, the Labyrinth, everything I'd ever known. But Reev wouldn't be there waiting for me. None of those things meant anything without Reev, who had given me the sense of safety that Ninurta's walls couldn't.

The Gray shifted beneath me as Avan increased our speed.

"You know what you're doing?" I shouted over the wind. Probably should have asked sooner.

Avan didn't answer, but I imagined his self-confident smile.

The Watchman on the left waved the scout at the front of the line forward. Both guards stepped aside to give it room.

A jerk of our Gray to the right. A burst of speed. My stomach dropped.

The Watchmen didn't expect us. They shouted, diving out of the way, hands slapping for the metal grate. Too late. We blew through the gate into the barren darkness of the Outlands.

We'd done it. We were fugitives of Ninurta.

CHAPTER 10

IT WAS IMPOSSIBLE TO SEE BEYOND THE FLAT, DRY EARTH illuminated by the energy stone. Avan checked the map every once in a while to make sure we hadn't gone off course, but we could have been anywhere and nowhere. So far, there was no sign of gargoyles, but anything could be lurking beyond the wall of darkness. It was like riding through empty space, only the sound of metal hooves striking dirt and the wind tugging at my clothes to remind me we were moving at all.

With nothing to focus on but the red glow of the Gray's chest and the windblown smell of Avan's shirt, I slept in intervals. Lucidity was never far out of reach, though. Falling off the saddle and breaking my neck wouldn't help Reev.

Being this close to Avan was a practice in contradictions. His body heat and the solid comfort of his back soothed me. I could relax against him and feel secure enough to sleep, even if only lightly. It was almost like being with Reev.

But Reev didn't also make me hyperaware of every point of contact between us. The shift of his muscles beneath my cheek.

The backs of his thighs. The way our hips aligned on the seat. For the first hour, my heart pounded so hard, it was like a battering ram against my ribs.

It didn't help that, surrounded by nothing but the pressing dark, it was as if we were the only two souls in the world.

Stupid. The dark could also be hiding a pack of gargoyles closing in. I glanced over my shoulder, but I couldn't see anything except the vague line of the horizon in the blackness.

I pushed down the paranoia and rested my head against his shoulder blade. I closed my eyes.

The next time I opened them, daylight had begun to filter in through the clouds, giving my first clear view of the Outlands. Flames of light licked across a flat brown landscape. Low, craggy rock formations rose haphazardly to our left, interspersed with yellow-green cacti.

My instructors at school said most of the Outlands was desert, and I could see now that this was true. All around, patches of dead grass and copses of skeletal trees marked miles and miles of dry earth with no recognizable roads. Without the map, we would've had no idea where to go.

The wall of darkness was gone, but the world didn't feel any less empty.

I leaned a bit in the saddle to try and see Avan's face. "You should rest," I said.

"I'm okay," he shouted over the wind.

"I could take over while you sleep. Can't be that hard. I'm a quick learner." It was too bad I couldn't speed up the threads to make the hours go by more quickly. I watched the terrain pass in silence for a few minutes before saying, "Hey, do you think it's true that there's nothing out here but dust and gargoyles?"

"Looks like it."

"But seriously. You've seen the archived maps. We can't be the only ones left. It's just not possible." Not to mention it'd be incredibly lonely. The maps in the records hall showed whole countries spread across vast lands, filled with cities.

"If enough people around here survived to rebuild, then it's likely the same thing happened somewhere else," he said.

I had to agree. The alternative was too depressing. But if there were other cities hidden within the expanse of the Outlands, then the people had never tried to make contact. Maybe they believed they were alone as well. Maybe there were even other *mahjo* out there.

It made me wonder about those scouts leaving and entering the city. What exactly were they doing? Scouting for habitable land? Harvesting natural resources?

Either way, it was possible to survive out there if the Black Rider had set up a base somewhere in the Void. Especially if he was sustaining an army of kidnapped Ninurtans.

When we found Reev, would he still be himself? Or would the Rider have already . . . I chased away the thought.

"If there's anyone else out there," Avan continued, "they're too far away to get in contact with. I doubt we'll run across anyone. Look." He pointed ahead.

The terrain was so flat that I could make out a strip of brown and green far in the distance. The border of the forest. It looked like moss growing against the horizon. I couldn't be seeing that right.

"We're almost at the forest already? But it's only dawn. We can't have been riding for more than eight hours. How fast are we going?" I looked down, watching the Gray's hooves practically fly over the ground.

I could hear the pride in Avan's voice when he said, "Pretty sweet, right?"

"But Grays can't go this fast in Ninurta."

"We're not exactly in Ninurta anymore."

"But I didn't think they were even built to reach this speed."

He turned enough for me to glimpse the dimple in his cheek. "I made some modifications to this guy."

"Illegal ones."

"Says the fugitive."

I preferred not to think about that. Anyway, I was grateful for the "modifications." Not only would we get to Reev sooner, but I'd have to spend less time plastered to Avan's back. I wasn't used to being physically close to anyone for so long, not even Reev.

"How much farther until we reach the forest?" I asked.

"About an hour."

"We can rest then," I said. "You need sleep."

"I'll be okay. I've stayed up longer than this."

I didn't want to know why. But the curiosity remained at the back of my mind.

"Nervous?" he asked.

I was. Our knowledge of forests came strictly from school. The trees in Ninurta bloomed for one week a year, but they were sickly and yellow, nothing like the green leaves in the history books.

White Court experts theorized that there was either a vast

source of water hidden inside the forest or an underground reservoir that fed it and kept it alive. But their theories had never been confirmed because they couldn't get a team of researchers past the gargoyles.

"I've read about the forests. They're dangerous. Lots of places for wild animals to hide," I said.

"What do you really think, though?"

"I can't wait to see it," I admitted. Had the Rider given Reev the chance to appreciate the forest?

The air became steadily hotter as the hour passed. Moisture gathered where our bodies touched, and although the feeling wasn't exactly unpleasant, I tried inching back to give us some space. When it grew difficult to swallow, I twisted around to rummage in Avan's bag for one of the canteens I'd seen him pack. I had forgotten to pack water myself. If Avan had let me go alone, I would've died of dehydration before ever finding Reev.

I hated feeling so incompetent. With a sigh, I maneuvered the open canteen between his arms so he'd see it.

"Drink?"

"Thanks," he said, taking it from me.

I relished the wind against my face. I drank from a second canteen, taking even more sparing sips than I would have in Ninurta. We didn't have a pump out here. I took another deep breath of hot, dry air before putting away the water. Something dark flickered at the corner of my eye.

I jerked my head to the side and scanned the line of rocky outcroppings. Maybe it had been a trick of the li— There it was again!

A figure darted between the rocks, keeping pace with the Gray despite our speed. I squinted. The figure ran on all fours, with a long tail whipping behind it.

"Avan," I rasped, my hands flattening against his stomach.

A gargoyle.

CHAPTER 11

GARGOYLES HAD BEEN NATIVE REPTILES ONCE, BEFORE REBIRTH happened more than two centuries ago. But the mass collision of magic and technology during the war had changed them and killed off their major predators. Then, Kahl Ninurta I had taken their evolution a step further by combining them with other lizards to create monstrous chimera. But something had gone wrong—I didn't know what; I assumed the Kahl lost control of them—and he'd abandoned the project, killing those he could and unleashing the rest into the Outlands.

"They've been following us for a while," Avan said evenly. "I didn't want to alarm you."

Several more figures darted into view. Their powerful legs carried them over the jagged rocks with little trouble. My heart jumped. Of course—they traveled in packs. They must've been aware I'd seen them because the one on the rocks jumped off and continued along the flat earth, less than twenty feet away and in full view.

"Well, I'm alarmed," I snapped, and then felt immediately guilty. "Sorry. I didn't mean—"

"Don't worry about it."

I'd heard plenty about the gargoyles but not much about how they looked. The creature following us had a broad head with frills extending over a thick neck and a spiny back. It was lean and long, with sinewy muscles stretching beneath brown skin that looked as hard and dry as the earth.

Seeing a gargoyle for real made me think about the demons they were whispered to be. The creature looked like something that might have crawled out of fire and brimstone, breathing shadow and smoke.

"What are they waiting for?" I asked.

"Not sure."

The Gray's hooves stumbled. I tore my gaze from the gargoyles and held on tight as Avan maneuvered the Gray into a steady gallop. I peered over Avan's shoulder at the controls. I didn't know much about Grays, but I could figure out what a frantically flashing light meant. Even in full daylight, I could tell the energy stone was considerably dimmer.

"Hmm," Avan said, sounding a lot calmer than I felt. "Definitely smarter than I expected."

I connected the dots. The gargoyles had been biding their time, waiting for our energy stone to die out. I tried not to panic but didn't do a very good job.

"I thought you said the stone would last us to the Void," I said.

"That was my optimism talking."

I dug my fingers into his stomach and felt his muscles contract. I slid my hand higher, my palm pressed to his chest, and was somewhat relieved to discover that his heartbeat wasn't nearly as steady as his voice.

"Hold on," he said.

He bent lower over the Gray's neck, and I followed suit. I turned slightly to keep an eye on the gargoyles as the Gray burst forward. My arms tightened around Avan. The wind stung my face and tugged at our clothes.

Every sense sharpened as we raced closer to the tree line. The gargoyles picked up speed along with us. But we were faster. They slowly fell behind.

The forest was less than a mile ahead. We could make it.

The gargoyles must have realized this as well because they abandoned their strategy to bide their time and began aiming their claws for the Gray's legs and flanks. I could hear their snarls and guttural snorts. Clicks and grunts.

"I think they're talking to each other," I said. Maybe the Kahl had combined them with other creatures we didn't know about.

Up ahead, the trees were a blockade of brown bark and dry branches, rushing to meet us. I didn't see enough space for the Gray.

"Drek," I whispered, and clenched my eyes shut.

We crashed through the forest. I held on as the Gray galloped along, jarring us back and forth. Bark scraped my arms. Branches raked across my skin and ripped through my hair. I tucked my face between Avan's shoulder blades as he forced the Gray through. I dared a glance behind us but couldn't see the gargoyles. I heard them, though. They mowed through the underbrush with the coarse sound of claws tearing through roots and dirt and scoring the trees.

The Gray stumbled again.

I gasped as its front legs rammed into a raised root, the noise screaming in my ears. Or maybe that was me. I lost my grip on Avan, and we flew off the saddle, sailing into the branches. Brown and green whirled in dizzying and painful confusion. I brought up my arms to shield my head as something smashed into my back and shoulder. The air rushed from my lungs. For several excruciating seconds, I couldn't move or breathe.

Then I groaned, prayed nothing was broken, and pushed up onto my hands and knees. A few yards away, the Gray lay on its side, metal warped and chest smoking. I blinked through my burning eyes and found Avan also lying nearby. His arm didn't look right.

My ears were ringing. I tried to say his name.

A huge gargoyle burst through the trees and landed on top of the Gray. The metal groaned beneath the gargoyle's weight. The creature looked at me and then at Avan. It pounced.

Time crept to a near stop. I heaved forward, fighting against the threads that tied me to its flow. For the first time, I felt them snap around me. My limbs moved quicker, more easily. I focused on Avan's prone form and the gargoyle—its body extended mid-leap, its open mouth exposing two sets of serrated teeth, and its curved claws aimed at Avan. The threads brushed against me but didn't drag. I was free of them.

I scrambled for the rear of the Gray, reaching for the prostitute's knife that had fallen from my strewn bag. Then I threw myself in front of Avan and brought up the knife, slashing at the gargoyle's chest just as my grip on time slipped. Time sprang forward.

All the air left me again when the gargoyle crashed into me. My back hit the ground, the creature crushing me. I couldn't even shout.

My hands came up as I braced for the pain of claws and teeth—but the gargoyle slid off me, slumping to the forest floor. Blood from the knife wound pooled around its chest.

More gargoyles broke through the trees, pausing near the Gray to take in the scene. They growled, coming closer. I forced myself to my feet, standing between them and Avan. I gripped the knife so hard that my hands hurt.

Don't think. Don't think. I could move free of time now. I could do this.

I reached again for the threads.

CHAPTER 12

THE GARGOYLES STOPPED.

It wasn't me—I hadn't touched time yet. Since I couldn't hold on to the threads for long, I had to plan it just right.

One of the gargoyles lowered its head, luminous yellow eyes flicking between me and the dead gargoyle at my feet. A tremor went through its frills, and the other gargoyles backed away. The rest of them lowered their heads as one.

I licked my dry lips, my bravado ebbing. They didn't look as if they were determining how best to eat me. If anything, they looked wary, but what did I know about reptiles?

Maybe they hadn't expected to lose one of their own. Honestly, I had no idea how I'd even killed the other one, because I was pretty sure I hadn't cut it deep enough. Their tawny gazes were unflinching. I held their stares. I couldn't show them weakness, even while my heart pounded in my ears and my breath came in frantic pants.

"Come on," I breathed, lifting the knife higher. The threads glittered around me. "If we're going to do this, then let's do this."

After a moment, it dawned on me that they weren't looking at me at all. They were looking at the knife in my hands.

Avan groaned behind me. I heard the rustling of underbrush.

"Stay still!" I shouted without checking to see if he listened. "You're—"

"Fine," he said.

He appeared beside me, brushing off his torn tunic. I didn't dare look away from the gargoyles to inspect his injury.

"What are they waiting for now?" Avan asked, raising a broken branch that I doubted would be much of an obstacle for their claws.

The gargoyles looked at Avan, then back at the knife. Suddenly, in unison, they slunk away. They kept their heads down and their bodies low, sliding over root and bush until they had melted into the forest.

I waited, fear and adrenaline still pumping beneath my skin. Why would they just leave? Was this a trick? Maybe they were circling to attack from behind.

"I think they're gone," Avan said. "That was pretty strange."

He lowered his makeshift weapon. I barely heard him.

"Kai." His fingertips brushed over my knuckles, coaxing the knife from my rigid hands. I had to remember how to uncurl my fingers.

Once Avan had the knife, all the energy drained from my limbs. My body folded. Avan caught me around the waist before my knees hit the dirt.

"They left," I said, sagging against him in disbelief. I didn't think I could have fought off a whole pack.

"You okay?" he asked, setting me down. "Hurt anywhere?"

Everything hurt. But I shook my head because I could still move, which probably meant nothing was broken. And we were alive. Amazingly.

"What about you? How's your arm?"

His hair was mussed, and bits of leaves tangled in the dark strands, but his expression was composed. I touched his shoulder tentatively. My hands passed down his arm, at the spot where I was certain it had been broken, but I felt nothing.

"What? I thought . . ." I ran my hand back up to his shoulder and then trailed my fingers down his chest, searching for injuries. I must have seen wrong—I had been reeling from the crash and panicking about the gargoyles.

He cleared his throat. My fingers stilled over his stomach. He gently pushed my hands away and stood. "I'm not hurt."

I gripped my shirt. My knuckles stung in protest. "Sorry, I didn't—" I'd practically groped him. "I was worried. I could have sworn I— I'm sorry."

He flicked hair off his face, leaving a streak of dirt on his forehead. "I'm glad you're not hurt."

I gathered my wits, which currently lay scattered with the debris from our crash landing. We'd have to leave the Gray behind. It was useless now. Same with the energy stone, which was all but spent. Avan kept the branch; a crude weapon was better than none. Then we gathered up our bags, and I took out the map to determine our location. But after our blind charge into the trees,

I couldn't be sure which direction we needed to take without a compass.

Looked like we were on our own.

We walked for hours. Even though I wasn't hungry, I ate to keep up my strength. Avan took the lead. I placed the knife in my bag, within easy reach.

The forest looked exactly the way the history texts described it. I was happy to know that some places had successfully recovered after Rebirth. Everything was green. *Alive.* The trees near the border with the Outlands had been brown and brittle, but the deeper we traveled, the taller and healthier they grew. These looked as tall as the towers in the White Court, and the branches grew so thick that they blocked out the clouds.

I drew in lungfuls of air, relishing the scent. The decay lingered here as well, but not like in the city. This kind of decay promised new life. I wanted to memorize the smells of the earth and the moss and the dampness, and keep them with me to revisit on nights when nothing but the rusting metal walls of the Labyrinth closed in around me.

That is, if I ever saw the Labyrinth again.

Once I found Reev, once he was safe, then I could deal with everything else.

The forest was humid. I wasn't expecting that. I had to braid my hair and tie the end with a strip of cloth torn from the hem of my shirt. But flyaway strands still stuck uncomfortably to my forehead and neck. Sweat blackened the hair at Avan's temples, and he pushed up the sleeves of his shirt, giving me an almost unobstructed view of his tattoo.

It snaked down his bicep, a jagged black bramble at once lovely and primal. I decided it was a tree. The lines on his neck were the branches—I assumed more spread across his chest— and the roots twined down his arm in deliberate knots and turns. Like the trees in Ninurta, its branches were bare. It probably meant something, but the symbolism escaped me.

I was letting myself get distracted again. My focus returned to the forest. I picked a broad, veined leaf and held it between my fingers. The texture felt strange: soft and rubbery, but delicate as well. Someday, I told myself, I would share these wonders with Reev.

I strained to listen to the forest and heard nothing but our footfalls. Not far ahead, Avan's foot snapped a twig, and the sound echoed in the branches.

I felt something, an aura pressing in around me as surely as the darkness had in the Outlands. Dread seeped beneath my skin.

Moments before, the canopy had been alive with the calls of birds, none of which I could identify. Now, the wildlife fell silent. Nothing moved, not even the leaves. The air was still, like when I grasped time.

Avan and I exchanged a look. He felt it, too.

We pushed on, breaking through the ferns and overgrown weeds, until both of us came to a sudden stop.

The forest ended abruptly, and the ground dropped four feet into a vast plain of blackened earth. For as far as I could see, nothing remained but a monochromatic landscape: black dirt and gutted gray trees. A few boulders peppered the plain, but it was otherwise empty. Dead.

The Void.

This was what Rebirth had done to the world.

After centuries of unchallenged power, the *mahjo* had felt threatened by the growth of science and technology. The advancements had spread into the world's armies, providing countries with weapons that, for the first time, were efficient enough in speed and scope to stand a chance against magic. In order to stop an industrial and military revolution, some *mahjo* leaders staged an attack on one of their own sacred cities. This became the perfect excuse to declare war against the industry as a whole. Nobody predicted what would happen next.

Both the *mahjo* and the military leaders, refusing peace, catapulted the war into something irreversible, a war so devastating that they wiped out each other and plunged the world back into darkness.

This particular patch of land remained the most prominent relic of the Mahjo War, renamed Rebirth by those who survived. It bore the deepest scars, gouged into the earth by powers beyond the imagining of anyone still alive. Nothing had grown here since.

"Looks inviting," Avan noted.

I adjusted my bag against my back and jumped down into the Void. The dirt was so loose and dry that a black cloud rose around me. I coughed and waved it away. "Like a bed of hot coals. But DJ said we'd find the Rider in the Void, so there has to be something out here."

"Hopefully nothing gargoyle-like," Avan said as he hopped down beside me and kicked up another black cloud.

"Don't worry." I grinned. "I'll protect you."

Avan smirked and started walking.

CHAPTER 13

I WASN'T SURE HOW MUCH TIME HAD PASSED BEFORE WE found the husk of a tree stump to rest against. Our feet had begun to drag, and I could tell Avan was exhausted even if he refused to say it. He still hadn't slept, but I didn't want to keep insulting him by asking if he needed to stop, so I asked for a break instead.

I ached all over. My left wrist had swollen to double its size. My ribs hurt when I breathed too deeply, and my face—already sore from my run-in with Joss's fist—throbbed again. I lowered myself gingerly to the ground, biting my lip to contain a groan. I didn't want to conduct a thorough survey of my injuries and alarm Avan. Still, I felt so bruised that I never wanted to move again.

We sat with our backs against the stump. The bark was sturdy despite its decay. I rummaged through my pack and found half a sandwich wrapped in wrinkled paper.

I fished it out and smoothed the paper. The message *"Eat only with a smile"* in Reev's handwriting greeted me.

Tears swelled in my eyes and choked my throat. I shoved the wrapper into the bag before Avan noticed.

What if Reev was dead? What if the Rider had turned him into a hollow? What if we didn't find him at all? What would happen when we ran out of water? There was no going back. We didn't have the Gray, and there was no crossing the Outlands on foot. I gave in to the fear for only a heartbeat. Then I swept it aside and firmly buried the doubts.

I'll find Reev. I nodded to myself, letting the simple motion strengthen me.

For a while, I nibbled on the sandwich as Avan ate an apple. The silence grew heavy, as oppressive as the heat in the forest. I wanted trees again. Why couldn't the Rider have hidden in the forest? It provided perfect cover. Why would he be out here in this emptiness?

Maybe that was why he called himself the Black Rider. Because he was coated in all this dust.

I would have chosen the humidity over this baked dryness. My lungs felt raw.

"I think we're lost," Avan said.

He didn't seem bothered by our circumstances. In fact, nothing had fazed him so far. I wasn't sure whether to be calmed or troubled by this.

"That's the idea," I said.

Avan paused in his chewing and looked over at me. A fine layer of dust had settled over his clothes and streaked his skin. It was kind of flattering, actually, like another tattoo.

"DJ said we had to get lost," I explained.

Avan dipped his chin and surveyed the drab landscape. "That doesn't make any sense."

I shrugged and, after a pause, put into words what each of us had avoided: "Neither does my ability to mess with time."

He shot me an inscrutable look. "Fair enough."

When he didn't say anything else, I sucked in my cheeks and picked at the bread of my sandwich. So he *had* seen. Why was he so casual about it? Not that I wanted him to freak out, but he didn't even seem surprised.

We finished our food and continued on. I didn't like being out in the open, and I seriously wished we still had the Gray. Who knew how long we'd be out here, completely vulnerable to whatever creatures might haunt the Void?

Daylight faded a couple of hours later, the sunset allowing us to determine which direction we were heading: northeast. The air grew chilly. With the summer heat in Ninurta, I hadn't thought to bring anything thicker to wear. By the time daylight dwindled to a faint glow in the west, I was shivering.

We had to find shelter. I was willing to bet the darkness in the Outlands, however bleak, would be nothing compared to a night in the Void. Already, nebulous shapes formed in the descending dark.

Some boulders were piled in a cluster about twenty feet ahead. I had no desire to sleep out in the open, so we headed for them.

I felt my way around the boulders, hoping to find any sort of opening. Once I found one, I sighed with relief. There was hardly enough space for me to wedge through, but I managed it, wincing as rough stone scraped my bruises. The space inside the rock cluster would be a narrow fit for both of us, but I wasn't about to let Avan sleep out there by himself.

I couldn't see him, but I heard him curse as he maneuvered himself in. I marveled that he fit at all.

"Here," he said from my left. I could hear and feel him getting situated in the cramped space. He took my bag, then his hand groped for mine.

Dirt made his fingers gritty, but I grasped them tightly. This was familiar.

For the second time in my life, I was crouched in the darkness with Avan, completely blind and grateful that he was with me. The first had been years ago when I'd gotten myself trapped in the sewer.

"Lay on your side," he said, helping me down.

I did, blushing fiercely as he molded to my back. My head touched fabric; he'd arranged our bags as pillows. His shoulders curved around me, legs cradling mine as his arm draped over my waist. I felt light-headed and a little flushed, my skin tingling everywhere we touched. I didn't even mind the hard ground. Or that we were both dirty and sweaty and covered in bruises.

"Sorry," he whispered, a low rumble in my ear. "This is kind of weird, isn't it?"

He started to get up, and I reached out. My hand landed on his hip, and I gripped it. There was no room for being embarrassed.

"It's okay," I whispered. After an awkward beat, I added, "Don't want you getting carted off by gargoyles."

He hesitated but eventually gave in. I guided his arm around me, the sound of my pulse in my ears. His body heat chased away the chill. I even dared to scoot back, eliminating any space left between us, and heard his sharp intake of breath. I closed my eyes.

The tight space was different from that night in the sewer. Then, there had been a metal gate between us. I had been thirteen and trying to find the latest underground club. Reev had forbidden me from going to them, insisting they bred "illicit and immoral" behavior, but I'd wanted to judge for myself. Reev probably had a twisted idea of what was "illicit" considering where he worked. And anyway, all the other kids went, so why couldn't I?

Some girls at school had given me directions and said the derelict building near the old town square was the entrance. Inside, I would find an open gate that led down some stone stairs into the sewage tunnel, and from there, all I had to do was follow the sounds. Well, I'd found the gate and the stairs all right. But the moment the gate shut behind me, the click of the lock echoed down the tunnel.

Everyone knew that the sewers were off-limits, but the girls had sworn this tunnel was open—how else would all those people get to the clubs? It had made sense. But they must have played me, because the lock was clearly still working, and I could hear nothing but my own quick breaths in the dark silence.

The only light came from a lamppost outside a tiny window. The light was too dim, though, and didn't reach very far into the building. I couldn't even see my fingers when I'd held them up in front of me. Fortunately, I had been more angry than scared. I'd squished myself against the topmost step, the stone wall against my back and the metal bars of the gate cold against my side.

Then as the minutes ticked by, my anger had melted into the darkness, replaced by a slowly building fear: What if the girls hadn't alerted the Watchmen? Nobody used this building anymore; how long would I be trapped here? What if no one found me?

I was vibrating with panic by the time the door to the building swung open. I'd expected Watchmen. Instead, Avan's voice called out:

"Kai?"

I had been so stunned I hadn't even answered. Avan hadn't spoken to me for three weeks, not since I'd kicked his dad. My fingers clutched the bars and the metal squeaked.

"Kai, that you?" He'd walked over. I could see only his silhouette, highlighted in pale gray by the open door behind him.

"Y-yeah." I'd pushed to my feet. "What are you doing here?"

"I overheard some of the girls. They said they sent you here instead of to the real location." He'd approached the gate and peered through at me. "You do realize even though we call them underground clubs, they're not *actually* underground?"

Well, I knew that *now*.

I had backed down a few steps into pitch-blackness, all my panic reverting to anger that made my heart pound. "Did you come here to make fun of me?"

He'd snorted. "Don't be dumb. I came to see if they were serious. You want me to get Reev?"

"No!" My shout had echoed in the empty space, and I lowered my voice. "No. He'll . . ." He'd be so angry and disappointed with me. I couldn't let him know. "Please don't tell him."

"Well, the Watchmen should be here soon to let you out. I alerted a runner." He turned, and I swallowed the urge to ask him to stay.

But instead of leaving, he had dropped his back against the bars and slid down, shifting against the floor to find a comfortable position.

"What are you doing?" I'd asked.

"I'm not going to leave you here by yourself in the dark. And I have to make sure someone gets you out, don't I?"

I hadn't known what to say, so I lowered myself down on the top step and leaned my head against the nearest bar. From this angle, I could see Avan's profile.

"Thanks," I whispered.

I thought I saw his mouth curve, but it had been hard to tell in the dark. His arm moved. When warm fingers reached through the bars, I hesitated only a moment before gripping his hand.

Even though we sat on opposite sides of the gate, with nothing but a yawning blackness behind me, I had known it would be okay. Avan would make sure of it.

The Watchmen arrived an hour later to let me out. I had put on such a convincing display of tears and remorse that they let us go with no tax out of sheer pity. Afterward, Avan and I had gone back to his shop where we hung around and snacked on dry fruit for another hour, talking about nothing I could recall now; all I remembered was the expressive and fluid way his hands moved when he spoke. I returned to the Labyrinth shortly before Reev's shift ended, and neither Avan nor I had spoken of that night since.

But I had never forgotten. In the same way that I knew Avan

would see me through the night, that was the moment I realized Avan and I would be okay—that our friendship, which had been in serious doubt for weeks, would be okay. It didn't matter how he spent his nights or that we rarely saw each other outside of school or my visits to his shop; he would still be there for me when I needed him.

Coming with me on this journey, however, wasn't something I'd expected. This was going too far. I never would have asked this of him.

But that's what was so great about Avan. I never had to ask.

The dusty fabric of my bag chafed my cheek, and I tucked my face against my shoulder. His arm tightened around me. I wished I knew what he was thinking.

As if he'd heard my thoughts, he whispered, "I was wondering . . ."

My eyes opened, even though I couldn't see anything. "What?"

His breath was a warm spot against my hair. "How did you and Reev meet?"

Avan knew about my missing memories, but I'd never told him that Reev and I weren't real siblings. It was obvious just by looking at us, though.

"By the river. Reev said I was unconscious. He picked me up, took care of me, and then decided he couldn't just drop me off on the street afterward. The earliest thing I can remember about Reev is his eyes. They were the first things I saw when I woke up." Considering I couldn't remember anything about where I'd been or who I was, they'd left an impression. "I had an ID with me, and when he checked it at the registry, we found out I had no living relatives to claim me. So he kept me."

"I've always admired the way you two look out for each other," Avan said.

"Even though he's not my real brother, we're still family."

"Yeah," he murmured. "Family should protect each other."

I bit my lip. "Avan, you're—"

"You don't remember your parents?" he asked, cutting me off. It was just as well. I didn't know where the words had come from. Or how he would have reacted to them.

You're my family, too.

"If I answer, do I get to ask about yours?"

His silence stretched for long enough that I figured he had no intention of responding. But finally, he said, "Someday."

His voice was quiet but not cold.

"Then ask me again someday," I said.

He gave an exaggerated sigh that made me smile.

A few beats later, he said, "I have a confession."

I grew tense, only for a moment, but the way his thumb swept soothingly against my cheek meant he'd felt it. With my stomach fluttering, I waited for him to go on.

"About six years ago, you came into the shop to buy lunch for Reev. I recognized you from school, but we didn't really talk then. Anyway, you were going around a corner, and your elbow knocked something over. I can't remember what it was. But you did it then—the thing with time."

I guess this explained why he hadn't been shocked by what he'd seen lately.

"I thought I was going crazy," Avan said. "I tried to move, to ask you what was happening, but I couldn't open my mouth. I didn't even know it was you doing it until I saw your face. You were completely focused on reaching for whatever you'd knocked over. And then everything sort of rushed forward, and you caught the thing before it hit the floor. You looked so relieved."

All this time I had assumed, because no one besides Reev ever reacted to my manipulations, that people couldn't sense them. They carried on as if nothing had happened. Of course, I didn't make a habit of doing it in crowded areas, but who else might have been aware? Who else hadn't I noticed *noticing* me?

He seemed to be waiting for me to say something, so I licked my lips and said, "Then you already knew."

I didn't know how some people could sense it, but I realized it didn't bother me that Avan was one of them. It made me feel less crazy. Less alone.

And I couldn't deny that I liked the idea that Avan had noticed me long before he ever gave me those apples.

"I should have mentioned it sooner," he said.

I tried to shrug, but it was difficult in our current positions. "Doesn't matter now. But it would have been good to know a few years ago."

"I waited for you to tell me."

He would've had to wait a long time. He probably knew that, though.

"Is it magic?" He sounded awed by the possibility.

"I don't know."

"Before Rebirth, there were plenty of *mahjo*. What if the Kahl isn't the last one?"

"I don't know," I repeated, quieter. I doubted there was anything he could ask that I hadn't already wondered myself. "I can't exactly send the Kahl a note saying, 'Hi, I think I have magic, too, and I'm dying to talk to someone about it. Let's have lunch.'"

He laughed, the slight motions pressing his body more firmly into mine. "So what do we do when we find the Black Rider?"

I appreciated that he said "when." "We save my brother."

"Good intentions aren't going to get us very far. We need a plan."

The problem was that we didn't know anything about the Black Rider: who he was, what he might do, how he might attack us. I couldn't risk Avan getting hurt or killed trying to protect me.

I slid my fingers into my bag and felt the handle of the knife that the prostitute had given me. I wished I'd gotten her name, but I hadn't thought to ask. I'd been so worried about what might have happened to Reev.

"The knife," I said. "There's something about it. It scared off those gargoyles."

"You can't fight the Rider's army with one knife," Avan said, his usual wry undertone entering his voice again.

I traced my fingers down Avan's forearm and wrist until I found the bumps of his knuckles. I could tell he was holding his breath. I pretended not to notice when I felt the light pressure of his lips against my hair. I imagined turning in his arms and meeting his mouth with mine.

I tried to will away the sensations spreading through me, the warmth and the ache that made it hard to think clearly.

"I'll figure something out," I whispered. Actually, I did have a plan, but I didn't want to tell him yet. I was pretty sure he wouldn't like it.

I had a gift. I had no idea why or how, but my abilities could be useful to the Rider. Hopefully, the Rider would be open to a trade.

CHAPTER 14

"KAI."

Avan's voice cut through my drowsiness. Fingers skimmed my cheekbone. I leaned into his touch.

"Kai, wake up."

Something in the way he said my name made my eyes open. Light streamed in through the cracks of our small shelter, muted like twilight or early dawn.

"You need to see this," Avan said, before maneuvering his way out into the open.

I rolled onto my back and immediately wished I hadn't. Every muscle in my body screamed.

"Drek." I pushed myself up. Once outside, I could see why it was so hazy. Fog had rolled in overnight, making the Void appear even more ominous and surreal. I couldn't see ten feet in front of me.

Goosebumps spread down my arms. Fog, especially this dense, required moisture. The Void was nothing but dry earth.

"Look," Avan said.

I followed his line of sight. Then I blinked a few times to make sure I was seeing this.

A bridge loomed ahead, a stone arch that rose out of the scorched earth and disappeared into the fog. The bridge spanned at least thirty feet in width, aged to the point of decay.

"Was that there last night?" I asked, even though I already knew the answer.

"I don't think so," he said grimly. I wished he'd pretend it was no big deal, like everything else we'd run into since leaving Ninurta.

I wrung the strap of my bag. Questions collided in my mind: *What if it's a trap? But how can we not take the bridge? It's practically an invitation.* "Well, we won't have to keep walking through all this dust."

"We'll have to thank him for being prompt," Avan added. "It's too bad we forgot a gift for the host."

"I'll improvise," I said, thinking about the knife.

Now that the path forward had literally been presented to me, I didn't know if I was prepared for it. My clammy palms suggested I wasn't. I had been so focused on just getting through the Outlands and then the forest and the Void that, aside from bartering with the Rider, I hadn't thought about what else I'd do when we found him. Or if I'd even get the chance to offer the trade.

Still, at the end of that bridge was Reev. That was all the reason I needed to move forward.

We approached warily. The bridge appeared solid enough. I had been half expecting it to vanish like a mirage.

I paused at the first step from black dirt to dusty stone, but Avan didn't hesitate. I followed, stepping carefully.

Holes blistered the stone, and whole sections had crumbled at the outer boundaries. We stuck to the middle where it seemed sturdiest, despite the fissures throughout. Tall unlit lampposts, more rust than metal, braced each side in intervals. We couldn't see where the bridge ended. I began to wish I'd had breakfast first.

Movement above made me look up. We hadn't seen birds, or any signs of life, since the forest. It was easy to lose all sense of direction in this fog. Maybe some pigeons had gotten caught in it. I scanned the edge of the bridge, following the vertical line of the nearest lamppost.

It wasn't a pigeon.

Atop the lamppost, where it bent over the bridge to form an inverted L, crouched a gargoyle. Its long body huddled above the busted lantern, wrapped in smoky threads. It watched us with wide, flat eyes, claws clacking against the flaking rust, tail twined around the post. Frills extended from the sides of its head, quivering as if caught in an invisible wind.

Avan reached for my hand, and I squeezed his tightly.

Something else moved on our left. My gaze darted that way. A second gargoyle sat atop another lamppost, its tail flicking behind it.

"The knife," Avan whispered.

I reached for it, afraid to make any sudden movements but just as afraid the creatures would pounce before I could grab it. We made our way slowly down the bridge, feet shuffling against dust and loose stones. The urge to turn and run seized me, but I forced my legs to cooperate. My quick breaths sounded deafening in the silence. Now I saw that one of the creatures occupied nearly every lamppost along the bridge. The gargoyles balanced at the tops, some straight and alert and others reclining on folded legs. All of them watched us.

It's true, I thought, horrified. The Rider did tame gargoyles. What if the rest of the rumors were true as well? What if he did feed them . . .

I had the hilt of the knife in my hand when a voice rang out: "You won't need that."

I jumped, yanking the knife from my bag. Avan stepped in front of me, blocking my view. I scowled and elbowed him aside.

A figure emerged from the fog—a boy, wiry and a bit disheveled and probably no older than Avan. He waved affably.

I looked between the boy and the gargoyles, my body still strung tight. I didn't lower the knife.

"The gargoyles are trained to identify Ninu's sentinels," the boy said, gesturing to the creatures guarding the bridge. "Which you're obviously not."

I looked at Avan, who lifted his pierced eyebrow as if to say "Your call."

Still hyperaware of the gargoyles watching us, I said, "We're looking for the Black Rider."

"I figured," the boy said. His eyes were bright blue in the muted light. "Why else would you be here?"

Then he turned and strolled back up the bridge. He didn't even check to see if we would follow. I lowered the knife to my side, shifting my weight from foot to foot as I watched his outline grow faint in the enveloping fog. Following him would be crazy.

"Kai?" Avan said. I realized that I still held his hand tightly in mine. He pulled me forward.

I nodded, and we hurried after the boy.

The fog was so thick that the fortress seemed to float in the clouds. It looked as if it had been carved from a cliff, jagged and impossibly high, with only a few windows far at the top. More gargoyles prowled along the battlements, pacing back and forth like the Watchmen along Ninurta's walls. Others were stationed on jutting perches, as perfectly still and menacing as their namesakes.

Amazingly, people patrolled the high ledges as well. Their figures looked small and indistinct as they stood guard alongside the creatures.

Avan gave my hand a reassuring squeeze, and I relaxed my white-knuckled grip on the knife. I didn't know if it was fear or anticipation that had my heart pounding in my ears.

A silver door swung open as the three of us approached, the dragging sound of metal on dirt climbing up the fortress wall. Once we'd stepped off the bridge, the ground was black, which meant we were still in the Void. I didn't know how the Rider was hiding this place, but I doubted we would've made it here if he hadn't shown us the way.

Inside the door, lanterns hung from the rafters on chains, lighting a cavernous hall, empty save for some broken benches pushed against the walls. A few of the lights quivered weakly. Our shuffling footsteps echoed around us.

The stone beneath my feet vibrated as the door swung shut behind us. I kept walking. I had to stay focused.

"I would introduce myself," the boy said, "but I haven't decided on a name yet. I was called G-10. Might as well go with that for now."

G-10. Not even a name. Was he a hollow, then? But he looked so normal.

My eyes scanned the shadowy corners of the hall. I saw only layers of dust and cobwebs. I kept expecting an ambush. I was glad it hadn't happened yet, but this strange welcome worried me.

I looked at Avan, but as usual, his face gave nothing away.

We passed through the hall into a corridor with a low ceiling and a sallow rug stretched over the floor. The corridor forked up ahead. The boy turned left, but I looked right.

I dropped Avan's hand, inching forward to see more. A glass door opened into a courtyard. The air here was bright and clear. It smelled different: warm and sweet instead of the cool dryness of the Void. The clouds hung overhead, bloated and yellow with no sign of the fog that cloaked the fortress and the bridge. Bushes weighted with flowers lined the swept path, and a single tree rose on a grassy patch at its center, its branches providing shade to a wrought-iron table and matching chairs.

My eyes fell on the blade of my knife, still clutched in my fist. What was I doing ogling a courtyard in my enemy's house?

Behind me, G-10 and Avan waited. G-10 smiled. I didn't see any malice in his eyes, but it had to be there. When he turned to continue on, the breeze from the open door shifted the high collar of his tunic and revealed a red tattoo at the base of his neck.

CHAPTER 15

I JOLTED FORWARD, MY HAND CLOSING ON THE BOY'S SHOULDER.

"That—on your neck," I stuttered, and then let go. I hadn't meant to touch him, but it looked so much like Reev's.

G-10's fingers brushed over the bright scar tissue edging the tattoo. He smiled, and this time, it didn't quite reach his eyes.

"My collar," he said. "Broke the leash, though."

"What does that mean?" I asked.

Instead of answering, he gestured to a door I hadn't noticed. The wood bore scars and scrapes and looked ready to fall off the hinges.

"The Rider is inside," he said.

I couldn't swallow. I kept seeing the gargoyles lined up on top of those lampposts. Wild animals transformed into perfectly controlled guards.

G-10 knocked briskly on the door—which didn't cave in— and pushed it open. He stepped aside to let us enter.

The study had peeling blue walls, brightly lit by an assortment of mismatched lanterns, and an oversize desk. In the middle of the room, a man stood bent over a round table, building an elaborate series of towers out of beige blocks. He murmured something and then snatched up one of the blocks and bit into it. It made a chewy sound.

Was this the Rider? I slid my hand behind my back to hide the knife.

The door shut behind us, with G-10 on the other side. The Rider straightened, half-eaten block in one hand. His other hand tugged at a strand of hair that stuck out from his head. He was tall, even hovering over Avan. And he was startlingly thin, his gaunt face topped with black hair that was peppered in gray. His eyes, deep set and shadowy against his light-brown skin, regarded us with mild curiosity.

Why would G-10 leave us alone, armed, with the Rider?

"Bread bite?" the man asked, holding up his bitten block. His voice was deep and resonant, and I felt it vibrate through the small room as if we stood in a much larger space. If emptiness had a voice, this was it.

G-10 had left us with the Rider because he didn't believe we were a real threat. Not to this strange-looking man who could steal people from behind Ninurta's walls and unsettle me with a couple of words.

I stared at the Rider's offering and didn't answer. He shrugged and shoved the rest of it—the bread bite—into his mouth.

"Mmm. Brilliant with honey," he said, indicating the amber moat surrounding his bread towers. At the forefront of the display was a pile of bread bites artfully arranged into what looked like a miniature horse and rider.

He moved over to a set of purple drapes hanging from floor to ceiling. He had to elbow aside standing lamps to get through. They wobbled on their uneven bases, the flames inside wavering, but didn't tip. He parted the curtains to display a pair of glass doors. Natural light joined the array of lanterns in the room. Beyond the glass doors, the view presented another angle of the courtyard.

He gestured to two chairs beside the doors. The upholstered seats were torn, and stuffing spilled out the sides.

"Welcome to Etu Gahl," he said. His voice made me feel empty, too. Adrift. Hopeless. "Please sit."

I didn't move. I didn't want to sit or eat or make small talk with him. Avan remained standing as well. The Rider didn't appear bothered by our refusal.

"My name, as it is now, is Irra," he said, and swept us a liquid bow. He wore a tattered suit, the tails of his untucked shirt fluttering around him.

As it is? I didn't know what to expect when we found the Rider, but this wasn't it. The friendly guard, the quiet threat cloaked in hospitality, the man's frazzled appearance—if this was a trick to throw us off, then it was working.

But I wasn't interested in whatever game the Rider was playing. "Where's my brother?"

Irra's lips curved into a smile. His eyes, golden brown and an odd match to his gaunt face, wrinkled at the corners. He bent over his table and began building a tower of bread bites again.

"And what brother might that be?" he asked, his voice like the wind sighing across the Void.

"Reev," I said, shivering. The weirdness of this place was getting to me. "You kidnapped him a few days ago."

"Did I?" His eyes cut to me, and I realized my initial thought had been right: Even armed, we weren't a threat to him. The moment we stepped onto his bridge, it had been the other way around.

I resisted the urge to step back and put the knife between us.

"You've been misled," he said.

A weight lodged in my stomach.

"Are you saying he's not here?" Avan asked.

Hearing the question made that weight grow unbearably heavy.

"That's correct. I like to stay on top of our new arrivals, and there have been none since G-10 five months ago."

That couldn't be true. "What did you do with my brother?" I demanded. If the Rider could turn gargoyles into guards, who knew what he could do to people?

"I assure you that your brother, whoever the unfortunate fellow might be, holds no interest for me."

"But what about the hollows?" I asked. "What about your war with Kahl Ninu?"

"DJ said you were kidnapping Ninurtans," Avan said.

Irra looked unimpressed, his eyebrows raised over hooded eyes. "DJ is not the most reliable of sources."

"You're lying," I said. He had to be. Because if he wasn't, then—I breathed in through gritted teeth. If he wasn't lying, everything we'd done to get here had been a waste. Leaving Ninurta, accepting the reality that we might never go home again, crashing into the forest, and nearly getting killed by gargoyles—this entire journey would have been for nothing.

Had I exiled myself and Avan to chase a lie? If Reev wasn't here, then what the hell was I supposed to do now?

Something nudged my hand. Avan pried the knife from my fingers. They'd been clenched around the hilt for so long that it hurt to move them. I covered my face, which felt hot against my cold hands.

"Not at this moment, no," Irra said. "Lying has always been a distinctly *human* trait."

Whatever that meant. All that mattered was whether he was telling the truth about Reev.

"If you're not kidnapping them, then who is?"

Irra pinched one bread bite between his thumb and forefinger. Then he popped it into his mouth. He straightened and approached us, his presence overwhelming as he drew closer. I had to crane my neck to see his face.

"Do you know why the Tournament is kept a private Academy event?" he asked.

"What does that have to do with anything?" My neck hurt, but I didn't look away. I wasn't ready to give up. I would never be ready to give up on Reev.

His smile was much too wide. "Everything."

"Almost everything inside the Academy is kept private," I said impatiently. "Cadets aren't even allowed to leave the campus until they've completed their two years."

"True," Irra said. "But the secrecy, particularly surrounding the Tournament, is because Ninu wouldn't want you noticing any familiar faces."

He couldn't mean—

"Ninu is taking them to play in the Tournament?" Avan said.

"But . . . ," I began. The Tournament was the final challenge that Watchmen Academy cadets had to face. It was their last chance to improve their ranking and placement after graduation. Ninu selected his sentinels from the cadets who won the Tournament. I'd read about it in school. Every year, a bunch of high school graduates left the district to join the Academy. I didn't know any of them personally, but once they left, the chances of seeing them again were slim. The Watchmen were rarely assigned to their home neighborhoods.

"Are you saying Ninu kidnaps his own citizens and puts them in the Academy? Or right into the Tournament?" I asked. "Why would he need to do that? It's not like they're short on cadets."

"The answer to that is a bit complicated," said Irra.

"Well, we've come all this way, so I think we can spare the time."

Irra scratched his cheek, looking thoughtful. Then he pushed past us and threw open the wooden door. "I'd like to show you something."

He disappeared down the hall. After a quick look at Avan, I hurried after him.

Irra led us down hallways that could have been pulled from

the Labyrinth, except the smell was musty instead of damp. Stained walls had progressed well beyond peeling, the puckered seams so brittle that they looked about to disintegrate at the slightest touch. The floor creaked and convulsed underneath us. We encountered a couple of girls in the halls. They both wore the same belted, faded-blue tunics with fitted pants, although one of them had altered her tunic by cutting the baggy hem and tying it tight above her hips so that the material hugged her curves. If these people were the Black Rider's hollows, then DJ was seriously misinformed.

The girls nodded politely to Irra and then to us. When I glanced back, the same red tattoos were visible at the bases of their necks, beneath their matching ponytails.

Irra came to an abrupt halt at the top of a staircase. I skidded on my toes to keep from running into him. Avan steadied me with a hand on my lower back.

It felt different here. That empty feeling returned, stronger, pushing beneath my ribs: gnawing, cramping, ravenous. It dipped cold fingers into my chest.

"You feel that, right?" Avan murmured. I nodded and leaned into his hand, focusing on the warmth of his palm and letting it soak into my skin.

"This is where the walls of Etu Gahl end. For now. It does change." Irra lifted his hand to indicate we should stay where we were.

We watched from the landing as Irra moved ahead and stood in the middle of a hallway that led to a dead end. I didn't know what we were waiting for until I looked at his feet. The floor changed beneath him. No, not changed—*aged*.

I looked around. It wasn't just the floor but the whole hallway. The walls turned from white to yellow to brown; paint bubbled and peeled; mold spread in a dark stain along the crease where the walls met the ceiling and then streaked down to the floor; an entire section of the wall sagged into the beams. In this narrow hallway, time had spilled forward at an unbelievable speed, nothing like what I could do.

But the threads remained undisturbed. Whatever he was doing, it was outside of time. Which didn't make any sense, but my thoughts were too jumbled to work out what I was seeing.

New objects winked into being as well: end tables covered in lace and then linen and then plaid, set with silver saucers that gradually darkened to brittle brass. Paintings and photographs fastened themselves to the walls, the images fading in and out with new faces until the glass shattered and the wooden frames dwindled to dust. Past the hall where Irra stood, the dead end had given way, and a completely new room had sprung from nowhere.

"The living go to my sister when they pass," he said. "But Etu Gahl is where ideas and objects come to die. My house is a place of forgotten things."

Irra glanced back, and I felt his stare inside me, like something alive.

"What are you?" I asked.

"The hunger that cramps your stomach. The decay that shrivels your crops." He dragged his fingers along the wall. It blistered and rotted beneath his touch. "The shadows that carve into your cheeks."

He folded his elegant, slender hands at his waist. His golden-brown eyes were soft and warm and terrifying.

"I have been known as Famine. But call me Irra."

CHAPTER 16

MY JAW SNAPPED SHUT. MAGIC WAS THE ONLY EXPLANATION for why he could do such extraordinary and inexplicable things. Like me.

But I had a feeling he *wasn't* like me. Or rather, I wasn't like *him*. This was way beyond my own abilities. Was this what a real *mahjo* could do?

"Wait," I said, stepping back and forgetting that I was standing at the top of a staircase. Fortunately, Avan's hand kept me from tumbling backward.

Irra chuckled. "Is it so hard to believe?"

After what I'd just seen him do? No. And *yes*. Because as much as magic remained a vital element in Ninurta, as much as I was reminded of it every time I watched a Gray in motion, I had never seen magic do *this*.

Suddenly, I could understand how powerful the *mahjo* must have been before Rebirth.

"How did you do that?" I gestured to the hallway still shifting around him, although the speed had slowed. "You just . . . How?"

I knew it was a difficult question to answer, but I still wanted to know. Even though, if someone asked me how I could sense the threads, I would say, "Beats me."

"I am Infinite," he said, as if that explained everything instead of confusing me more.

I shook my head. "What is that, like . . . immortal?"

"Generally, yes."

What the drek was that supposed to mean? "You can't really think you're immortal?"

"Among other things," Irra said breezily. "But no matter. Most of my hollows aren't sure what to believe, either. I suspect a few of them still think I'm simply a demented *mahjo* and that Etu Gahl is a lunatic's magic gone wild." He didn't seem bothered by that fact. If anything, he sounded amused.

"*Are* you *mahjo?*" Avan asked.

"No," he said. "But we are connected."

Seeing what he could do, I was tempted to believe him. But immortality seemed like something much bigger than wielding magic.

Avan's fingers flexed against my back. "What are you doing here," he asked, "hiding in the Void with a bunch of hollows?"

"*They're* human, right?" I added. I remembered G-10's smile, the girls we'd passed in the hallway, and the tattoos on their necks.

"For the most part," Irra said. "And I'm here because my brother—Ninurta, your Kahl Ninu—built his city to spite the laws of our kind."

The floorboards groaned beneath Irra's weight as he joined us on the landing again. Behind him, the hallway and the room had stopped changing, and settled into the same state of general disrepair as the rest of the fortress.

"The laws," Irra continued, "that forbid direct interference with humans."

"Kahl Ninurta the First?" Every Kahl took on the name of Ninu, and the current one had ruled since before I was born.

"There has only ever been one Kahl."

How was that possible? I didn't know what any of the Kahls looked like, but I'd been taught that each Kahl ruled for his lifetime, schooling his heir in relative seclusion until it was time to pass on leadership. Wouldn't *someone* have noticed if he was immortal?

"The Infinite are constant in number," Irra said as we followed him back the way we had come. All the turns and passageways made the route difficult to memorize. "We lost one some time ago—Conquest, as we knew him—and Ninu was chosen to succeed him. He is the youngest of us. When a child is given restrictions, he grows rebellious."

"Ninu created Ninurta because he was having a tantrum?" I said. "That's ridiculous."

Irra gave a delicate shrug. I suspected there was more to it—a lot more—but he wasn't sharing the information.

"Absurd or not, Ninu has fashioned himself into a leader of men. As to his sentinels, they are *mahjo,* the result of our dalliances with humans."

"Ninu isn't the last *mahjo*?" Avan asked.

"Ninu is not *mahjo* at all," Irra said. He turned a corner, and I hurried to keep pace with his much longer legs. "The *mahjo* are mortal descendants of the Infinite. Once, they carried our magic in their blood. But their petty war changed that."

"That 'petty' war decimated the world," I said.

Irra waved a dismissive hand. "And for what reason? To prove which side was the superior force? It was a conflict born of little more than pride and conceit. The Infinite decided it would be too dangerous to allow the *mahjo* to retain their powers. However, by stripping them of magic, their blood became poison to their Infinite parent. It was, I believe, nature's way of maintaining balance."

"So when Ninu discovers any descendants . . . ," Avan began.

"He snatches them up and transforms them into his toy soldiers, both to protect himself and as weapons against the rest of us. I've managed to recruit my own, mostly by stealing them from him, but I make do with my resources."

"Ninu has Reev?" I asked.

"Is that all you've taken from this conversation?"

I flushed, first out of embarrassment and then frustration. To think that Reev had never left Ninurta at all . . .

"Why would Reev's boss believe he sold him to you?" Avan asked.

"Ninu does have to keep up my reputation if he doesn't want an uprising on his hands."

We reached the hall where Irra's study was located, but he led us past it. I slowed outside the door to the courtyard again, lulled by flowers as big as my hand and the scent of grass—*real* grass, not the dry, straw-like weeds in Ninurta.

"There will be time later to explore," Irra said.

I looked away, annoyed with myself, and spotted the knife in Avan's hand. I had completely forgotten about it. He gave it back to me, and I stuffed it into my bag.

"Come," Irra said, "you must be hungry." He grinned, a dark, almost derisive gleam in his eyes. "Fed by Famine. What has the world come to?"

The mess hall was full. It was probably about lunchtime now, and there had to be at least fifty people gathered around the wooden tables and benches. They talked loudly, laughing and leaning into one another as if they were all old friends. Several of them waved when Irra dropped us off at the entrance.

In the food line, Avan and I received trays, and an enthusiastic chef allowed us to pick what we wanted to eat. I stared at the display of food. My stomach grumbled loudly, but I was completely at a loss. Our meals at school were picked for us and usually consisted of a clump of mashed potatoes, watery pea soup, overcooked carrots, and sometimes milk, if we were lucky. The vegetables tended to taste a little sour, but I was happy to eat. Food was food.

"Tell you what," the chef said, brandishing his spatula. He wore a blinding-pink apron, and his wavy brown hair was covered with a matching hairnet. He was almost as riveting as the mounds of food. "I'll let you sample everything, and you can decide what you like best."

Despite my objections, he piled my tray with enough food to feed a whole level in the Labyrinth. And then he did the same for Avan. I tried not to gape.

The chef winked at me and said, "Come back for seconds."

"So wasteful," I muttered as we searched for an open table.

I kept one eye on Avan and the other on my tray. The bread roll actually steamed—it was *fresh*. The beans were covered in a brown sauce that didn't look like mud. I'd never seen carrots that were so orange, and the corn glistened with what could have been real butter. I had tried butter once when a friend brought it to school, but it had been rancid.

How could the Rider afford these quantities of food? Where did it come from? I sniffed at my tray. Everything smelled delicious. My stomach growled again.

"Then we better eat up," Avan said.

We sat near the wall, and I hunched over my tray. Everyone around us was dressed in similar tunics. But like the girl from the hallway, many of them had altered the clothes to suit them. They also had no reservations about staring. I felt distinctly out of place.

"What do you think of Irra?" Avan asked, seemingly oblivious to the dozens of eyes on us. "Crazy or immortal?"

"Maybe both."

"You believe him?"

"I don't know yet."

If Ninu wasn't *mahjo* . . . If he and Irra really were immortal . . . then what did that make me?

The mess hall, like the courtyard, was spared the decay of

the rest of the fortress. Someone had swept the stone floors and dressed the walls with colorful drapes. Sweet and savory aromas and the heat from the kitchen wafted throughout. It felt comforting. Safe. Like Reev.

My chest tightened. I focused on my laden tray instead.

I took my time eating, sipping my soup and trying bites of everything. I wanted to relish each new taste.

"You know," Avan said, picking at a bowl of bright fruit slices, "after my final exams last year, I got an invitation from the Academy."

I put down my spoon, my eyebrows rising. This was news to me. Sometimes, if students did exceptionally well on their final exams, the Academy scouted them for enrollment. If we had stayed in Ninurta, I would have taken my finals at the end of the coming school year.

"And?" I said.

He looked down. "I considered it. I mean, I heard even the lowest-ranking Watchmen make about thirty thousand credits a year. My dad could close his shop."

That was probably more than what his shop made in *two* years.

"Why did you turn it down?" I asked. It was a hell of a deal, but no amount of credits could have persuaded me to devote my life to serving the city. I would rather be poor and free, but that didn't mean Avan felt the same.

His lips quirked. "I couldn't stomach being one of them."

I grinned and began to reply, but was startled by a clatter to our left, followed by laughter.

Two tables away, a group of women were talking animatedly.

One of them had her hair up in a ponytail, exposing her scarred tattoo—her collar, as G-10 had called it. From what I could tell, Avan and I were the only people in the mess hall without collars.

No one here displayed the same guardedness about it as Reev and that sentinel outside the Labyrinth. I guess there was no shame in something everyone shared. After the talk with Irra, it was easy to figure out what the collars meant. And what that meant about Reev.

Why hadn't he told me he was a sentinel? I didn't even know how it could be possible, but there was no other answer.

A heavy body dropped into the space beside me. G-10 beamed as he placed his tray next to mine. His held a modest portion of soup.

I gave him a small smile in greeting. He brushed his sandy hair out of his eyes and then thrust out his hand. After a moment's hesitation, I took it.

"We should have proper introductions this time," he said. The smattering of freckles on the bridge of his nose made him look young. "I'm G-10. For now."

"Kai," I said. "This is Avan."

He shook hands with Avan as well and nodded to my tray. "Best thing about this place: the food. We've always got more than enough to eat."

Considering Irra's unlikely claim that he was the personification of Famine, the irony didn't escape me.

"It's different than what I'm used to," I said. I bit into a green vegetable that resembled a tiny cabbage. Sweet juice spilled over my lip, and I licked at it. I never knew a vegetable could taste like this. "Mmm. In a good way."

When G-10 didn't say anything else, I glanced up. He was looking at my mouth. Warmth crept into my cheeks even though I couldn't tell what he was thinking. He could've been thinking about what a slob I was. I wiped my mouth with the back of my hand, glancing quickly at Avan. He was watching us with an inscrutable expression.

G-10's eyes lifted to mine. He looked amused by my reaction. "Did the Rider fill you guys in?"

"Some of it," I said. Maybe G-10 could fill in the many blanks that Irra's explanation had left. "Were you a sentinel?"

G-10 made a broad gesture. "We all were. Irra saved us. Severed the leash." He touched his neck. "But he couldn't take off the collar. The magic is too complex. It'd kill us to remove it."

DJ's information had been considerably off, but I couldn't blame Irra for keeping him in the dark. DJ wouldn't hesitate to spill Irra's secrets for the right price. It still irked me that I'd given him most of our life savings.

"You're all descendants of people like Irra?" Avan asked. He leaned against my side to talk to G-10, his arm pressed against mine.

Even now, after all the time spent clinging to him on a Gray or sharing his body heat on the cold dirt, his touch sent ribbons of warmth spiraling through me. I fixed my attention on what G-10 was saying.

"They call themselves the Infinite," G-10 said. "And yeah.

Finding out I was *mahjo* was hard to believe, especially since I don't have any real magic. Still, being a descendant of immortals does give us some pretty convenient abilities. Rapid healing. Strength. Superior reflexes, that sort of thing. It's the reason Ninu can brand us with collars. Normal humans wouldn't survive it."

The description fit Reev well—my indestructible big brother. Not once in all the years I'd been with him had I seen him hurt or sick.

"What does it do?" I asked, gesturing to his neck.

"The collars are like magnifiers. They seek out whatever traces of magic remain inside us and enhance them so that we can work harder and tire less. After Ninu is done with us—" His gaze slid away. "Can't really say how much of what's left is human."

"Of course you're human," I said. Because Reev was human, too.

G-10 looked as if he wanted to smile, but he smothered it behind a spoonful of soup. After swallowing, he said, "The collars also connected us to Ninu. He sent us commands with a thought, and if we disobeyed an order, he could kill us immediately."

"Charming guy," Avan said.

"Disobedience was rare. Most sentinels exist only to obey Ninu," G-10 said bitterly.

"My brother, Reev, who we came here to find, has a collar like yours. He never told me what it meant," I said.

G-10 looked impressed. "I've never heard of anyone escaping Ninu before, not without the Rider's help."

Reev had possessed a collar for as long as I could remember, which meant he'd been a sentinel since before he'd found me. He must have been so young when Ninu found him the first time. Then, somehow, he had escaped the Kahl on his own.

"If he was already one of them, what'll they do to him now that they've caught him?" The possibilities made me ill. If I'd known that Reev was in hiding, I would have been more careful. I would have used my powers less. Why hadn't he trusted me?

"Since he's already escaped once, Ninu will probably brand him with a new collar, one that'll completely burn his mind." G-10 said it so matter-of-factly, as if his words hadn't just shattered me. "Your brother will no longer exist."

The flimsy wooden spoon snapped in my hand. I dropped the broken pieces. Avan grasped my hand before I could hide it in my lap. He rubbed his thumb against the stinging skin—another mark to add to my collection—and I closed my eyes, letting the motion soothe me.

"But how did they find him again?" Avan asked. "Reev was pretty well hidden in the Labyrinth."

"Ninu found most of us through blood donations," G-10 said.

I grew still. "What?"

He gave me a shrewd look. "Ninu's energy drives. I didn't find out until I came here. The blood is used to create energy stones, but Ninu also has it tested for traces of magic. We have just enough magic to identify us, nothing we'd notice on our own."

My head spun. "But Reev has never . . ."

The day I was attacked, Reev mentioned an energy drive. But he wouldn't have— He promised not to— I covered my face, my

breath coming fast and broken against my fingers. He *promised.*
Why would he do it after promis—

And then it hit me. He'd done it for the same reason I had
considered it: to pay the tax. The tax notice I couldn't find, because Reev had gotten it first.

I finished eating on autopilot. Avan noticed the shift in my mood,
but I brushed away his questions. Keeping my promise to the
prostitute, I asked G-10 if he knew anyone named Tera, but he
said he didn't. It made sense. If Reev wasn't here, then there was
little chance the other kidnapped people were—unless, like G-10,
they'd been rescued from Ninu's ranks.

After lunch, G-10 offered to give us a tour of the fortress.
The tour lasted hours because G-10 lost his bearings in the new
wings that were constantly popping up at the edges, like what
we'd seen earlier with Irra. Once G-10 found a familiar hallway
again, he scratched his head, embarrassed, and took us to the
dormitory floor above the mess hall.

He gave us neighboring rooms. Mine felt like a cave. The
walls were rough stone, and only a few tattered rugs covered the
floor. Against the wall were a narrow bed and a standing lamp. A
sliver of a window had been set too high up for anyone to look
through, but it brought in some natural light.

The room was half the size of my place in the Labyrinth, but
it felt far emptier.

I grabbed my bag and left. Avan opened his door after the first
knock.

"Can I stay with you?"

At first, he didn't react. Then his mouth curved into a slow smile that made my heart jump to attention.

"Not like that," I said. "I just . . . I . . ." I felt stupid admitting I didn't want to be alone.

Still looking amused, Avan swung the door wide. His room was identical to mine, including the narrow bed against the wall.

"I'll sleep on the floor," I said.

"You can have the bed." He pulled some clothes out of his pack and wadded them against his stomach. "I'm going to wash up."

I waited until he'd left before digging out my own clothes and heading for the girls' bathhouse on the floor below. There was an aisle with private stalls on either side, closed off with sliding curtains. The bathhouse had a pleasant humidity from all the steam and was filled with the raised voices of girls trying to have a conversation above the sound of running water.

A girl wrapped in a towel with dark-red hair piled on top of her head was coming down the aisle. I moved aside, but she stopped when she saw me.

"Hey! You're the new girl," she said. She had pretty golden skin and a warm smile. "I'm Hina."

"Kai," I said. Apparently, word of new arrivals spread quickly.

"Nice to meet you, Kai." Hina propped her arm against a stall divider, looking perfectly comfortable talking to a stranger in nothing but a towel. "You and your friend are the first people to make it out here without Irra's help."

"Really?" I tugged at the collar of my tunic. The humidity was beginning to make my clothes stick to my skin. "Does that mean we're the only ones here who weren't . . . you know, sentinels?"

"Pretty much," Hina said. "We're not really sure if others have tried, but we've found remains. The gargoyles get everyone who isn't riding a scout."

They almost got us, too.

"Anyway, catch you later?" she said, brushing a damp red strand from her cheek.

"Sure," I said, and squeezed to one side of the aisle to let her pass.

I found an open stall and snapped the curtain shut. Then I undressed, bent over the spotted tub, and peered at the knobs.

Once the tub was full, I braced my hand against the slick wall and climbed inside.

There was only room enough to sit with my legs crossed, but the hot water felt heavenly. The water in the East Quarter bathhouses was either lukewarm or frigid depending on the time of year. I'd mastered the art of washing quickly. But here, I decided to take my time. The amount of dirt that had accumulated since leaving Ninurta was embarrassing, even by the Labyrinth's standards. I dragged a soapy rag across my skin, scrubbing even after the dirt had been washed away.

The heat soothed the bruises, but it also made every scratch sting, including the new welt on my palm from when I snapped my spoon. Still, it was all easy to ignore as I rested my shoulders against the lip of the tub.

This didn't seem like such a bad place. Etu Gahl. G-10 had said it meant "to exist in darkness" in whatever ancient language was native to the Infinite. I hoped it referred to the way the fortress could remain hidden from outsiders, but I doubted it.

My house is a place of forgotten things.

I wasn't sure what Irra meant, but the memory sent a shiver through me despite the hot water. Still, the hollows seemed to be happy here. They had full stomachs, a roof over their heads, plenty of water, and a community of people who understood one another. I wished Reev *had* been brought here.

I dunked my head beneath the water, my eyes squeezed tight.

I'm sorry. I didn't know who my apology was meant for. Reev? Definitely. But maybe also for the woman who attacked me in that alley. Because if I had known then that it would lead to this—Reev kidnapped by Ninu, and Avan and me stuck outside Ninurta's walls—I don't know if I would have alerted the runners. It scared me to think it: that I might have left her to die instead.

Avan was wrong. *I don't always do the right thing. I'm sorry. I'm sorry.*

Back in Avan's room, he had stacked the rugs into a makeshift bed on the floor and settled in with a threadbare blanket. His hair, still damp, clung to his neck in dark tendrils like the lines of his tattoo.

Without a word, I crawled onto the bed, on top of the covers, and leaned over to switch off the lamp. My stomach grumbled. I hadn't been hungry when it was time to go down for dinner, and then I'd spent a long time in the bath.

"Kai," Avan said, "have you . . ."

"Have I what?"

After a moment, he continued. "Have you considered the possibility that you might be like Irra?"

"I'm not like him. I can't do anything like what he did." I recalled how the walls shriveled at his touch. "And I really don't want to."

"What if you could find out for sure? Would you want to know?"

Something in his voice sharpened my attention. "Yes," I said. "But what are you getting at?"

It was so quiet I could hear him breathing: slow, uneven breaths.

"Nothing," he murmured. "I'm just thinking about everything Irra said."

"A lot to take in," I agreed.

"Yeah. You okay?"

No. Reev had been found because of me. I should have just told him about the tax.

I reached over the edge of the mattress and was met by Avan's fingers. Strong and reassuring, they laced through mine. I clutched his hand, afraid he'd let go. But he didn't. Even after my body finally relaxed and my fingers grew slack, he held on.

"Kai," Avan whispered sometime later.

My name sounded different when he said it: a tender, velvety quality that I wanted to wrap around me. But maybe that was just the film of sleep. I fought the drowsiness that curtained my eyes.

"Do you know what tomorrow is?"

I thought about it but couldn't seem to focus on much more than the timbre of his voice. "No."

"The first Day of Sun."

I counted back the days. How could I have forgotten? Tomorrow, the clouds would clear for the first time in a year, just enough to get genuine sunshine.

The texts told of a time when the Sun had been a constant in the sky—when the weather had been both varied and volatile. After Rebirth, a pall of clouds had taken control of the sky. The storms grew more violent, the nights darker. For decades, the Sun became nothing but a memory for the people left behind. Maybe that, too, had been punishment from the Infinite.

Then one day, the clouds broke and sunlight slipped through— only for a minute. And every year after, the Sun had appeared a little bit longer. Now, the Sun remained for a week. I liked to think that someday it would stay.

During the Week of Sun, Reev and I would climb to the roof of the Labyrinth, the highest point in the East Quarter. We'd lay on top of the metal freight containers, warm from the Sun. When it grew too hot, we climbed down to the bridge to watch the light skip across the river, heat shimmering above the surface. At night, we returned to the roof to observe the stars, a billion little suns more beautiful than anything I'd ever seen, more beautiful even than the White Court with its ivory walls and silver banners.

That this week should happen now, without Reev to share in it, didn't seem right.

"We'll meet with Irra again in the morning," Avan said. "Figure out what to do next. Then we'll find a place to watch the Sun."

The courtyard. I wanted to go *there*.

"Kai?"

I whispered, "Okay."

CHAPTER 17

A RED BIRD LANDED ON A LIMB TOO HIGH FOR ME TO REACH.
I didn't even know birds came in red. I watched it hop along the
branch, a clear tune warbling from its beak.

Beside me, Avan tilted his head to get a better view and said,
"I didn't know they came in red."

I smothered a laugh. We stood beneath the tree in the courtyard, waiting for the clouds to clear. Nearby, Irra flitted from
flower to flower like a frantic bee, watering can in hand, talking
to the plants too quietly for me to hear. I wouldn't be shocked if
the plants *could* hear him. In his other hand, he held clippers. He
had yet to use them.

The sound of wheels rumbling over stone stole my attention
from the red bird. A hollow wheeled a silver trolley up the path.
The trolley looked ancient, all the corners rusted. The decay had
eaten through the metal in some spots, leaving holes in the mottled
silver bars. The trolley held a steaming kettle and three dainty cups.

Avan helped the hollow, a woman with gray-streaked hair,

place the tray with kettle and cups on the table. She thanked him and then left with a fond glance at Irra.

"The hollows are servants, too?" I watched the woman as her trolley rattled away. Despite her apparent age, she walked with a straight spine and smooth steps. I'd noticed that about all the hollows—whether barely Academy age or silver haired with weathered skin, they looked to be in great physical shape.

"They do only what they wish," Irra said as he put the tin watering can beside the path. "I make no demands of them."

"We're supposed to believe you're a philanthropist?" I didn't mean for it to be an accusation. "That is, I mean—"

"You have a right to your questions. I give my hollows a choice. Sanctuary and, to be frank, a chance at revenge—or return to Ninu and his sentinels."

"The choice is obvious," I said.

"Is it?" Irra asked. "Not everyone has accepted my offer to switch allegiances."

Irra pulled out the wrought-iron chairs for us. As Avan's hand touched the back of his seat, Irra's clippers swiped at his forearm.

My gut lurched. Avan jerked away, shielding his arm with his body.

"What the drek are you doing?" I shouted at Irra before turning to Avan. "Let me see."

He moved out of reach. "I'm fine." He extended his arm to show me. His skin was perfectly unharmed. "See?"

I whirled on Irra. "What is wrong with you?" I snatched the clippers from him and tossed them into the grass.

Irra looked down at his empty hand, as if surprised. "My hand slipped. Forgive me."

"Like hell."

Avan sat, his fingers around my wrist tugging me down into my seat also. "It was an accident."

With an apologetic smile, Irra poured the drinks. I glanced between the two of them, but they both seemed to have put the incident aside. Something was going on here.

Irra placed a cup in front of each of us. "Tea," he said, and then began heaping piles of sugar into his own.

The tea smelled sweet and inviting, and although I had never had tea before, right now I didn't want it.

"Your citizen IDs," Irra said. "We're going to replace them."

"What?" I blurted. All Ninurtans were required to carry an ID—a metal card issued by the registry. Mine was at the bottom of my bag in the room Irra had given me. "Why?"

"You're the first civilians to leave Ninurta in a century. They'll do everything they can to identify you. The safest way to get into Ninurta is with a new identity."

"You can get us back in?"

Irra blithely dumped more sugar into his cup. His demeanor had changed from when we'd first met. He still seemed a bit frayed, but the silent threat hidden beneath his peculiarities felt dampened. If I hadn't known who he was, hadn't seen and felt his power compressing around me and *into* me, I might have believed he was as unremarkable as any human.

"Well, of course," he said. "Unless you'd prefer to stay here?"

"No! I— If you can get us in, that would . . . that would be great." I wasn't trapped here. I could still find Reev. Hope swelled inside me, but I had to be sure of what he was offering.

"What do you want in return?" Avan asked. His question cut short my inner celebration.

"Not much," Irra said. "Just information."

I tapped my fingernail against the side of my cup. "What kind of information?"

"G-10 has filled me in on the details of your brother's situation. Whatever knowledge Reev might have from his time with Ninu would be adequate. And since I imagine Ninu will rebrand him, I should like to study his new collar. If you return successfully, of course."

He meant to treat Reev no differently than he treated the other sentinels who'd joined him. I couldn't see any reason not to take the deal. Besides, what else could I do? I wasn't exactly swimming in options.

With a glance at Avan, who didn't object, I said, "Okay. I'm in."

"Won't they know if a new ID shows up in the registry?" Avan asked.

"Not," Irra said, holding up his spoon, "if it's one that never left."

"That doesn't make any sense," I said.

"It will."

My mouth pinched at his dismissive tone. "How am I supposed to find my brother if he's in the White Court?"

"My hollows will place you among the cadets performing in the Tournament."

"Wait, wait," I said, putting up my hands. "What do you mean, 'the Tournament'?"

"If you want access to the areas in which Reev is most likely to be, then you can't be civilians. And we can't throw you in as Watchmen, either, because the ranks are meticulously run. Entering you as cadets is the safest route."

Avan leaned forward. "But that would mean—"

"Yes!" Irra said, brandishing his spoon in excitement and sending flecks of tea flying. "Training. Better start now."

"We have to wait until the Tournament begins?" I said. Who knew how much damage Ninu would do to Reev before I found him? Who knew what he had *already* done?

"It's only two more weeks. And we have the time. Whatever Ninu decides to do with your brother, any alterations with permanent damage would require months to complete. Delicate organ." He gestured at his head.

"Permanent damage," I echoed.

"You keep focusing on the wrong details," Irra said. "As to training—Kai, you possess unique abilities rooted directly in the River. It would be best not to showcase them."

I stared at him from above the rim of my cup. How could he have known? I hadn't done anything since the gargoyles chased us into the forest. I looked at Avan, who mirrored my wariness.

Admitting I was different still felt dangerous. Even if I was no longer in Ninurta. But I wanted to know what he meant— what if he had answers to the questions I'd always been afraid to ask?

"What river?" I asked cautiously. The only river still running that I knew of divided the East Quarter and the North District like a natural wall. And it wasn't as impressive as the one made of stone and metal surrounding the White Court.

"*The* River," Irra said. "The steady current over which Time keeps watch, in which all things flow. You must have been born of it."

The threads. I brushed my mind against them. Yes, they flowed evenly, at the same pace—reliable, constant, ever present. Still, it remained a mystery how I could grasp and manipulate them.

My confusion was plain, because Irra added, "I don't understand it myself."

"How can you tell? That I'm different, I mean."

"We each have our own gifts," he said. "And you reek of the River."

"I *reek*?" I tried not to sniff my shirt.

"Not literally," he said. "It's in your eyes. I can see the River reflected there."

I stopped feeling self-conscious about the color of my eyes a long time ago—Reev made me realize that everyone was too caught up worrying about their own insecurities to see mine—but now I wanted to duck my head so Irra would stop staring at me.

"Does that mean I'm *mahjo*?"

But Irra had said they no longer possessed any real, usable magic, and I couldn't do any of the things G-10 mentioned: I didn't heal fast, I was too scrawny to have much muscle strength, and I was fast but not superhumanly so. Reev had never gotten sick, but I had, plenty of times.

Irra leaned over the table to peer directly into my eyes. Avan leaned forward a little as well. I tried not to move despite the awkwardness.

Then Irra shifted away and spooned more sugar into his tea. "No," he said decisively.

I waited for him to continue, but he didn't. Beside me, Avan slowly relaxed into his seat.

"Then what am I?" I prompted.

"You," he said, lifting his cup to his mouth, "are a conundrum." He took a happy sip.

I slumped into my chair and sighed. "So you don't know. Shouldn't being Infinite mean having infinite knowledge?" I muttered.

"Eternity would be quite dull if that was true."

"Can you at least tell us where to find Reev? Is there a sentinel barracks?"

"Unfortunately, Ninu keeps that sort of information to himself. I can't break those particular enchantments without alerting him to my interference."

The disappointment felt heavy in my chest, but I pushed it down. I'd find Reev the old-fashioned way: by searching. Inside the White Court, I'd have a better chance at success.

"I'll find him," I declared.

"And I'll leave you to it. However, I do feel the need to repeat this again," Irra said, and suddenly, his presence vibrated around me like an echo, plunging me into that same chilling emptiness of the Void. "In the Tournament, do *not* use your powers. No matter what."

CHAPTER 18

AFTER HE FINISHED HIS TEA, IRRA LEFT US IN THE COURTYARD to await the Sun. The courtyard was enclosed on four sides by the dusky walls of the fortress. Moss and vines spotted in blue flowers had taken hold of the stone.

Since the tree blocked our view of the sky, we relocated near a fountain at the back, nestled between overgrown rose bushes. I knew they were roses from the history texts and because, rarely, I'd seen them shipped from their special gardens in the White Court and sold on the street for fifty credits a stem. I imagined sunshine would smell like this.

The fountain itself was a sad thing. Cracks threaded the stone, and water trickled from the top where green moss clogged the spout. It reminded me of the slime that grew on the walls in the Labyrinth. Definitely not something I missed. Weeds had crawled up the sides of the fountain, creeping over the rim to dip into the murky inch of water at the bottom of the basin.

I sat on the fountain's overgrown rim, watching Avan. He took a seat beside me, his hand lingering on his arm where Irra had almost cut him.

He noticed me watching and dropped his hand. "Irra's a little off in the head, isn't he? Maybe that's what happens when you're immortal. Living forever must mess with a person's mind."

Maybe insanity *was* the price of eternity. Nature's way of keeping balance, as Irra had said. I could see this gloomy sort of balance reflected in this entire place: Etu Gahl was a fortress of perpetual deterioration that could expand by pulling whole rooms and floors from who knew where. And this sliver of a courtyard, which Irra kept green and alive despite what I'd seen his rotting touch could do.

Growth and decay.

"It's all so impossible," I said.

Faced with truths I never would have imagined, I still had no idea what I was. I had tried so hard to remember, to pull images and thoughts from those years of my life before Reev, questions I had finally forced myself to bury. But those questions rose again to the surface. What did Irra mean when he said I'd been born of the River?

And he'd spoken of Time as if it was a person—which, considering Irra had called himself Famine, maybe it was.

"Yeah, but I've seen what you can do. Nothing is impossible after that."

It was still disarming having other people know about me. For so long, this had been my secret. Mine and Reev's.

But Reev had other secrets.

"Do you think Irra is being honest with us?" I asked. "He's pretty quick to offer up help."

"We're his guests," Avan said. "He's given us food, shelter, and protection. And now he's going to get us back into Ninurta. We're not exactly in a position to question his motives."

"I didn't realize you were so blindly trusting."

Avan's expression darkened, and he regarded me coolly. I didn't know how he could go from warm to cold so quickly. I'd seen a lot of Avan's "faces": the polite but distant shop clerk, the beautiful boy with a smile that could spin fantasies, the friend unwilling to leave me alone in the darkness. And the kid from the Alley who hid behind a cool exterior when anyone tried to peer past his walls.

I didn't understand why he felt he needed those walls with me. After what we'd been through, I thought our friendship had gotten past this.

Maybe I should have chosen my words more carefully. I thought of those rumors about Avan accepting anyone's bed to keep from going home. Guilt stung my chest.

"I didn't mean it like that," I said. "You're right. I should be more grateful. I *am* grateful." And I was. I had no illusions about where we'd be now without Irra. "It just worries me that he's help-ing us without asking for much in return. Information is great, sure, but is that really it?" In my experience, there was always a catch.

But maybe I was being paranoid. Maybe this was what the Infinite did when they weren't . . . building human cities to spite one another.

Avan's fingers plucked at the weeds clinging to the fountain. "I don't trust him. But we don't have any other options."

I tucked my hair behind my ear. "I know."

He sighed heavily. "Do you think maybe Reev knew about all this?"

I looked at him. "About what? The Infinite?"

He shrugged. "He was a sentinel. He must have escaped for a reason. What if it wasn't coincidence that he found you?"

"What are you saying? That Reev had something to do with me losing my memory?"

I had told Avan years ago that I couldn't remember anything from before I was eight. At the time, he said he envied me.

"I'm not saying anything. I'm just . . . thinking out loud."

"Reev took care of me," I said. Whatever Reev had kept from me, I'm sure it had been in my best interest. "I trust him completely."

Avan's dark eyes locked on mine. "Exactly. I've seen the way you look at him, Kai. The way you talk about him." He dropped his gaze. "You love him so much that it blinds you to his faults. You won't even consider—"

"I love him *in spite* of his faults. He's my brother."

Avan's lips curved, but it was a mockery of a smile. "Yeah. Your brother. You don't even realize it."

"Realize *what*?" I demanded.

He ran his fingers through his hair, and the look that darted across his face made something wrench inside me. "He has so much of you already," he said, the words stilted as if they were being forced from him. "Is there anything left for—" He cut himself off and shook his head. "For anyone else?"

I didn't understand why he was saying this—*of course* Reev would always hold a part of me—but the answer seemed to matter to him. So I said, "Yes."

He didn't look convinced. "Have you ever asked him about his past?"

Only a few failed attempts about his collar. But I wanted to. I never stopped wanting to. Fear had kept me silent—insecurities and doubts that haunted me over the years despite everything Reev had done. Someone had abandoned me on a riverbank. There was no blood to connect me and Reev, and if I pried into things he wanted kept secret, what if he decided to leave me, too?

Avan didn't wait for me to answer. "Or about your own past. Why are you so content not knowing?"

"Not every family has to be broken, Avan."

I regretted the words the moment they were out. My lips tightened, and my hands curled in my lap. Avan remained still, his hair shielding his eyes from me. He began to rise. My fingers latched on to his forearm.

"Please stay," I said, ducking my head. "I don't . . . I don't want to argue with you."

I held my breath and didn't release it until he sat again, his face turned away. I scooted closer so that our sides touched. He nudged my shoulder, and I relaxed against him.

I didn't tell Avan that he had it wrong. I wasn't content not knowing. I'd never told Reev, but the reason I wanted to be a mail carrier was because it allowed me to explore the North District beyond his restrictions. And because maybe one day I'd find someone who looked like me. Or recognized me. *Someone* must have taken care of me before I was eight.

Maybe this was the universe's way of punishing me for wanting to know about my past. Reev had taken me in, cared for me, loved me like his sister, and still I had wanted more. Having Reev should have been enough. Why couldn't that have been enough?

I tilted my head, resting my cheek against Avan's shoulder. Right now, the most important thing was rescuing Reev. Everything else could wait.

Closing my eyes, I listened to the wind rustle the branches of the tree. Much nicer than the clang of metal walls. I would miss this place when we left.

"Kai," Avan said. "Look."

I felt it first. Spreading across my face. Warmth. Radiant, natural warmth. I raised my eyelids, slowly. There it was.

The Sun. It hurt my eyes, so I squinted at the clouds around it instead. They were yellow—not in the usual stark, chemical way, but vibrant and muted at the same time—and highlighted in gold where beams of light filtered through. Sometimes, the clouds held beauty in their own way.

I closed my eyes, letting the heat and light soak in. The Sun shone on my face for the first time in twelve months, but I couldn't help thinking that the best part of this moment was being able to share it with Avan.

I leaned against his side and felt his arm circle my shoulders. Even though I knew it wasn't true, I imagined his warmth like a Sun that shone just for me.

CHAPTER 19

OUR LESSONS WITH G-10 PROVED HOW LITTLE I KNEW ABOUT fighting. And G-10 transformed into an unrelenting jerk in the training circle. When I remarked on this, he gave me a look that made me cringe and said, "In the arena, you're not going to win with kindness."

I didn't care about winning, just making it through so I could find Reev. G-10 replied to this by knocking me on my already-bruised ass.

He had made his point. And now I had no qualms about breaking his nose. Or trying to, anyway. Having survived in the North District our whole lives, Avan and I had pretty good reflexes, and Reev had taught me basic self-defense.

But we were still no match for G-10.

Avan landed on his back. Then he set his jaw and shoved himself to his feet. G-10 had given us new tunics and fitted pants that matched what the others wore. The clothes were much tighter than what we were used to, and as Avan brushed off his backside, I had to admire the view.

"Again," Avan said.

G-10 attacked. He was fast, faster even than Reev, although I was pretty sure Reev had held back when he taught me. Avan blocked a punch, avoided a kick, and then swung for the ribs. G-10 caught his wrist, but Avan's foot came up, connecting with G-10's shoulder. G-10 didn't even stagger before sliding close and striking beneath Avan's chin. Avan grunted, stumbling.

I winced and rubbed my chin in sympathy.

G-10 crossed his arms. "That was good. You landed a hit."

Avan opened and closed his jaw to make sure it still worked and then swore under his breath. "Again," he said, straightening.

"You don't have to defeat me," G-10 said wryly. "Your opponents in the arena won't be trained sentinels. Most will be normal cadets. They'll have two years of combat training, though."

Two years next to my paltry skills sounded intimidating. But one day, those cadets would become Watchmen, and fighting them now would almost be like hitting a Watchman without worrying about the consequences.

"Will we be able to tell if one of them is a descendant?" I asked.

"They always rank at the top by the end," G-10 said.

I rested my elbows on my thighs. Avan didn't budge, stubbornly facing G-10, and I stifled a laugh. He'd never struck me as the competitive type.

"Sit. Kai's turn." G-10 motioned for me to join him on the floor.

Oh boy. I stood, and Avan relented, taking my place on the sideline.

The indoor training yard, another area thankfully without decay, spanned an entire floor. An array of weaponry lined the walls like an armory, and tall windows allowed plenty of light into the expansive room. Numerous broad, gray circles marked the rings where the hollows sparred. Aside from two boys throwing knives at the other end of the room, we were the only people using the training yard.

I took a position in front of G-10. For the first few days, he'd taught us combinations, and how to hit, kick, and block. He'd forced us to repeat the motions for hours until each move was committed to muscle memory. I spent more than an hour each night in the bathhouse soaking away the aches. Now we had to use what we'd learned.

I nodded to indicate that I was ready. I didn't even have time to be surprised before pain shattered my jaw. I found myself on the floor, staring up at the ceiling. My face and neck throbbed. I blinked lights out of my eyes and didn't move.

"You hit her where she was already injured," Avan said, his voice tight. I focused on his voice, drawing strength from it.

"Yes, I aimed for her weaknesses." G-10's feet appeared in my range of vision. I groaned and rolled onto my stomach. "Kai, if you expect to fool the Tournament judges into believing you're a cadet, then show me you're better than this."

Drek. Something savage and angry clawed up my gut. Gritting my teeth, I pushed to my feet. I *was* better than this. Reev had taught me better than this.

"Good," said G-10.

His leg blurred, and I dodged, rolling away to avoid the kick that swung over me, snagging the end of my ponytail. From the corner of my eye, I saw Avan stiffen at the strike. My speed was my main advantage. Reev had always said so. When G-10 came at me again, I ducked and jabbed, driving my knuckles against his ribs.

He grunted. Then he smirked and dived in close, strikes coming fast. It was all I could do to block. He dropped low and then sprang upward, his palm crashing into my chest. I fell, landing on my back with a breathless gasp.

"In the arena, use that speed," G-10 said. "End the match with as few strikes as possible."

I drew a breath. *Ow.*

"That's enough for today. Same time tomorrow morning."

Avan tried to help me up, but I brushed away his hands. I would do this on my own. I was pretty sure my bruises had bruises, but I managed to keep from groaning as I stood. I averted my face so they wouldn't see me grimacing.

"Kai!" G-10 called after me. "I need to talk to you."

I rolled my shoulders and then fixed on a smile as I turned to look at him. "What about?"

G-10 walked past me. "Come with me." He glanced at Avan, who was leaning against the door frame. "You can leave."

"Sure," Avan said. "I'll just go wander aimlessly through the corridors."

G-10 snickered. "Don't get lost."

I gave Avan a shrug as I followed G-10 out into the hallway. "Where are we going?"

"To see Irra."

My feet faltered, but I caught up to his side again. This didn't sound promising, but maybe Irra just wanted to share another cup of tea. "Why?"

He didn't answer. I chewed on my bottom lip. I hadn't seen Irra for a couple of days, which, according to G-10, was nothing unusual. He tended to disappear into his study or the nether regions of Etu Gahl for periods of time, the reasons for which no one quite knew.

When we reached Irra's study, the door was cracked open. The rusty doorknob was held in place with a single half-screwed nail. G-10 knocked before pushing the door open wider.

Irra sat cross-legged on the carpet in front of a lantern, his long legs bent like a spider's. He was facing the glass doors that led to the courtyard, but the curtains were closed.

G-10 and I stepped in, and he closed the door behind us. The wood scraped shut. I didn't ask what Irra was doing.

"How is your training?" Irra asked, unfolding his legs and standing in one fluid movement.

"Fine," I said warily.

"Is that correct?" He directed the question at G-10 as he circled his table piled with bread bites. They were now arranged into a circular wall, surrounding a tall bread fortress. I wondered if it was supposed to be Ninurta.

Behind me, G-10 slumped against the wall, eyes downcast and arms crossed. I frowned at him. "What is this about?" I asked.

"I'm worried about the starting point of your skills," G-10 said.

Irra had arranged for G-10 to train us, for which Avan and I were both grateful. And while G-10 had complimented my speed,

I knew I could be faster. I wasn't used to pushing through the pain of unhealed abrasions and sore muscles, and nobody felt that frustration more keenly than I did.

Irra plucked at the frayed sleeves of his black tunic, which hung so loosely on his frame that it looked like a curtain. "Matching the proficiency of the cadets within two weeks is impossible. I don't expect you to be their physical equals. However, your success depends on your ability to blend seamlessly into the Tournament. You can't let your lack of training show in your matches."

"I won't," I said, my shoulders hunching. I didn't like where this conversation was leading. "This was the first day of actual fighting. I'll get better."

"Kai," Irra said, his voice reaching across the space between us. I shivered. "If you can't pull this off, I'm canceling our deal."

"You can't!" I said, my back snapping straight. Outrage flushed my cheeks. "You—you can't give me hope and then take it away."

I looked at G-10, but he was staring at the floor. No help there. Irra scratched his wild thatch of hair.

"Consider the risks," Irra said. "I'm sending my hollows into the heart of Ninu's city, first to get you in and then to bring you out. If Ninu discovers that I can sneak someone inside his walls, he will completely restructure his security. He could even weed out my spies, some of whom have been undercover for years. All the information I have worked to acquire, that my hollows have risked their lives to acquire, would have been for nothing. I would have to start over again."

His voice grew steadily softer until it thrummed in the room, vibrating through my skin. I wanted to flee, but I stayed where I was. Irra moved closer, bending over to meet my eyes. The low lighting sharpened the shadows in his cheeks.

He said, "Prove to me how much you want this."

CHAPTER 20

G-10 CAUGHT UP TO ME IN THE STAIRWELL LEADING TO THE dormitories.

"Kai, wait." He reached for my hand.

I slapped away his fingers. "I don't want to talk to you."

"Wait." He darted in front of me, forcing me to stop or bowl him over—or, more likely, hit his brick wall of a chest and tumble down the stairs myself.

I stopped and glared. What did he have to be upset about? *"What?"*

"Why are you *really* mad?" he asked, using his instructor tone. It made me want to hit him. "Because you don't like that he doubts you or because you're afraid he's right?"

I already knew the answer, and judging by the shrewd look in his eyes, so did he. My shoulders sagged.

What if I can't do it? What if Irra decided that the information Reev might have wouldn't be worth the risk? I could leave Etu Gahl, but walking back to Ninurta wasn't an option unless I wanted to be eaten by gargoyles or get lost in the Void. Again.

G-10 pulled me against the wall as a pair of hollows passed us in the stairwell. He greeted them with a smile before nudging me up the steps. "Come on. We shouldn't talk here."

He led me to the floor above my room and then down the hall to a door identical to all the other dormitories. Inside, however, his space was markedly different from my own drab, empty room.

On his cot lay a blanket that had been sewn from a mix of fabrics and patterns. A colorful, braided rug covered the stone floor, and a shelf ran along the wall, its frame weighted down with random bits of metal contraptions.

"Wow," I said, crossing the room to get a better look at his shelf.

In one corner was a rusty box with two narrow, rectangular slots at the top and a short lever along the side. G-10 had stuffed a handful of colorful feathers into the slots.

"What is it?" I tried to read the words carved into the spotted metal, but they were too faded.

G-10 shrugged. "Some sort of appliance. I haven't figured out the actual purpose yet. I found it while exploring some unused rooms around Etu Gahl." He let me look over his odd collection for a moment longer before he said, "Kai, listen. I had to tell Irra. I can't let you go if I think you're going to get caught."

I turned to face him. "You don't think I can do it, either?"

"I do," he said. "You landed a hit, but that was because I made you angry. I shouldn't have to provoke you to get you moving properly."

"I know," I said, sinking to my knees on the rug. The colors were beautiful and the threads tightly woven. My fingers traced a purple thread. What was the point of having the gift to delay time if it couldn't even help me find Reev? "I can't leave my brother with Ninu. I *can't*."

G-10 dropped down next to me on the floor. "And you can't save him without Irra's help."

"Drek." I tilted my head back. I had to stop panicking. I hadn't come all this way to fail now. I had to prove to Irra—and myself—that I could do it.

He sighed. "Look, if Irra cancels your arrangement, I'll—"

"No. You won't do anything. You won't need to."

G-10 smiled. "And why's that?"

"Because I can do this," I said. I would be strong enough. I *was* strong enough.

I returned to my room to bathe and change, and headed for the courtyard, where I knew Avan would be waiting. When I spread out on the grass with a wince, Avan insisted I see the medic, but I ignored him. If I let myself get hit, then I deserved to deal with the aftermath.

I closed my eyes, savoring the warmth. Everything in the courtyard, including me, seemed to stretch upward, reaching for that rare and cherished bit of sunshine. Eventually, I heard Avan lay down beside me, and his nearness was enough to make my breath grow thin. A twitch of my arm and we'd be touching. Seconds passed in silence before I cracked open an eyelid and glanced over.

He was watching me. The moment our eyes met, he looked

away, his neck turning red from having been caught staring at me instead of the sky. I could feel my own blush rising hot in my cheeks.

I wanted to say something, but my mind had gone utterly blank. I felt aware of every blade of grass prickling my arm, of the cool air against my burning face. I stretched out my fingers and touched his wrist.

Avan cast me a sheepish smile. My heart jumped. Neither of us spoke.

We remained there until sunset. Then I peeled myself off the grass, joints and muscles aching, and we joined G-10 in the mess hall for dinner. My jaw still hurt and chewing food felt like torture, but I wasn't going to let that stop me. G-10 had a lot to teach us, and I couldn't give him any more reason to think I was weak.

Hina had spotted me in the mess hall a couple days ago and had since joined us for meals. She lugged her boyfriend over as well, but other than a couple of ambiguous grunts, he had yet to talk to us.

At the moment, he was spoon-feeding her soup. It was sweet. In a "What the drek?" kind of way.

"Irra wants to see you after dinner," G-10 said to Avan.

"No one talks to Irra as much as you guys," Hina said with a look that was part curiosity, part sympathy.

"Lucky us," I said. "Why does Irra want to see him?"

Avan just nodded, his fingers fiddling with his eyebrow piercing.

I tapped my fork against my plate. "Well?"

"He didn't say," G-10 answered. He switched topics to his plans for tomorrow's training, including bringing Hina in to assist with sparring. Then Hina brought up the various hobbies that the hollows had formed out of boredom, such as building scrap models out of the junk constantly popping up around the fortress. They drew Avan into a discussion about Grays and their construction as I mulled over what Irra might want with Avan. Would he give Avan the same warning he'd given me?

When Avan excused himself from the table, I gave him a half-hearted wave and watched him go. G-10 mentioned he had patrol duty in a few hours.

"Does that mean with the gargoyles?" I asked. With everything else going on, I'd almost forgotten about them. "Are they safe? Where do they live?"

He grinned, his blue eyes sparkling with anticipation. "I'll show you. Come on."

He rose from the table and bounded for the door. I had no choice but to follow him or risk looking like a coward. I waved to Hina and her boyfriend, who didn't look up from his tray.

G-10 led me around a corner to a staircase that spiraled up and up into the darkness. The metal handrail wobbled, so I kept to the wall. The stairs were littered with paint chips and rust that had flaked down from the underside of the steps above. They creaked as we climbed, the sound echoing so loudly that it felt as if the whole structure was about to crash down around us.

To distract myself, I said, "Irra mentioned you're the newest recruit."

"Yep," he said with a nod. "Ninu sent my team to the Void to scout out where Irra might be. We split up to cover more ground, and I got cornered by a group of hollows."

"What about the rest of your team?"

His mouth dipped at the corners. He had a tiny beauty mark on the right side of his chin, and I found myself studying it as he talked. "They left without me. All sentinels work in teams of three, and we do pretty much everything together, so most of us grow close. I asked to be sent back to Ninurta to get them out, but Irra couldn't justify the risk."

Even though his teammates had left him behind, G-10 still seemed loyal to them. I wondered what he'd do if he had to face them in a fight.

"Why are you called 'hollows'?" I asked. "You're not exactly the empty shells I was expecting."

"It's supposed to be ironic," he said. "Ninu's sentinels are the hollow ones. Not us."

I thought about Reev and prayed that wasn't true.

"Do you remember much from before you were a sentinel?"

"Bits and pieces."

He didn't sound winded at all, even though we seemed to have climbed a thousand rickety steps. I, on the other hand, sounded like I had run the entire length of the Void.

"Ninu doesn't remove our memories. He erects walls in our minds, locking away our memories a little at a time. Too much at once can be overwhelming and interfere with our training. It takes months. I was about two-thirds of the way into my cleansing when Irra took me. He hasn't been able to break through the walls yet."

"That's awful," I wheezed.

"We're almost there," he said, and pointed up.

I tipped back my head to see. He offered to carry me the rest of the way, but I chose to keep my dignity. Or what was left of it, anyway, as I practically crawled the last few steps to the landing.

G-10 walked over to a door, but I remained sprawled on the floor until my breaths slowed.

"You ready?" he asked.

"Ugh." I forced myself to stand. My knees wobbled but held.

We went through a narrow passageway that ended abruptly in swirling gray mist. We were outside.

To be accurate, we were on the roof, standing at the peak of Etu Gahl. Surrounded by gargoyles.

I gasped, jumping, and collided with G-10. His hands came down on my shoulders to keep me from fleeing. His voice was soothing against my ear.

"It's okay. Irra enchanted them. They're completely tame. Except if there's an intruder, of course. Which hasn't happened yet, but we like to be prepared."

I repeated his words in my head. *It's okay. They're tame. No eating humans. I think.* I imagined my fingers skipping along the threads, just in case.

One gargoyle slipped from the pack. Its tail swept in an arc across the stone as it neared us, its head raised and its eyes looking straight at me.

"Say hello," G-10 told me.

"Can it understand?" I inched forward. They were obviously intelligent creatures.

"Irra says they can." He moved past me and offered his hand to the gargoyle.

The gargoyle touched its nose to G-10's knuckles, and then bobbed its head, its tongue flicking out to lick his fingers. It was almost . . . cute.

G-10 laughed, his whole face lighting up. "No, I didn't bring you any scraps today. Just wanted to show Kai the nest."

When G-10 smiled like that, his sandy hair blowing across his forehead, he could've been just another boy from the Alley instead of a trained sentinel. How old had he been when Ninu put the collar on him?

The gargoyle snorted, sounding disgruntled. I noticed something on its neck, half hidden behind its frills: a series of red lines carved into the leathery skin.

I reared back. "It has a collar!"

G-10 nodded. "It's not like Ninu's collar. It just allows Irra to communicate with them."

"How do you know he's not lying?" I looked around at the gargoyles sprawled across the rooftop. "How do you know he's not putting his own brand on you when he removes Ninu's?"

G-10's eyes grew hard and distant. "I know what being controlled feels like."

I pressed my lips together to keep from arguing further. Irra's hollows certainly didn't act as if they were being controlled. But did that mean the same for the gargoyles? How could you tell with animals?

G-10 pointed over my shoulder. "The nest is in there."

I looked. A tall structure rose over the rooftop, its large opening spilling heaps of straw. Inside, sleek figures rustled about. They seemed tame, but whether that was a result of the collars or not, I still didn't feel like getting any closer.

"Want to see more?"

"I'll pass." I slipped back into the passageway. The gargoyles were fascinating, and I liked seeing G-10 interact with one. But I still had the image of them stalking us through the forest.

As we headed for the stairs, I glanced at the back of G-10's neck. "Could I . . . maybe look at your collar?"

He turned to face me. "Are you flirting with me?"

The laugh that burst from my mouth surprised me. "I wouldn't know how."

"And here I was hoping 'collar' was a metaphor for—"

"Hey!"

His smile was devilish as he said, "Kidding." He presented me with his back. "Have at it."

Rising to my toes, I braced my hands on his shoulders and peered at the tattoo. Reev had never allowed me such a close inspection.

The tapered rectangle shape wasn't actually outlined. Instead, the overall design was created by tiny symbols. Geometric shapes with lines or arcs cutting through them. Half circles. Swirls and dots and sharp angles that twisted in all directions. The shapes must have been sigils or runes of some kind, but there was no pattern and no meaning that I could discern.

I brushed the pads of my fingertips against the tattoo. The raised skin felt unnaturally smooth.

"Weird, right?" G-10 said, his voice soft. He rocked on his

feet, and my fingers tightened on his shoulder, feeling the lean muscles shift beneath my touch.

Suddenly, I realized how close we were standing. My breath rustled the hair above his collar. I stepped away, lowering my hands awkwardly to my sides. G-10 looked back at me.

Before he could say anything, I hurried past him and asked, "What's Irra doing with all these gargoyles? And you guys? I mean, I know, revenge and all that, but why is he even here? Doesn't this contradict the whole 'don't interfere with humans' thing?"

G-10 followed me, and we began the long descent down the stairs. "I asked him the same thing when he offered me a place here. He said this was only temporary—just until Ninu left the humans and restored balance. He said that"—G-10 rubbed at the side of his collar, his footsteps light as we descended—"interference with the humans isn't necessary because, eventually, we'll find our way to the Infinite. All things wither with Time."

G-10's words stayed with me after he left me at the bottom of the stairs.

All things wither with Time.

It was kind of depressing, and I didn't know what to make of it or what it meant about Irra's decision to help us. I wished I could be certain of his intentions instead of relying on faith.

Either way, I didn't want anything to do with Irra's revolution. I would prove my determination to him, but once I saved Reev, my only concern would be how to keep him safe.

I made my way through a dim corridor, smiling politely at a

hollow who passed. I'd memorized the paths around the mess hall and the dorms. Apparently, once the new additions to the fortress settled in, they stopped changing.

As expected, I found Avan in the courtyard.

"So what did Irra want?" I asked, dropping onto the grass beside him.

"Where'd you go?"

I noted his avoidance of my question, but I gave in for now. He would tell me eventually. I hoped.

When I told him about the nest, he wanted to see it for himself. He'd have to find G-10 to guide him, because there was no way I was climbing those stairs again. He agreed to wait until tomorrow to see the gargoyles, and we spent another couple of hours watching the stars in silence.

I could stare at them forever. They didn't hurt my eyes the way looking at the Sun did. The school library held numerous books on stars and constellations, which meant people had once been free to study them. Now, nothing could penetrate the ever-present clouds except a special device that my school instructor had called a telescope. It was located in the White Court in what was called an observatory. I'd seen its dome during my routes through the barracks, but it was on palace grounds. I wondered if Ninu opened it for public use.

As my eyelids grew heavy, Avan nudged my shoulder. I rolled onto my side, toward the sound of his voice.

"Irra's making us new IDs at the end of the week," he said.

I nodded drowsily. "If he doesn't call everything off."

I told him about Irra's warning.

"You'll do great," Avan said without a hint of doubt. "You're a fast learner."

I appreciated his words even if I didn't fully believe them.

"Are you okay with getting a new ID?" I asked. Honestly, I wasn't sure myself. My ID wasn't just a proof of citizenship, it was proof that I—me, Kai Adahnu, not some fake identity—belonged somewhere. Of course, a scrap of metal and my name in a registry didn't represent all of me, but my ID had always been with me. It was the only thing I had from my life before Reev, my only link to my past.

"He gave me the choice of returning home to my family."

My mind went from sluggish to fully alert. I pushed up onto my elbow so I could see Avan's face. As usual, it was maddeningly blank.

"I still have to get a new ID, but it wouldn't belong to a cadet, just someone from the Alley."

This might be Avan's only chance to go back to the life he'd given up for me. But how would I—

I banished those selfish thoughts and gave him a smile.

"That's great, isn't it? You can go home. I mean, you'd have to be careful not to attract attention from the Watchmen, but you've always been careful about that."

"What about you? If Irra gave you the choice—"

"No." Without Reev, there was no going back.

"I figured," he said quietly. "What do you think I should do?" His dark eyes watched me.

I lay down again. "Why are you asking me? It's your choice."

He didn't say anything else, and I didn't know how to fill the silence. After a few minutes, Avan stood and offered me a hand to help me up.

We went to his room. I had tried to drag my bed in here so we could each have one, but its legs were bolted to the floor. I wasn't sure why. Maybe Irra didn't like the hollows rearranging the furniture. So instead, I'd just brought the mattress and Avan used it.

Lying on my side, I reached over the bed, and Avan's hand found mine. Even with everything on my mind, heat danced down my spine as warmth crossed from his fingers to mine. Not for the first time, I wanted to tug on his hand, to pull him into the cot with me.

I wanted him beside me the way we'd been that night in the Void. Close enough to feel his breath against my skin. The weight of his arm around me. Maybe this time I'd be brave enough to kiss him.

But I doubted it. I didn't know how to kiss, and with Avan's experience, I'd just embarrass myself.

Besides, I had no idea if he'd kiss me back.

Anyway, this wasn't important, despite what my body was telling me. What mattered was why we were here, and I wouldn't have made it this far without him.

"You should go home," I whispered, even though it hurt to say the words. "You've done so much for me already. And you have a family, real parents. You should go home to them."

Avan didn't respond for a long time. I was almost asleep when he broke the silence.

"The night before we left, I got into a fight with my dad."

I held my breath and didn't move, afraid to interrupt.

"Actually, it wasn't much of a fight since it was just Dad shouting. He told me I abandoned them when I moved out, and that was why Mom's condition got worse." Avan said it so casually, but I could hear the hurt beneath his words.

My fingers tightened around his. *It's not true,* I wanted to say. *You know that, right?* But he wasn't telling me this for sympathy. I clamped my lips together and remained quiet.

"Maybe part of why I left with you was to spite him. I wasn't thinking it at the time, but now . . . Maybe this was the only way I could stand up to him—by doing exactly what he accused me of."

I shifted on the cot, resting my head against the edge so I could see him. Avan lay on his side, facing me, our fingers twined in the space between us. I couldn't make out his features in the dark, but my eyes traced his silhouette against the mattress.

I whispered, "Then you should go home and fix things. I'm sure they're waiting for you."

Avan didn't reply.

CHAPTER 21

WHEN I AWOKE ON THE LAST DAY OF SUN, AVAN'S SPOT ON the floor was empty. After washing up, I made my way down to the mess hall and ran into G-10 outside the door.

"Avan's up in the nest," he said.

Maybe his observation skills came from his superior abilities. Or maybe I was just that easy to read.

"By himself?"

"I keep telling you, the gargoyles are tame. They won't hurt him."

I flushed, nodding. "I know."

G-10 shouted at my back as I walked away: "Don't be late for training!"

Since our meeting with Irra, G-10 wouldn't talk about my progress with me. Yesterday, I had kicked his leg and gotten him down on one knee. Of course, then he'd flattened me, but I still got in a hit. Hina was helping as well by sparring with me in the afternoons.

When I reached the bottom of the staircase, I looked up at the endless spiral of rust and wood rot. Did I really want to go up there again? I groaned and started climbing.

Halfway up, I plopped down on a step to catch my breath. The sound of creaking steps echoed through the shaft. I could see Avan descending. He pulled up short when he saw me.

"What are you doing?"

"Resting," I said, and patted the step beside me.

Avan sat, stretching his long legs over the steps and crossing them at the ankles.

"What were *you* doing?" I asked, leaning against his arm. "Besides communing with gargoyles."

"They're interesting animals. G-10 says they're enchanted, but I'm not sure that's it. Or at least that's not all of it. They're too smart."

"Did you make a new friend up there?" I teased.

His dimple appeared briefly before he turned serious again. "I guess it got me thinking about what might have been done to them. Back when they were first created by Ninu and then changed by Irra. You can't will loyalty through magic."

"Every sentinel trapped by Ninu's collars says you can."

"But that's not *real*. They've lost all sense of self. The gargoyles aren't like that. Real loyalty is a decision you have to be able to make for yourself. Like how the hollows choose to stay here and fight for Irra."

"Avan, for all we know, the collars Irra put on them might not be just for communication."

Avan shrugged and fell silent.

I stared at a large scratch in the wood beneath my feet, the random creaking of joints the only sound between us.

At last, I said, "If this is about the decision you have to make today—"

"I've already decided."

"Oh." I pushed my hair behind my ear, waiting for more.

He stood up. "Come on. If we're late, G-10 will probably punish us by making us climb these stairs again."

After training, Avan and I spread out on the grass beneath the tree in the courtyard to enjoy the last of the sunlight. Already, the clouds had begun to close in, thick plumes flaring orange. We stayed there for what felt like hours, until the shadows grew long and the Sun made its final, valiant fight, beams of light pushing through the crowding sky. But eventually, the last of its rays diminished.

G-10 had informed us that Irra would see us in the hospital wing as soon as night fell. So Avan and I picked ourselves up and made our way there.

The space was strangely cozy. Lively drapes in all colors separated the cots, and patterned rugs cushioned the floor. I tilted my head to study one of the patterns. The geometrical shapes looked a bit like gargoyles.

Irra instructed Avan to wait as he took me into a well-lit room. He pointed me to a padded chair beside a metal counter. Nearby was an operating table, which we hopefully wouldn't need, and various instruments, the purposes of which I didn't want to know.

I extended my arm across the counter, palm up. Irra sat on a stool opposite me. G-10 had told us that each ID contained threads of blood through the metalwork—a simple enchantment that allowed Ninu to trace people. We were too far away from Ninurta for Ninu to trace us now, so I didn't know if the Watchmen had identified us as the fugitives. But in case our new IDs were given close scrutiny in Ninurta, Irra would have to re-create the fusion of blood and metal.

"G-10 is pleased with your improvement," Irra said as he felt along the bend of my elbow.

I smiled, proud of myself. It had been only a few days since we began real fighting, and every training session left me more bruised than the last; but I was learning to tolerate the pain. Anything less was unacceptable. With another week left to train, I could only improve. The true test of my progress would be in the arena.

"When new hollows join, do you break their connection to Ninu yourself?" I asked.

"Certainly," Irra said as he picked up an ominous-looking needle. "Ninu also works on his sentinels himself. The branding requires a careful touch. The human brain must be handled with precision."

His hair was especially wild today, sticking out from his head like wires. When I didn't look into his eyes or hear the emptiness in his voice, he might have been just a peculiar man. If he was Infinite—was this his real form?

"Why 'the Black Rider'? What is it supposed to mean?"

Irra glanced up at me, the needle in his hand hovering above my skin. "You know the temples they once built to worship me?"

I shook my head. "There's a temple in the North District, but I don't know who it's for."

"You've seen one just for me, though," he said.

"I have?" I asked, racking my memory and coming up with nothing.

"The day we met."

I snorted softly. "Are you talking about your bread . . . model thing?"

He almost smiled. "I'm working on the details of my replicas. But yes. The defining feature of my temples was the image the humans painted of me: a rider with black robes."

"Was sugar their signature offering?"

He did smile then, but there was something darker hidden behind it that I couldn't identify, like trying to see beyond the mist that cloaked Etu Gahl.

"Everyone has their weakness," he said. "Yours is human emotion. Mine is the brief rush of sweet, if false, happiness."

The way he said "happiness" snagged against my thoughts. "Why is happiness a weakness?"

"Look at who I am," he said, without an ounce of sarcasm. His eyes searched mine, and the room slipped away, plunging me into blackness. Then he blinked, and the moment ended. "Happiness is not my natural state."

I didn't think he was trying to intimidate me—just drive his point home. So I shook off the lingering sensation and tried for a light "But horse rider is?"

The pall over him lifted. "I wouldn't be much of a rider now."

He sounded wistful. "I was much younger then. And I haven't seen a horse in ages."

"How old are you?"

"Even the Infinite are tied to the River's flow. And its current has carried me a very long ways. This may sting."

I winced as the needle pricked my skin, sinking into the vein. The vial attached to the end began filling with blood. It looked like magic, but Irra insisted it wasn't. Drawing blood by magic would hurt more.

After a few seconds, he removed the needle and pressed a clean bit of gauze over the small wound.

"Hold this," he instructed.

I did, watching as he reached across the counter and retrieved a slim piece of metal. My original ID, which I'd tossed into my bag that day we left Ninurta, lay beside my arm. He picked it up and held both against the light.

"See how yours has a red tint?" he asked.

I studied the way the light slid across the metal. My old ID held the barest tint of red. I nodded, slightly unnerved.

"I can re-create my own version of the enchantment, one that should pass a cursory inspection. Ninu will only seek out a trace if he's given reason."

"If every ID is created with a bit of blood, why does he need energy drives to find the *mahjo*? Wouldn't it be simpler for Ninu to snatch away babies and raise them as his soldiers?"

"Even before Rebirth, *mahjo* only came into their powers as they matured. The blood of a newborn would contain no magic for Ninu to detect."

The words *newborn* and *blood* used together made my stomach turn.

"I'll have the new IDs ready soon. You will, of course, have to leave your old one here." He took the gauze from me and examined the red spot on my arm. The skin around it had begun to bruise.

I almost snatched back my ID. "Thanks. For doing all of this."

He only nodded. "This will be your new information," he said, pulling out a sheet of paper. "Name: Nel Souin. Age: Seventeen. Born May twenty-third in the North District. You lived with your parents until you were fifteen, when the Academy offered you early admittance based on exceptional scores on your aptitude tests. After completing the preliminary exams for graduation, you were ushered into the Tournament with quick approval. Congratulations."

I gave him a weak smile. "Can't wait."

"If anyone asks about your time at the Academy, be as vague as possible. Their enrollment numbers are high enough that no one should question not having seen you before."

"Got it."

"Next!" he called abruptly, and I stood.

Outside, Avan lounged on the nearest cot. He looked too relaxed for it to be real. What was he thinking? Was he regretting his decision, whatever that was? I hoped he had chosen to go home. I truly did.

Despite the ache inside me, I did.

I swept my arm to the side to indicate it was his turn. Once he was in the room with Irra, I sat in the slight indentation left on the cot. It was still warm.

G-10 had briefed us in training this morning. He would lead us into Ninurta, all the way into the White Court. I didn't know how he planned to get us in, and with G-10 in full-on instructor mode, I hadn't dared to ask. Our false identities had already been added to the citizen registry by Irra's spies.

If Avan chose to go home, then G-10 had designated a hidden location for him to surface in the North District. We would arrive the night before the Tournament, allowing me to slip easily into the preliminary rounds.

Weapons weren't allowed in the matches, but G-10 had shown us his torch blade. Torch blades were the exclusive weapon of the sentinels. It was a beautiful sword, forged with subtle traces of magic that transformed the metal into something lightweight and iridescent. The silvery blade moved with silken ease in G-10's practiced hands.

He taught us a few ways to block it. Then he showed me how to strike with my knife, quickly and deadly. Hopefully, I wouldn't need to use these skills. But if things didn't go according to plan, I'd have to use all my abilities to get us out of there.

I lifted my arm, studying the bruise.

Nel. I reminded myself I wanted this. Logically, I knew that switching my ID was a smart tactic. It didn't change anything about me. But I couldn't help feeling as if I'd left a bit of myself behind in that room. More than my blood.

My house is a place of forgotten things.

Giving up my name felt like, this time, I was letting my identity be taken from me—everything I'd been, everything I had become. Would that bit of me wither away, merge into the ever-growing walls of Etu Gahl?

I rubbed my hands down my arms. How long had it been since Avan went in? Twenty minutes? He should have been done by now. Remembering the incident with the clippers, I suddenly wasn't sure if leaving Irra with Avan and an array of sharp tools had been a good idea.

I stood and paced the aisle between the cots. Another twenty minutes passed before Avan emerged.

"What's wrong?" I asked.

Tension pinched the corners of his mouth. "We had some complications," he said. "But it's done now. My ID says I'm Savorn."

He held his arm against his side, hiding the bend of his elbow. I reached over. "Let me see."

He showed me his arm. It was completely unmarred. I swept my thumb over his skin. His muscles jumped beneath my fingers.

"Did he even . . . ?"

"Yes," Avan said, lowering his arm. "I told you it's done."

"Avan—"

"I'm joining the Tournament with you."

I stepped back. "I can't believe you gave up your chance to go home."

"There will be other chances after we save Reev. And it's my choice. I made a promise to myself when we left Ninurta. I'm not leaving you."

I wanted to yell at him. I should have. He'd made the wrong choice. I could have done the rest of this without him—I was determined enough to try. But . . . despite how much I wanted to push Avan away from this mess, a part of me was glad he'd chosen to stay.

He put up a hand. "Don't. It's over. I'm not doing that again just to get another ID."

My gaze cut to his arm. "What were the complications?" It was a needle in a vein. What could have gone wrong?

"Nothing worth repeating. I'm going to do some extra training," he said, and brushed past me.

I watched him go, his shoulders stiff.

G-10 had said that the descendants of the Infinite healed rapidly. I had yet to see any injuries on Avan, even after our tumble off the Gray. If Avan was *mahjo*, it would also explain how he sensed my manipulation of time.

Have you considered the possibility that you might be like Irra?

Maybe that first night here, Avan hadn't been talking only about me. Maybe, even then, he'd suspected.

What if you could find out for sure? Would you want to know?

I was willing to bet that he had figured out the answer for himself. And he didn't seem thrilled about it.

CHAPTER 22

ON OUR LAST DAY WITH IRRA AND THE HOLLOWS, WE TRAINED
in the courtyard. G-10 had warned us that for our final lesson
he wouldn't hold back, because he felt we could handle it. Still, I
winced through Avan's fight.

Avan was growing into a good fighter, fast and powerful, but
G-10 was a fully trained sentinel with a collar that enhanced his
already superhuman abilities. When Avan finally landed a kick
that knocked G-10 down, G-10 flipped easily to his feet and
congratulated him. No one mentioned how Avan's brief limp improved almost immediately.

In my fight, I dodged more often than not but managed to
land a few quick jabs that made G-10 bare his teeth in approval.

Afterward, I sprawled on the grass, exhausted. But it was a
good sort of exhaustion. I had gotten used to the insane training
regimen. I was almost sorry it was over. A few minutes after G-10
left, a hollow I recognized as a medic from the hospital wing
joined us in the courtyard.

Seeing as it was our last day, I let her prod my skin and feel along my bones while asking if it hurt. "Nothing's broken," she announced once she finished. "But this is some impressive bruising."

She fished in her bag and withdrew a vial. She held it up and swished its contents. Then she popped open the top and offered it to me.

I gave the vial a dubious look.

"It's a healing tonic," she said, pushing the vial into my hand. "We developed it from studying our own increased healing abilities."

"Why would you need tonic?" Avan asked. He was sitting beneath the tree, looking attractively mussed but not the least bit tired.

"Some of us heal almost instantly, but a few of us don't seem to have increased healing at all. It's different from hollow to hollow. This just makes things easier for everyone, especially whenever Ninu sends sentinels into the Void to look for us."

I tipped the contents into my mouth. It tasted bitter. I coughed, grimaced, and handed back the empty vial.

"G-10 told me you guys are leaving tomorrow for the White Court," the medic said. "You should be all healed by morning. Can't have you going into the Tournament looking like you were trampled by a Gray."

"Thanks," I said, dropping onto the grass again. Was it my imagination or did I already feel a bit better?

The medic didn't bother checking Avan before she left. Did everyone know? More importantly, was Avan ever going to tell me?

I watched the clouds through the branches for a while, listening to the sound of the birds bustling around in their nest. The metal legs of Avan's chair raked across the ground as he stood. My eyes closed, and the grass rustled as he lowered himself beside me. Neither of us spoke.

After sleeping next to each other for more than two weeks, having him so close no longer felt awkward. Well, not entirely. That fluttery feeling in my stomach had grown stronger, along with a constant desire to touch him, even if it was just my fingertips against the lines of his palm. There was a comfort in knowing that if I reached over, he'd be there.

And then there was the part of me that whispered every night to lie down beside him. To curl against his side and drape my leg across his hip. To place his hand on my thigh.

What would he do? Would he push me away or wrap his arm around my waist and grip me closer?

The next time I opened my eyes, the sky had grown dark, and I was alone.

I rubbed my face and rose to my elbows. Lanterns along the path confirmed that the courtyard was empty. My stomach rumbled. I hadn't eaten since breakfast. I stood and glanced at the curtained glass doors leading to Irra's study. Last night, Irra had met with us long enough to present us with our new IDs. I hadn't seen him since, and I doubted he'd be there to send us off tomorrow.

In the mess hall, I was surprised to find that the clock said it was after nine. At our usual table, G-10 and Avan waved me over. The other hollows murmured greetings. They were polite, but G-10 and Hina were the only ones who consistently sought us out. I didn't mind. I would probably never see these people again, and there was no point forming connections.

Forgotten things. I pushed the thought away.

I picked up a tray of food, overflowing again—the enthusiastic chef had eventually introduced himself as Rennard—and sat down at the table. "Why didn't you wake me?" I asked Avan.

"You needed the rest."

"But now the day's been wasted." It had been my last chance to explore Etu Gahl.

"You look good," he said, his eyes roaming my face.

My cheeks grew warm.

"I mean your skin," he said, and then broke into a smile as my face grew hotter. "I mean your bruises. They're almost completely healed."

I carefully chewed my bread. "Yeah. Thanks."

G-10 cleared his throat. "I have a surprise for you both tomorrow morning."

"Parting gift?" I asked, twirling pasta around my fork, glad for the distraction.

"Sort of. But I have another surprise for you first. There's a reason Avan left you in the courtyard. He was in the kitchen with me." G-10 brushed crumbs off his fingers and pushed aside his tray.

"You were cooking? Is that a skill we'll need in the Tournament?"

G-10 waved at someone across the hall.

The doors to the kitchen swung open, and a flurry of hollows rushed out, carrying trays filled with drinks. Hina was wheeling a giant cake.

I stared, mouth open in confusion. G-10 rolled his eyes.

"Your good-bye party. Couldn't let you leave without proper fanfare, could I?"

"This is for us?"

"No, it's for the gargoyles," G-10 said.

"Maybe we should have invited them." Avan nudged my shoulder.

I didn't know what to say. No one had ever done something like this for me before.

The hollows around us stood and pushed their tables against the walls to clear the floor. Avan helped to arrange the drinks on our table. I eyed the cake as Hina rubbed her belly and pretended to take a big bite off a frosted end.

Along one wall, a group of hollows set up battered but functioning instruments. Lilting music with a quick beat filled the room. Hollows, young and old, converged into the cleared space, arms linked, the air buzzing with excitement. I awkwardly tried to push into a corner, but G-10 grasped my hand before I could get very far.

He tugged me out into the middle of the crowd and began . . . I don't know what he was doing. Dancing, I think. I'd never been to a party; and music in Ninurta, outside of the underground clubs, was a rare treat. I didn't know how this dancing thing was done.

What I did know was that I had no interest in trying. It looked silly.

"Oh, come on, Kai!" G-10 swept me up in the air, hands at my waist, and spun me around with a breathless laugh.

His enthusiasm drew a laugh from me as well. All around me, hollows shouted encouragement. Hina whistled from behind her boyfriend's beefy shoulder. For the first time since we'd gotten here, I felt like one of them.

I swung around, looking for Avan, and the smile grew stiff on my face.

Avan held a pretty hollow in his arms. He drew the stares of more than a few people around him. On full display, his beauty reduced even trained soldiers to helpless admiration. The girl with him leaned in closer.

Gentle fingers touched my jaw and directed my attention back to G-10's blue eyes. He smiled ruefully. "He's just having fun."

"It's none of my business."

"I don't think he'd mind if you wanted it to be."

I didn't want to think about what that meant. "Avan is my friend. And my only interest right now is to find Reev."

G-10 pushed his fingers through his tousled hair. Then he took my hand and led me over to the drinks. He plucked a green one that smelled of citrus.

"Well," he said, pushing the cup into my hands, "hard to compete with that, isn't it?"

What was he talking about? I examined the green liquid before taking a sip. It tasted sweet and a little tart.

"What is this?" I asked, watching the way the green liquid caught the light.

"Fruit juice with a touch of magic for flare," he said, and then nodded at some glowing blue drinks farther down the table. "Those are alcoholic if you're inclined."

"I'm not."

"Come on." He pulled me into the crowd of dancers. The hollows shouted happily at us as we passed.

It amazed me that they'd done all this for us, and I appreciated it, but I couldn't stop thinking about what lay ahead of us. G-10 turned around to face me. In the light of the lanterns overhead, I could see the way his eyes searched mine.

"Tomorrow, you leave us," he said. "But tonight, be here. For a little while."

"I *am* here," I said, lifting the drink in my hand.

He rubbed his thumb against my temple and stepped close enough that I could count the pale freckles on his nose.

"No," he said. "Be *here*. Quit thinking about what's going to happen when you get to Ninurta." He touched my jaw. It didn't hurt anymore. "For now, be *here*."

I sighed softly. He had arranged all this for us. "All right."

His eyes lit up. They were really very nice eyes.

"Good," he said. "Now dance."

I did, but not very well. He laughed at my attempts, and I laughed along with him. Around us, people twirled and swayed to the music with no embarrassment. I could disappear here. For a little while.

Avan spun by, the pretty hollow clinging to his shoulders. He looked at me, then at G-10, before looking away. The girl's lips hovered at his ear. I couldn't tell what she was saying—Avan showed no reaction.

I closed my eyes and let myself move to the beat that vibrated through the floor and into my body.

CHAPTER 23

WE DANCED UNTIL MY FEET HURT, THEN G-10 CUT ME A SLICE of cake as big as my head. It tasted like nothing I'd ever had: moist and sweet with a hint of lemon. It practically melted in my mouth. G-10 took inordinate pride in detailing how he and Avan helped Chef Rennard prepare it while Hina shouted unproductive suggestions. Afterward, other hollows took my hand and guided me around the floor a few times before returning me to G-10. I collapsed onto a bench and downed another of the tart fruit drinks. Beside me, G-10 looked flushed, his blue eyes bright.

"I think," he said, "I've settled on a name."

"I was growing fond of G-10."

He made a face. "Ninu assigned me that name."

"Oh, well, then it's a terrible name. What should I call you now?"

"Mason," he said, and waited for my response. He seemed uncertain.

"That's a great name. Very strong."

"Mason it is, then." He reached out and nudged the hair sticking to my cheek. His knuckles were light against my skin.

In the training ring, he was brutal. Away from it, he was deliberately careful with me. He didn't hide behind different faces like Avan. Mason was just Mason—whatever his name: serene, controlled, disciplined.

"Excuse me."

We both looked up at Avan. Mason's hand fell away.

Avan regarded Mason for a moment before he turned to me. "Dance with me?"

Mason's fingers brushed my elbow, urging me to stand. "Go on."

He waved at the musicians, and the song ended with a screech of strings. When the music started again, the notes were slow and silvery. I didn't know how to move to this. Avan pulled me close with a hand at my back.

"Are you having fun?" I asked, resting my hands on his shoulders, where the other girl had held on to him.

"Yeah. It's been a while since I've been to a party."

Avan had been a fixture at the underground clubs. I knew this because everyone did—up until a couple of years ago when he'd stopped going. And somehow he had still managed to open his dad's shop every morning. Bleary-eyed and rumpled, but there all the same.

The girls at school liked to corner me for details, convinced that because I was Avan's friend, I had insider information on him. But Avan didn't talk about his private life, and I never asked. I didn't want to know.

"The clubs—are they like this?"

He smirked. Someone had dimmed the lanterns, and the low light stained his eyes black. His hands seared my waist. The shadows cut his dimple deeper into his cheek.

"Yes and no. Lots of people, some music and dancing. But mostly it's just an excuse for kids to screw around without fear of the Watchmen."

"I've wondered about them."

"Don't. The clubs wouldn't have been right for you," he said. At the look on my face, he added, "That's a compliment. Trust me."

I wasn't sure what to make of that. Avan's past made me intensely curious—and maybe a little unreasonably jealous—but no one in Ninurta was innocent, and Avan had turned out better than most.

When I'd first met him, I'd treated him brusquely because of my assumptions about him. But even after we became friends, I kept my distance. Not because I didn't trust him, as he probably still assumed, but because I refused to let him sweep me into that category of people: those who'd slept with him and then spoke of him afterward with smug words and vulgar smiles. As far as I could tell, the gossip didn't bother him.

But it bothered *me*, and I wouldn't have him thinking I was like them.

If there was ever to be any sort of "us"—the sum of much more than just him and me—I wanted to be different. I wouldn't accept just one night.

"And I like this better," he said, smiling—not the blinding

smile used to charm people but a private one, even though people surrounded us on all sides. "What about you?"

"Not bad for my first party." I closed my eyes, feeling strangely light-headed. I could smell the soap the hollows had used to wash our clothes, and his skin—citrus and vanilla from the kitchen, and an earthy warmth from dancing. His breath, warm against my temple, smelled sweet like the cake. Would he taste sweet as well?

I didn't know what was happening between us—what *had been* happening between us—but his friendship was worth more than all of Ninurta. I couldn't do anything to mess that up.

My fingers tightened against his shoulders before letting go. "I'm tired," I said, looking at his chin. "I'm going to clean up and go to bed."

"I'll come with you."

"No," I said, pressing my hand against his chest. "You should stay and enjoy yourself. I doubt we'll get another chance after tonight."

I gave him a light shove to stay put. Then I backed away, and, with a wave, I wove through the crowd, heading for the door. Hands brushed my shoulders as I left, words of parting and well wishes shouted over the music. I responded to them with rushed thanks that I hoped conveyed how glad I was to share this night with them. I had lost Hina in the crowd, but I'd see her tomorrow.

At the door, someone grabbed my wrist. I looked back, expecting Avan.

Mason gave me a half smile. "Can I walk you up?"

"I'm not going to get lost."

He laughed quietly. "Can I walk you anyway?"

"Sure."

We didn't talk as we climbed the staircase, but it felt nice to have him there beside me. I realized how much I would miss him. When we arrived at the dormitories, I glanced between Avan's door and mine. Remembering the way that girl had whispered in his ear, I decided I should sleep in my own room tonight. After Mason left, I would just slip into his room long enough to retrieve my mattress. I ignored the ache in my chest, as well as that inner voice urging me to claim my space on his cot instead.

"I'll see you in the morning," Mason said. He looked like he wanted to say something else, but I was glad when he didn't.

I gave him a hug, then mumbled good night and shut my door.

I was swimming in the place between dreams and awareness when a knock jolted me awake. For a moment, I almost expected to see Reev lying on his cot across our little freight container. A lump in my throat, I went to answer the door.

Avan stood in the hall, hands shoved into his back pockets and shoulders hunched. His whole body seemed to unfurl in relief at the sight of me.

"You weren't—" He gestured at his room. "I thought maybe you . . . had gotten lost. Or something." He rubbed the back of his neck, looking embarrassed.

I was too tired to try and make sense of what he was saying. I made vague motions between my door and his. "You're alone?"

He checked over his shoulder as if someone might have crept up behind him. "Pretty sure," he said awkwardly, as if confused by my question.

"Oh. Well." I gave a small yawn and rubbed my eyes. "Okay then."

His embarrassment seemed to melt away as his mouth curved into a crooked smile. He moved closer. His scent enveloped me.

I found myself leaning forward. Blinking, I grasped the door to keep steady. My pulse quickened as his face drew nearer. My hand tightened around the doorknob. I stared at his mouth and shivered.

"Did *you* want to be alone?" he murmured. His fingers skimmed my jaw and rested just beneath my ear.

No. I wanted to reach up and guide his lips down to mine. I knew my reaction was due in part to the lingering gauze of sleep, but I didn't care. I didn't want to be rational. I closed my eyes and leaned into his touch, savoring the way his palm cupped my neck. My thoughts felt muddled, drowned out behind the veil of darkness and the haze of warmth spreading through me.

"Kai," he whispered, and even though my name was like a sigh in the silence, I could hear the question in it.

My eyes opened and sought out his in the scant light. I wasn't sure what he was asking—why I hadn't kept our usual arrangement and slept in his cot or . . . if I wanted him to join me in mine.

So I gave him the easier answer of the two. "I figured you'd want your privacy tonight."

His confusion lasted for a second before he realized what I meant. I caught a glimmer of surprise in his eyes.

"I see," he said, and backed away.

Drek. I was instantly wide-awake. What was wrong with me?

Idiot!

I stepped into the hall and watched him push his own door open. I wanted to reach out, but I didn't know if my touch would be welcome now. "Avan, wai—"

"Sorry for waking you," he said, and shut his door before I could say anything else.

CHAPTER 24

IN THE MORNING, WE GATHERED OUR THINGS AND MET Mason at the front entrance.

Like the day we arrived, the dense fog was a physical presence. The smoky gray wrapped around our legs and crawled up our sleeves. High above, the obscure shapes of the gargoyles hopped along their rocky perches as they patrolled. My fear of them felt distant. I was stronger than that now.

Mason waited at the base of the bridge with Hina, who would be joining us on the trek back to Ninurta. She had her long red braid coiled into a tight bun. Beside them on the black earth were two Grays, one of which I recognized. It was the Gray we'd crashed. A seam scarred the neck where the metal had been welded together. Several other metal sheets along its body had been replaced.

"Surprise!" Mason said, patting our Gray's head. "We made some cosmetic repairs and replaced the energy stone with a more efficient one. I improved on your modifications as well. She's as good as new. Even better."

Avan looked genuinely pleased. He mounted the Gray, flexing his hands on the grip. Then he tugged a lever along the neck. The Gray's chest lit up, and the metal rippled to life, much more smoothly than the first time we'd ridden it.

"Nice," he said. "Thank you." His gaze felt heavy when it fell on me. "Riding with me or Mason?"

I dropped my bag into the compartment on top of Avan's and pulled myself into the saddle without his help. Pressed thigh to thigh and chest to back, I could feel the moment he exhaled.

"What about the gargoyles in the Outlands?" I asked Mason. "They aren't exactly as well behaved as the guards here."

"We've had a few skirmishes in the past, and I think they know we're not easy prey. They've learned to leave us alone."

Mason and Hina, who flashed me an encouraging grin, mounted the other Gray, which looked like a mix between an enormous dog and a bear. My hands gripped Avan's hips as our Gray gave a jarring shimmy and stomped its feet. The metal shifted beneath me. This was it.

I'm coming, Reev.

We followed Mason over the bridge. It didn't feel as long as it had on foot.

Above us, the gargoyles leaned forward on their lampposts, their claws scraping the rusted metal as they watched us pass. On impulse, I waved. They didn't respond.

After we crossed into the Void, the fog thinned. I looked behind us. The fog consumed the bridge and dissipated in the dry air until nothing was left but the black stretch of dead earth. I understood now why Ninu couldn't find Irra's fortress.

The Grays lifted a trail of billowing dust as we raced across the Void. Avan pulled up alongside Mason to avoid choking on dirt. Judging by its speed, Mason's Gray must've had the same kind of modifications as ours. We would be out of the Void in a few hours. I was happy not to have to spend the night here.

The bleak emptiness reminded me of how I'd felt standing at the fringe of Etu Gahl. The familiarity was probably why Irra had chosen this place to hide.

My hands tightened at Avan's hips. He turned his head.

"It's weird," he said, "how we can still feel the aftermath of what happened here."

"Do you think this is how everyone felt after the war?"

"It's no wonder Ninu took advantage. People would have been desperate for leadership."

I rested my head against his shoulder. I must have dozed, because Avan's shouts woke me. I peered over his shoulder to where Mason pointed. The border of the Void ended at vivid green underbrush and tall trees. I blinked and scanned the forest line. The trees were within reach, but Mason and Avan showed no signs of slowing down.

"How are we getting through?" I asked.

"We trust Mason," Avan said just as the other Gray veered to the right.

Mason aimed for a gap between the trees. I held my breath, but there was no clamor of metal scraping bark, only the whisper of air through the leaves as the Gray passed through. Avan lowered himself over our Gray's neck and followed suit.

We fit perfectly through the gap. I dared to look up. Mason

led us through the trees, weaving in a precisely executed pattern. I eased my grip on Avan.

Some gaps were so narrow that leaves and twigs snagged my hair. I had tied it back but realized now why Hina had chosen a tightly wound braid.

The temperature had risen since we entered the forest. I drew a deep breath of the humid air. The weight of it was welcome after the emptiness of the Void. Seeing the colors here, everything else paled in comparison. Even Mason's rug and the drapes in the hospital wing lacked the same sort of life.

Watching Mason and Avan dodge trees made me nervous, so I pressed my forehead to Avan's back. I trusted him to stay close to Mason and get us through. We traveled slower now. The trees grew closer together here.

Moisture gathered where my body met Avan's. I blew at the hair sticking to my cheek and thought how unfair it was that even the back of Avan's neck looked attractive.

Judging by the drops that scattered over us as we passed, it had rained recently. I wished it would rain now. The longer we were in the forest, the less bearable the humidity became.

I kept my head down and tried not to squirm too much even though my leg had fallen asleep. I didn't want to distract Avan. I wasn't looking for another crash landing.

After a couple of hours, I was panting as if I'd been running from gargoyles. Avan breathed a little heavier than normal, but his heartbeat remained steady against my hand. Finally, Avan nudged me with his elbow, and I looked over to see Mason pointing ahead.

The trees had gone from lush and green to brown and brittle. Bright light filtered through the branches. We hit a wall of dry heat as we broke through the forest, leaving the humid, leafy maze behind. We picked up speed, the Grays' legs blurring across the earth. I pictured the prostitute's map in my head and mentally tracked our progress. I would have offered the map, which was currently squashed at the bottom of my bag, to Mason; but he seemed to know where he was going.

I dug into my bag to find the large package of food that Rennard had left outside our doors this morning. It included everything from bread and cheese to leftover cake from last night. I wish I'd had time to thank him. With the steady meals and Mason's training, I felt stronger physically than I ever had in Ninurta.

I picked up a roll of sweet bread stuffed with cream. I offered half of it to Avan.

His fingers brushed mine as he reached for it. "Thanks."

The bread had hardened a bit, but it still tasted delicious. I downed it with a few gulps of water and then let Avan finish the canteen.

After putting away the empty water container, I pressed a tentative hand against his chest. My other hand skimmed over his ribs to rest on his stomach.

I curled my fingers against his shirt, his heartbeat strong against my palm. I closed my eyes, finding comfort in the way his breath grew shallow at my touch. By now, I had memorized the feel of his back: the shift of muscle, the slope of his shoulder blades, the curve of his spine.

I craned forward in the saddle, my arms tight around his torso, until my lips grazed his ear. "I'm sorry. For last night. I was wrong to assume anything."

I wasn't sure if he'd respond. But then he turned his head so that my lips skimmed his cheek.

"I don't blame you for making assumptions," he said. "Besides, I should apologize, too. I didn't know what to think when you weren't asleep in my room."

"You thought I was with someone?" I couldn't help feeling the slightest bit insulted. But also a little flattered.

"The thought did cross my mind, even though I knew better."

I eased back so I could rest my cheek against the line of his shoulder. "I should have known better, too. I just figured I shouldn't . . . get in your way."

He surprised me by laughing. I felt the rumble against my chest and my hands, but it was so quiet that the wind stole the sound.

"Your consideration is a little misplaced," he said. "You should get some rest. I'll make sure you don't fall."

I bit my lip. "I'm not tired."

He glanced at me. Then he covered my hand on his chest, thumb smoothing over my wrist before he laced his fingers with mine.

CHAPTER 25

DAYLIGHT WAS FADING FAST BY THE TIME NINURTA'S WALLS came into view. Mason stopped us behind an outcropping to wait until complete darkness before we approached. Seeing the wall twisted my insides into anxious knots. I had thought, maybe, coming back would feel like coming home, if for no other reason than because Reev was there. But instead, all that greeted me was a prison.

A few gargoyles had spotted us along the way, but they had merely glanced in our direction before carrying on. Was Ninu aware of how intelligent the creatures he'd released into the Outlands were? Even without hollows, Irra could build a formidable army out of the gargoyles. Maybe there weren't enough of them to do that.

We shut off our Grays, and Mason dismounted. He consulted a map that he drew from beneath the knife sheath strapped around his thigh. Hina went about replacing the energy stones on both the Grays.

"Since you won't need it once you get into the tunnels," Hina said, peering into our Gray's chest, "you'll have to leave this one out here. Mason will ride it to Etu Gahl when he returns."

"You're not coming with us?" I asked her.

"I only came this far to make sure the gargoyles didn't get bold. They leave hollows alone, but you two probably wouldn't scare them. Mason will guide you the rest of the way."

After she finished replacing our energy stone, she switched it back on so we'd have the light to see by. The Gray provided the only light source aside from the distant glow of torches along Ninurta's walls.

Before leaving, she pulled me into a hug. I found myself hugging back. We hadn't spent much time together outside of meals and sparring, but aside from Avan, she and Mason were the closest thing I'd had to friends in a long time.

"Thanks," I said, "for your protection. And for making the Void feel . . . not so lonely."

She playfully punched my shoulder. "Stop trying to tell me good-bye. I'll see you when this is over."

I smiled gratefully. "Yeah."

With a final wave, she jumped onto the other Gray and rode off. Her red light faded into the darkness.

Mason, who hadn't bothered saying good-bye to Hina, studied the map, turning his head left and right as he oriented himself.

Avan sat nearby, eating a handful of dried fruit, as I watched over Mason's shoulder. Unlike the prostitute's map, Mason's was in good condition, but it didn't show much beyond the familiar boundaries of Ninurta. Mason pointed to a spot on the map outside the walls, above a series of zigzagging lines. "This is where we'll enter."

"The sewers." So that's what Hina had meant by "tunnels." Neither Mason nor Irra had given us details about how they planned to get us into the city. "But they're patrolled. And there are locked gates," I added.

"I've arranged for someone to meet us inside to unlock the gates," Mason said. "And our source was able to supply the patrol route. I memorized it."

"It still sounds risky."

"I know." He grinned. "Most excitement I've had in two months. Ninu's reconnaissance teams have pulled back and left us with nothing to do."

"I'm glad you're enjoying this."

He looked at the map. "We'll go the rest of the way by foot. It's not far."

We grabbed our bags and switched off the Gray, leaving it in the dark. I hoped Mason would be able to find his way back here.

Strong fingers grasped my hand. Warmth shot up my arm and through my chest. But instead of Avan's voice, Mason's said, "To keep you from wandering off."

Flustered, I didn't say anything as I reached out and felt for Avan's hand as well. I touched his stomach first, then he took my hand in his, squeezing lightly.

"Can you see?" Avan asked Mason. The darkness felt less oppressive with the two of them on either side of me, but it was still pitch-black.

"Yes," Mason said without further explanation. Maybe the collar improved his night vision.

We walked for about ten minutes. Even after my eyes adjusted to the dark, it was unnerving being able to see only a few feet of dirt and black shapes. It didn't help that the only sound was our footsteps—mine and Avan's, because Mason had the eerie ability to move without sound. Mason pressed my hand when we reached another outcropping, and we stopped.

Mason released me and knelt in the dry earth. I heard a *click*. He grabbed something and yanked roughly. Dirt cracked and skidded off the lid of a manhole cover as he raised it from the ground. It sounded like a rockslide in the silence. I looked around uneasily. What if the sound attracted gargoyles?

Avan and I knelt around the opening as Mason descended into the sewer. All I could see was the uppermost rung of a disintegrating metal ladder. A moment later, Mason called for us to follow him down.

With a glance at Avan, I went first.

Rust along the ladder's rungs dug into my palms. I couldn't see where to put my hands and feet. When my foot finally hit solid ground, I eased off the ladder, brushing my hands against my pants, and retreated a few steps to allow Avan room. Light burst through the darkness. I shielded my eyes. Had we been caught already?

But it was just Mason. The light was coming from his arm, bright enough to illuminate the tunnel. I shuffled forward, blinking.

"What is that?" I asked, looking at his arm brace. It was made of metal, darkened to a dull finish that wouldn't reflect the light. A few buttons lined the seam alongside some roughly cut details.

"I'm not sure. It's Irra's creation." Mason aimed the light into the space in front of us. "Better than a lantern."

The light revealed a walkway that ran along the side of the tunnel. The sewage pit in the middle had long since dried up. Didn't smell that way, though. I wrinkled my nose.

Two passages branched ahead; the left side had collapsed, blocked by crumbled stone and distorted metal.

Avan dropped down beside me, and Mason gestured for us to follow with a twitch of his head.

"We're still a ways from the wall, but Ninu keeps the sewers patrolled for a couple of miles out," Mason said. "They'll have passed by this area already. We should be safe. I don't think the gargoyles have found their way down here yet."

"You don't think?" I asked.

I could hear his grin as he said, "I've learned not to underestimate them."

"Fantastic," I muttered.

"There are a lot of unused sewer passages in Ninurta," Mason continued. "Most of them are left from before Rebirth. They still patrol the unused ones as well, but most are caved in. That's why we can't use them to sneak an army inside. Too unstable."

"This just gets better and better," I said. How pathetic would it be if I died in the sewer before I ever got to Reev?

Mason chuckled. "Step lightly."

I tried to do as he said.

We walked along, every sound making the fine hairs on the backs of my arms stand on end. At least in the Outlands, we were in the open. Here, aged stone surrounded us on all sides, reinforced only by metal liable to collapse at any time. After a while, Mason's light fell on a gate and an ancient-looking padlock on the other side. Mason tapped the metal gate three times and then switched off his light.

We waited in the dark for several long minutes until clumsy footsteps approached on the other side. Someone responded with three knocks. Then I heard shuffling feet, a mumbled curse, and a screech of metal as the lock turned. Mason switched his light back on. DJ was peering at us through the open gate.

I shouldn't have been surprised. DJ *had* said he was the Rider's gatekeeper.

DJ looked us over. "You two still human?"

"Define 'human,'" Avan said.

DJ rolled his eyes. "Wasn't expecting to see you again. How the drek did you get to the Rider and back in one piece?"

He stepped aside so that we could pass through. Then he pulled the gate shut and locked it behind us.

"You were wrong," Avan said as we followed DJ through more tunnels. The smell grew damper, moldier, and more bitter. "You said the Rider kidnapped people and turned them into hollows against their will."

"Hey," DJ said, his voice uncomfortably loud. "I tell you what I'm told to say, and it still got you there all right. Anyway, Mr. Hollow over there isn't proving me wrong."

Mason smiled—not his usual smile but a fake, vacant version. "Lead us forward," he said in a monotone.

When DJ turned away with a shudder, Mason's smile cracked into a real one, and he winked at me. I almost laughed.

According to Mason's map, we stood directly under the Labyrinth—which explained the familiar smell—following an outside route to the White Court. The tunnels here were in worse shape than the Labyrinth above. We wedged through caved-in passages, making our way around the active sewage pipes, and had to travel in the dark for stretches when we drew too close to a patrolling Watchman. A few times, the entire passage quaked as a heavy Gray passed overhead, and we flattened ourselves against the wall to avoid any loose debris. I wasn't claustrophobic, but I had begun to change my mind about this by the time we reached another locked gate.

"This one leads into the White Court. I don't know what business you two got in there, but good luck. You'll need it here even more than in the Outlands." DJ jabbed his thumb in Mason's direction as he turned away. "He'll take you in."

This would be the farthest I'd ever been inside the White Court. *Somewhere up there is Reev.*

The sewers here were noticeably different. The dampness and the odors remained, but the tunnels were sturdier. They must have been reinforced sometime in the last century.

We walked for another ten minutes before Mason abruptly killed the light. His hand gripped my shoulder and pushed me up against the wall. I heard Avan hit the stone beside me. Mason leaned in, pinning us both with a whispered *"Quiet."*

I remained still, Mason's body like a furnace compared to the damp sewage air. My ears strained for whatever he had heard. There was nothing but the sound of dripping water.

Then I heard it. Footsteps, along with the hum of voices echoing off the tunnel walls. The footsteps sounded hurried. The glow of a lantern wavered through the metal grate of another tunnel to the left of us.

"Keep looking," a voice said.

Mason eased back, and I could practically feel the energy rising off him.

"Listen," he whispered. "Your exit is down that tunnel and to the right. There will be a ladder like the one we came down and a symbol beneath the manhole cover that looks like one of the marks on my collar. That'll open up to an alley behind Zora Hall, the Tournament dormitories. Go in through the back." He sniffed at me. "And try to clean yourselves off."

He began moving away. I grasped his wrist as more footsteps reverberated through the tunnel, closer now.

"What about you?" I asked, feeling Avan's hand on my arm.

"We must have tripped an alarm somewhere," Mason said. "I don't know how I missed it, but it doesn't matter now. I'll lead them away. You two get to Zora Hall."

"But, Mason—"

"Unless you hurry, I won't have enough time to get them chasing each other in circles." He sounded *excited* to have been caught. I wanted to smack him for enjoying the danger.

"Don't do anything reckless," I said, releasing his wrist.

I couldn't make out his face in the dark, but I imagined he was smiling. "Remember what I told you. End your matches as quickly as possible. Try not to let your opponent knock you off your feet. And remember, when you find Reev—"

"Go back to the manhole at noon. Flip the cover. Meet there twenty-four hours later," I finished for him. He grunted his approval.

I felt Avan brush past me as he reached over to Mason. "Be careful getting out."

"Take care of each other," Mason said quietly. Silence followed for a beat too long. Were he and Avan having a staring contest in the dark?

Finally, Mason's fingers found my cheek, and he leaned in so that his words were only a breath against my ear.

"I'll be waiting for you in Etu Gahl when this is over."

I touched his shoulder. "Thank you for everything."

CHAPTER 26

WE CREPT INTO ZORA HALL THROUGH THE BACK AND ENTERED a hallway. All the doors were identical except for the room numbers etched into the wood. I leaned closer to one, trailing my fingers against the woodwork. The curling lines had been carved with care.

"I don't suppose Mason forgot to give us our room assignments," Avan said. He dusted off his shirt, which sent a cloud of powdery dirt onto the gleaming floor. I looked down at myself. My clothes weren't much better. Mason had suggested we clean off, but he hadn't said how. Had he made it out safely?

"Hey!" someone said from behind us.

I jumped away from the door I'd been studying. A Watchman came up the hall, looking stern. I lowered my eyes, my pulse quickening. I hoped we just appeared lost.

"Lights-out was an hour ago." Her nose wrinkled. "What were you two doing? Crawling through the sewers?"

"We're a bit lost," Avan said, giving his best "I'm harmless and pretty" smile.

The Watchman shifted her feet, flustered, but dutifully demanded to see our IDs.

"Ah!" she said as she studied them, and returned Avan's smile—too enthusiastically. "I was told there would be late arrivals." She removed a book from her pocket and began flipping through the pages. "Your rooms are on the second floor. Nel, 204. Savorn, 207. Go on now. Cadets have lights-out at sunset."

We thanked her and headed for the stairwell. When she stared after Avan, I fell behind enough to block her line of sight. Honestly, you'd think a Watchman would have better self-control.

Our rooms turned out to be a few doors apart, on opposite sides of the hall. Avan paused, then he said, "Guess this is it," and disappeared into his room. With a fortifying breath, I walked into mine.

After I shut the door, I remained where I was, needing a minute to take in everything I was seeing. My room wasn't much larger than the one in the hollows' dorms; but the rug felt soft and full, and two sconces braced each of the walls, which were a soothing shade of butter yellow. The curtains were drawn on a window above my bed. I even had a real closet and my own washroom.

As incredible as the room was, I wanted to go out and search for Reev immediately. But I knew I couldn't risk it. I'd have plenty of time tomorrow when they released us for the Tournament.

I sat on the narrow but thickly cushioned bed that extended from the wall, and gave an experimental bounce. It felt like sitting on clouds. Beside the bed, a sign had been adhered to the wall. The top of the sign displayed four names: *Nel – 204, Grene –*

205, Tariza — 206, Savorn — 207. My teammates. Irra had said the entire team needed a high collective score to continue on.

Beneath our names was a list of rules:

1. No intermingling between teams.

2. Cadets caught outside their dormitories after lights-out will be subject to disciplinary action and potential expulsion from the Tournament.

3. Training is restricted to dormitories and the training center during the hours of 7 a.m. to 7 p.m.

The list went on, but I skimmed down to the bottom where it announced that the first fights would begin in the morning an hour after breakfast.

Little pulses of anxiety shot through my skin. I had to remind myself that both Irra and Mason had been satisfied with my progress. I could do this. I couldn't touch the threads for help, and yeah, Mason could make quick work of me; but he was a trained sentinel. In the end, I had managed a few hits against him, so I figured I would do better against a cadet. I just had to fit in. Winning didn't matter.

I washed up, dawdling as I admired the shiny fixtures and the overall sense of cleanliness. Then I dimmed the sconces and climbed into bed.

Last night had been the first time in more than two weeks that

I'd slept alone, but now, not having Avan here with me made all the unexpected comforts feel . . . cold. Did he feel the same or was he already asleep, grateful for the solitude of his own room and a proper bed instead of a mattress on the floor?

I yanked the blanket over my head and tried to convince myself it didn't make any difference.

A loud knock and a booming voice in the hallway woke me. I pulled the pillow over my ears. I couldn't identify the scent on the sheets, but I liked pushing my face into them and inhaling deeply. The smell reminded me of the courtyard: sunshine and warm breezes. Avan lying in the grass, close enough to touch.

"Good morning, cadets," boomed the cheerful voice outside my room. I groaned. It had taken hours to fall asleep last night. "Welcome to the opening day of the Tournament. Breakfast will be served in the cafeteria in thirty minutes. Please see the schedule, updated hourly, in the common room to avoid any confusion or delays, which could result in mandatory forfeit." The speaker grew alternately louder and softer as she paced up and down the hall. "Please read all rules and regulations. Violators will be subject to immediate disciplinary action. And remember, cadets, we are proud to be Ninurtans. Good luck!"

I rolled my eyes. Sitting up, I drew back the curtains on the window. I squinted against the light. I was looking down on a water fountain. Mosaic stones radiated in a pattern around the fountain, and despite the early hour, a few cadets were already outside milling about.

I kept the curtains open, and cleaned up. The washroom had a mirror, but I had been too busy studying everything else last night to pay much attention to my reflection. I was taken aback to see myself looking so . . . healthy. My cheeks had filled in, and the shadows beneath my eyes had faded. Although I was still too pale, I no longer looked on the verge of starving. I had Irra to thank for that. Another curious contradiction. Like the hollows', Famine's name barely captured who he was.

I leaned in closer and studied my eyes. I tried to find what Irra had seen: the River or whatever it was he had called the threads. But all I saw was a cool-blue iris around a dark pupil.

In the closet, I found a dozen identical outfits folded along two shelves. They consisted of form-fitting black tunics with green trim and dark-gray pants. Three sets of black boots were on the floor. At least it was all practical.

I changed, appreciating the tight but comfortable fit, and added a braided black belt I found in the dresser under the shelves. Then I drew the knife from my bag and slid it into my boot. We weren't allowed to use weapons during our matches, but I wasn't about to walk around the arena, bursting with Watchmen and likely a few sentinels, with only fists to protect myself.

Out in the hall, cadets dressed in the same style uniform as mine headed toward the staircase. I knocked at Avan's door.

"He's already gone down," a boy said, pausing beside me. He stuck out his hand. "I'm Tariza. Are you Nel? I saw you come out of 204."

I nodded and took his hand. He was short for a guy, only an inch or so taller than myself, but he made up for it in brawn. His upper body bulged beneath his tunic, stretched across his shoulders. I forced my face to remain neutral despite his crushing grip on my hand. I was glad I wouldn't have to fight him.

He offered to walk down to the cafeteria together. Since he seemed to know where he was going, I let him lead.

"Got in late? You and Savorn weren't at the opening ceremonies."

"Last-minute paperwork."

We passed through bright hallways with elegant metal sconces that ran the length of the wall. All around, cadets blew past us in their hurry to reach the cafeteria. Some of them looked to be about my age, although most were a few years older.

Two metal doors stood open at the entrance to a large cafeteria lined with polished wooden tables. It looked nothing like the mess hall in Etu Gahl, which had been dark and rustic but still cozy. If anything, the cafeteria resembled the one at school, only bigger and cleaner. Tall windows framed the Ninurtan emblem—the sword and scythe—embossed in silver and red on a plain white wall. Cadets lined up along another wall to retrieve their prefilled trays.

Each table had four seats, which probably meant they were assigned by team. I searched for Avan.

I spotted him sitting a few tables down with a blond girl. Tariza and I joined them.

Avan wore the same black-and-green uniform as everyone else, and he'd removed the steel bar in his eyebrow; but he still managed to stand out. And he'd already charmed Grene, judging by her helpless smile and flushed cheeks.

We made our introductions and went to retrieve our trays. Each meal held the same portions: A dollop of lumpy mash. Lentil soup. Steamed vegetables and a carton of milk. It was just like at school.

I didn't really mind. Having a meal at all was enough for me.

"Did you guys see the brackets in the common room?" Grene asked when we returned to our table.

I shook my head, but Tariza said, "Yeah. Savorn is up first from our team." He looked at me. "Nel, you're at three."

"Do you know who I'm fighting?" I asked, swirling my spoon through the soup.

"Didn't recognize the name."

"So where are you from?" Avan asked Tariza.

"Upper North District. My mom didn't want me to join the Academy, but now that I'm up for the Tournament, my parents are trying to get permission to visit." Tariza straightened, pride filling his already sturdy chest.

"What about you two?" Grene looked at me and Avan. "You seem like you know each other."

We had prepared responses for these questions, so I let Avan answer.

"Lower North District," Avan said. "We grew up in the same neighborhood."

"The familiar face must be nice," Tariza said, his eyes roaming the cafeteria. "And getting on the same team? What were the odds of that?"

"Yeah, do you guys have an uncle on the inside or something?" Grene asked, grinning with too much teeth. She talked with such enthusiasm that every word out of her mouth should've ended with an exclamation point.

"Just luck," I said. I ate fast, without needing to taste the bland fare. Eating only enough to fuel my body was like second nature.

"Slow down there, Nel," Tariza said, eyeing my tray. "The food isn't going anywhere."

Heat filled my cheeks at the insinuation. Because Avan had told them we were from the lower North District, the worst section of the Alley, they would assume that we had been poor and underfed. And they were right, for the most part, but I still didn't like his tone.

"Grene is from the South Quarter of the White Court," Avan said. The South Quarter was where the Watchmen headquarters and the Academy were located. "She was telling me about how her aunt was a sentinel."

Grene twirled her slender fingers through her blond hair as she ate. Even her smallest movements bounced with energy. Either she was nauseatingly upbeat or she was buzzing with nerves.

"She died on a mission to the Outlands a few years ago," Grene boasted, in the same way that someone would announce she had won a trophy.

I had to wonder if she wasn't dead at all but had joined Irra instead. Maybe we had eaten with her in the mess hall or danced with her at the party.

I hadn't considered it before, but the disappearances worked both ways. Ninu kidnapped people such as Tera, the prostitute's sister, while Irra could very well have taken Grene's aunt. Either way, families were left broken.

"Ever since, my father has been betting on me becoming a sentinel. I completed the courses at the Academy with top scores."

I wished I could tell whether or not she was *mahjo*. Magic must not manifest in every descendant if her aunt had been a sentinel but not her father or mother. And since neither of Avan's parents had been taken for the Tournament, they didn't have any *mahjo* blood, either, since I knew both of them had donated at the energy clinics.

"He insists he can't live without the honor of having a sentinel in the family, even though it means never seeing me again," Grene explained. She said it so airily that I couldn't tell if she agreed with her father or not.

"What do you know about the sentinels?" I asked.

"Not much more than the rest of you," she admitted. "But I like the secrecy. Makes them seem all mysterious or magical or something."

Or suspicious. But Grene obviously hadn't considered that.

I polished off my tray, while to my right, Avan ate slowly, forming his potato mash into a tall peak and then demolishing it.

"You okay?" I asked.

Avan gave me that lopsided smile that made my chest tighten. He didn't try to manipulate me like he did Grene. This was genuine.

He looked at me and murmured, "Perfect."

I held in my laughter.

"Nervous about your match?" Tariza asked Avan.

"Kind of."

"You'll do great," I said, because I believed it. We had yet to see these cadets fight, but, like me, Avan had managed against a fully trained sentinel. And he healed fast. I didn't need to worry about him, I told myself.

The others finished eating, and then Grene showed us to the prep room. All the cadets reported there first, where we would be called out to the arena. Observers to the matches were restricted to the judges and the participating cadets' teams to avoid scouting out another cadet's strengths and weaknesses. Personally, I was glad. I didn't relish the idea of being scrutinized by strangers and potential opponents.

Other cadets with early matches joined us in the hallway as we headed for the bright-red door. Avan entered first.

I saw the way his body tensed before he moved into the room. His hand found my wrist, pulling me close to his side. The intimate gesture caught me off guard. I pushed against his chest, but his hand tightened around my wrist, and, a moment later, I saw why.

Three sentinels stood in the middle of the room, facing away from us. It was jarring to see his collar on display, but I recognized him all the same. I would have recognized him anywhere.

Reev.

CHAPTER 27

I STARTED FORWARD. AVAN HELD ME BACK, HIS OTHER HAND gripping my waist.

"No," he said so softly that his words reached only my ears. "Look around. This room is filled with Watchmen."

I couldn't look around. Reev filled my vision. His reassuring back; the breadth of his shoulders; his hair, shorter now, curled around his collar.

I tried to wrench free of Avan's grasp, but Reev was already moving away. He followed the other sentinels through an entryway. Panic rattled my rib cage. He was getting away. He was *leaving* again. I had to stop him.

Strong hands seized my shoulders and spun me around. Avan's dark eyes met mine. He smoothed down my hair, his fingers cupping my face.

"*Kai,*" he whispered. "Get ahold of yourself. We've got time."

Another hand waved tentatively at me. "Nel, you okay?"

It was Grene. I pushed away from Avan and drew in a slow breath. And then again. I had almost reached for the threads to delay Reev. I could have blown our cover. I turned to face Grene.

"I'm just . . . a little tired," I said lamely. I looked at her chin to avoid her eyes.

"Well, don't let it interfere with your match," Grene said. "We're scored as a team."

"Maybe you can nap after Avan's fight," Tariza suggested.

I doubted I could sleep at all now that I knew Reev was within reach.

A man in a high-collared black tunic and green cravat appeared from the entryway through which Reev had left. He moved into the center of the room, clasped his hands at his waist, and scanned the cadets.

The chatter stopped.

"Welcome, cadets, to the first round of the Tournament," he said, his thick brows drawn together into a severe line. He had a nasally voice, made more pronounced by how loudly he was talking. The White Court really needed to find a way to make announcements without shouting. "This marks another year in which our young warriors rise to the duty of defending our great city. Let us once again give thanks to Kahl Ninurta I, who gathered the scattered peoples of the land, stricken and floundering in the dark, and built them a haven. The only *mahjo* to survive the devastation, who dedicated his life and his magic to restoring order and providing safety behind the protection of our mighty walls."

Avan and I shared exasperated looks. We already knew the story. Every Ninurtan did. It was retold every year on Founding Day.

More than two hundred years ago, Kahl Ninurta I—who Irra had referred to as Conquest and claimed was the same person still ruling today—had led survivors of the Mahjo War into the ruins of an abandoned city and declared it his own.

I glanced around. Some of the cadets looked bored, but others clung to his words. I wondered what they would think if they knew other *mahjo* were still around, enslaved by the Kahl.

"Kahl Ninu thanks you for your service," the man continued. "All matches will be overseen by a jury of sentinels. The sentinels may award the victory to either opponent based on skill and execution, regardless of the match's winner. Do your best, and you will succeed." He paused for dramatic effect before announcing, "Cadets, let the Tournament begin!"

The cadets cheered. I pumped my fist so I wouldn't stand out.

Once everyone had quieted down again, Avan led our team over to a bench along the wall. My mind flashed through scenarios: confronting Reev, rescuing him, hugging him, talking to him. I had to force myself to stop, to think of nothing, to focus only on the flicker of the candlelight inside the curling metal sconce across the room.

Tariza and Grene talked excitedly about something I didn't care to overhear. Avan sat close enough that his shoulder warmed mine. I let his touch anchor me in the moment instead of reeling forward to chase after Reev in my mind.

A few minutes later, a Watchman called for Avan. We stood with him, offering encouraging pats on the back. The Watchman ushered Avan through the entryway, while the three of us were directed toward a separate exit.

We walked down a hallway and then emerged in an outdoor arena. Our viewing box was at ground level directly in front of the fighting area, sectioned off by a waist-high partition. Three other cadets occupied a similar box across the arena.

The arena itself wasn't much larger than Irra's courtyard, with high walls that cut us off from the other matches. A mass of yellow clouds provided our only ceiling. About ten feet in front of me, Avan stood with his back to us, his feet apart and shoulders relaxed. In seats across the arena I spotted Reev and the two sentinels from the prep room.

Like the other sentinels, Reev was dressed all in dark leather. Practical pieces of clothing that would offer some protection and movement. He looked far too much like them.

I pressed my palm to my racing heart. Reev was watching the two in the arena. It was hard to read his face from here, but I didn't see recognition. He *knew* Avan. He had to recognize him. Reev was smart, though. He was probably pretending so he wouldn't give Avan away.

Look at me. I wanted him to see me so badly.

Then he did. He looked right at me.

Reev held my gaze for the span of a breath. My body went numb. Then his eyes slid away as easily as if he'd been looking at a stranger.

I bit down on the insides of my cheeks, letting the physical pain override the ache in my chest. Reev was pretending. He had always been good at hiding his thoughts. Even from me.

He had recognized me. Of course he had.

I had to get Reev alone.

A voice boomed around the arena, and we looked up to see the announcer, a plump woman in a red-and-white tunic, standing on a platform jutting from the wall. "Match number six: Elsin versus Savorn."

She struck a bell to signal the beginning of the match. I searched for Avan's opponent, angry with myself that I hadn't bothered to check sooner.

He was a young man, similar in build to Avan, with dark-red curls. I wasn't sure what to make of him. He sized up Avan as they circled each other.

Elsin attacked first. They were both fast on their feet, blocking and striking and unable to get in a clean hit as they moved around. Elsin dodged a kick and then stepped in for a punch. Avan blocked, grabbing Elsin's wrist and twisting it around to plant a knee in his back.

My attention darted between the fight and Reev. Reev watched the match with complete focus. I'd seen the way he was at work, when he had to be menacing to ward off the desperate folks who haunted the docks. But this was different. Colder. Emptier.

He couldn't already be rebranded. Irra had said whatever Ninu did would take months.

Tariza leaned over. "What are you so worried about? Savorn is winning."

I glanced back at Avan. Elsin lay on his stomach, his nose bleeding into the packed dirt of the arena floor. Avan had him pinned, his arms secured painfully behind him. A layer of dirt covered them both.

The bell sounded again. Avan released Elsin, and Elsin slumped into the dirt with a groan. His chest moved with rapid breaths, and blood still oozed from his broken nose.

Avan straightened and dusted off his tunic.

Tariza and Grene whooped, shouting "Savorn!" and pumping their fists. I tried to smile for Avan's sake, but his triumphant grin slipped a fraction when he saw me.

"Nel, come on!" Grene tugged my arm, and I reluctantly went with them through the corridor. I took in one last glimpse of Reev before the doors blocked my view. He hadn't even glanced my way.

After a hearty round of congratulations, Tariza announced he was going to train, and Grene wanted to explore the arena grounds.

"Want to come with me?" she asked, turning her wide blue eyes on Avan. When she realized I wasn't going to run off the way Tariza had, she glanced at me and added, "You, too, of course."

"I need to talk to Savorn about something."

"We'll see you back here at three for Nel's match," Avan said.

Grene looked embarrassed. "Oh, okay! Sounds great."

We waited until she'd cleared out with an energetic wave. More cadets streamed in for the next round of matches. It didn't look like Reev was returning, so we finally left. We found a quiet alcove down the hall, and Avan pulled me inside.

"Reev didn't recognize us," he said.

My jaw hurt from clenching it so tightly. "He was pretending."

"Kai," Avan said.

It made me angry the way he said my name, as if I was something delicate. Breakable. After everything we'd been through, he should have known better. I wasn't weak, and I wasn't giving up, especially not with Reev right here in front of me.

"You have to consider the possibility—"

"No," I said louder. I jabbed a finger against his chest. "And don't you dare, either. I just need to get him alone."

Avan regarded me. Then he nodded. "Okay. How do you plan on doing that?"

I scowled. "He saw us. He'll come looking for me."

Avan's blank expression was infuriating. "You're right," he said, but I couldn't tell if he really believed me or not. "We should make it easier for him by learning where everything is. I'm going to poke around. Join me?"

"I'm tired. I'm going to my room," I lied.

"If you want to be alone, just say so," he told me, which made me drop my gaze guiltily. "And be careful."

Before he turned away, I touched his arm.

"Do you think Mason made it out all right?"

"He's probably having breakfast in Etu Gahl as we speak. He's not the one you should be worrying about."

True, but it made me feel better that he believed Mason was safe.

I nodded. "Nice match, by the way. Are you hurt?" I already knew the answer but figured I should ask. Whenever Avan came to terms with the fact that he was *mahjo*, I hoped he would talk to me about it. I could tell him that it wasn't so bad being different.

Avan gave me his crooked smile. "Not a scratch."

• • •

Instead of going to my room, I did what Avan had suggested and wandered around the facility until noon. Unfortunately, Reev was nowhere to be found.

Cadets lingered everywhere. From what I knew of the Tournament, only a handful made it to the final rounds. According to Irra, more than a hundred cadets entered the Tournament. The judges culled half during the preliminary brackets. After that, another half were eliminated in teams until they reached the single-elimination matches, which were presided over by Kahl Ninu himself.

Mahjo naturally rose to the top, making it easy for Kahl Ninu to award them the rank of sentinel. The citizens of the White Court didn't seem to know what becoming a sentinel really meant. The sacrifices required. Grene had said they weren't allowed to see their families anymore, but had she ever questioned why Kahl Ninu had sent her aunt into the Outlands in the first place?

I returned to Zora Hall and headed to the back entrance where Avan and I had sneaked in. The alley where we'd emerged from the sewer was empty, but I made a sweep of the area. Then I reached down and heaved the manhole cover from its position. The top of the cover had a looping design engraved into the metal. It looked like flower petals extending from the Ninurtan emblem in the middle.

With a grunt, I flipped over the cover, careful to grasp the rim before it could clatter on the ground. The other side bore the same design, except instead of the emblem, there was what looked like an elaborate *A*, but I doubted it was a letter. It matched one of the designs carved into Mason's collar—a mark or sigil of some kind that Irra had added to sever the link with Kahl Ninu.

If Mason's information proved accurate—and he had yet to fail us—then Irra's spies would see my signal. In twenty-four hours, we would meet here and an escort would see us out.

I should have talked to Avan before going ahead with the signal, but his skepticism over Reev annoyed me. Lack of faith wasn't going to get my brother out of here. *I* was.

Now it was simply a matter of finding him. Reev was probably still overseeing matches, so I'd have to keep checking the prep room or try to locate the sentinel quarters before lights-out.

As soon as I talked to him, things would be okay. I would get him to the sewer and out of Ninurta. Irra would be able to help him, the same way he'd helped Mason and all the other hollows.

Reev would be okay. I knew it. I clutched that certainty close—it was the only thing I had left.

CHAPTER 28

AFTER A FEW WRONG TURNS AND SEVERAL EMPTY HALLWAYS, I came to the conclusion that I was lost. I didn't mind not knowing where I was going. I'd memorized the streets in the Lower Alley by first getting lost and then navigating my way back to familiar ground. I wandered a bit farther and discovered a huge lobby. Everything gleamed, from the silvery filament in the stone tiles to the gold and stained-glass accents in the mural on the ceiling. High-backed chairs with brocade upholstery were lined up all along the walls, a few of them occupied by people reading or sitting quietly as if they were waiting for something, but I couldn't imagine what that might be.

I crossed the lobby hesitantly. The ceiling rose as tall as the rafters in Etu Gahl, but the metal sconces holding hundreds of glowing candles were a far cry from drafty wooden beams dressed in cobwebs.

A pair of Watchmen stood at the entrance, but the lobby was otherwise unguarded. The Tournament, and much of the Academy, was kept private from the rest of the city. I had read that cadets were allowed to see their families only once a year until graduation, unless the families received special permission to visit.

Beyond the double glass doors, I could see a throng of people outside. The traffic in the White Court was as crowded as in the North District. The Watchmen guarding the doors gave me suspicious looks, but I just waved as if I knew exactly what I was doing and stepped outside. I doubted I'd find Reev out here, but I couldn't contain the curiosity that guided me forward. I had never seen the White Court from anywhere but the barracks.

As soon as I reached the sidewalk, I was overtaken by the flow of people. A hard shoulder knocked me off the curb. I gasped and clutched a lamppost right as a Gray barreled past, the ensuing gust of wind snapping my hair across my cheeks. I brushed it out of my face and continued down the sidewalk. I didn't like the crowds in the North District, but at least there I could feel invisible. The differences here confused and fascinated me at the same time.

I pushed forward, keeping closer to the buildings. As I'd seen from the barracks, colorful posters plastered the walls. They promoted an endless supply of goods that I supposedly couldn't live without: two-headed Grays, highly impractical clothes, and gadgets the purpose for which I had no idea. Only the food looked remotely appealing. On the cobblestone road, riders steered enormous Grays in the shapes of long-extinct animals: creatures with three-foot horns, lumbering feet, spiny backs, or long, slender necks that bobbed as they moved. Their massive chests glowed in two spots, indicating they needed two energy stones. They were passed on either side by sleek, compact Grays or the occasional scout.

Men and women were dressed in vibrant tunics and lovely patterns, billowing sleeves and elaborate collars and bustled dresses and boots made of buckles and leather. But amid the extravagance were some who didn't look so different from those in the North District—with plain tunics in muted colors.

I wondered what sort of work the people did here. The White Court controlled all Ninurta's resources, but nobody was allowed into the Production District aside from workers and Watchmen.

A few women walked past with horrifically cinched corsets that made me wince just looking at them. What a strange idea of beauty these people had. Not that their clothing wasn't beautiful, because even I couldn't deny that; but it was all so . . . *much*. Too many trappings and not enough simple, human imperfection.

Of course, Avan came to mind. I was hard-pressed to find any imperfections on him, but there had to be *something*. Like a weird birthmark he'd hidden beneath his tattoo or . . . something less stupid.

I studied the brocade boots of a woman with a large bustle. My eyes followed the dramatic dip of her corseted waist up to her metal choker and full, smiling lips. It wasn't until I met her gaze that I noticed she was smiling at me.

I looked away—only to realize other people were smiling at me as well. I slowed, shrinking against the nearest wall. I hadn't realized how much I stood out.

To be accurate, they smiled at my uniform, then at my face. Someone behind me called out, "Good luck, cadet!"

I nodded awkwardly. I scanned the street ahead and found a path leading away from the busy sidewalk, down to what looked like a food market. Smells both savory and sweet drifted from the smoky stalls.

I followed the scents, bouncing on my toes and peering over shoulders to get a look.

The offerings looked nothing like what had been on my tray this morning. My mouth watered just watching one of the stall owners ladle a thick soup into a bread bowl.

At the next stall, a woman basted an actual strip of meat on a fryer. I'd tasted meat only once, and it hadn't been that impressive. This sizzling meat smelled wonderful, but I didn't know that I'd try it again even if Rennard was the one to prepare it. The texture was too unusual.

All of Ninurta's crops and livestock were locked away in the Production District. I didn't think even Kahl Ninu ate meat on a regular basis.

One young chef caught my eye and began waving. I glanced around. When no one else reacted, I looked back to find him motioning me to come closer. I approached cautiously.

"Cadet," the man said. He grasped my hand before I could pull away and shook it vigorously. Flour dusted my fingers. Then he selected a plump roll of bread from his warming plate and shoved it at me. "Good luck in the Tournament. I'll look for your face when the victors are announced."

My eyes flicked from the roll heating my palm to the man beaming at me like I'd already won. "I-I can't take this." I tried giving back the bread, but he batted it away. "And what makes you think I'll win?"

"You have that wildly determined look," he said. He peered far too closely into my face. "I'd wager lower North District, possibly even the East Quarter." He nodded decisively. "Joining the Academy to better your station was a good decision."

What did I say to *that*? I wasn't ashamed of living in the Labyrinth. I extracted myself as politely as I could, thanking him for the bread. Everywhere I stopped, people waved and tried to offer me free food. This wasn't at all what I'd expected.

Everyone, save for a harried-looking few, seemed to be in good spirits. I suppose not having to worry about their next meal or their credit balance meant they could focus on things that seemed frivolous to me. It looked like a nice way to live, but it didn't feel real. They had no idea that Ninu kept them as effectively leashed as he did the rest of us.

I didn't want to see any more. I didn't want to like these people. I had to get Reev out of here, back to what was real, even if that reality wasn't as bright and happy as this one.

I had to get him home. Wherever that was. Once we left Ninurta, we'd figure it out.

CHAPTER 29

BY THE TIME I NEARED THE OPEN STREET, THE FREE ROLL OF bread had been joined by a package of sweets and a pear.

"Nel!"

I twisted around. Avan was weaving his way through the crowd, looking both worried and amused.

"I see you've been productive." He looked at my full hands.

"They gave these to me," I said, and followed him toward the street. "I couldn't give them back."

"And here I thought I was special," he said.

When I realized what he meant, my face grew warm. "I guess I've learned not to turn down free food."

"I don't blame you. Looks a lot better than what they served this morning."

"You can have them," I said, pushing the bread at him.

He shook his head. "You're not supposed to leave the hall. Didn't you read the rules? What are you going to do if we're expelled?"

I had read the rules. Just not all of them.

"You left, too," I pointed out.

"I've never had very good judgment."

Once we were safely inside the arena lobby, I let myself relax and considered the food in my hands. "I wonder if I could mail this to the Labyrinth."

"Would they even eat it?"

My neighbors in the East Quarter were notoriously suspicious, especially of anything and anyone outside its claustrophobic walls. Usually, that was a good thing. "Maybe if it came with my name on it."

"Probably not a good idea to broadcast where you are."

"Fair point. Guess you'll have to help me finish it, then."

I dropped off the sweets and fruit in my room but took the bread with me. Avan and I shared it on the way to the training center, and we agreed it was the best bread we'd ever eaten. Even the bread delivered daily to Avan's shop was a few days old and sometimes bordering on inedible.

The bakeries sold fresh bread only to those living in the Upper Alley, the sort of neighborhood Tariza had come from. Once the bread grew stale, they sold it to the rest of us for twice the amount of credits.

The training facility was made up of a series of rooms, closed off from one another to maintain privacy between teams. We found Grene's and Tariza's names written on the door of Room 8 and went inside. Two horizontal wooden beams were mounted in the center. Grene stood balanced on top of one, twirling on one foot, her arms poised over her head. She did a neat flip along the beam, her body bending like a blade of grass. If I tried to bend like that, I'd break. Tariza, meanwhile, did one-hand-ed pull-ups on the other beam. His bicep and neck muscles bulged.

"Glad we're not fighting them," Avan said, echoing my earlier thoughts.

I laughed. It drew Tariza's attention as he dropped to the floor and massaged the corded muscles in his arm.

"You're awake!" Grene said, flipping off the beam and landing on her feet.

Avan must have told them I'd gone for a nap. "Yeah. I need to warm up for my match."

"Me, too. Let's spar. I'll bet you're really good." She led me over to an open space near the wall.

Avan and Tariza went off to spar on the opposite side of the room. Avan almost looked excited.

Grene was a good fighter. She struck and then danced out of reach, as fluid and slippery as a fish.

She wasn't as fast as I was, but it still took all my concentra-tion to block her kicks. I hit back with only partial effort. I didn't actually want to hurt her.

"So you and Savorn were childhood friends?" Grene asked, blocking my punch. She slid sideways, leg arcing up in a kick. I caught her leg and shoved, but she was too nimble to lose her balance.

"Yeah," I said.

She beamed and darted back in. "You joined the Academy to-gether? That's so sweet."

Even had that been the truth, I didn't see what was so sweet about it. And anyway, she had the wrong idea about me and Avan. *Maybe.*

"I guess."

"It's great that you guys made it so far," she said in that perky voice. "I mean, how generous is it that the opportunities of Watchmen are given even to those of your standi— *Oof!*"

My fist connected with her stomach. She flew back, skidding across the floor, blond hair flying all over her face.

I immediately felt guilty. Because of where she grew up, Grene couldn't help thinking the way she did. I hurried over and knelt at her side. "Are you okay? I—"

"Great hit," she said, grinning up at me as she rubbed her stomach. She winced. I felt even worse. I helped her up. "Again?" she asked.

"I'm going to head to the prep room," I said. "You guys can stay here and train if you want."

"No way. We have to come support you," she said, patting down her hair. "Guys!"

Avan and Tariza were circling each other, their expressions intense. I couldn't tell if they were taking their sparring seriously or if they were angry about something. It must have been the first one, because at Grene's shout, Tariza broke into a smile and slapped Avan across the back.

The whole way to the prep room, my heartbeat felt as if it was trying to shatter my rib cage. I rubbed my palms against my pants before I entered the room and scanned the occupants.

Reev wasn't there. Disappointment replaced my anxiety. Three sentinels I didn't recognize waited near the exit doors.

On second thought, I was glad Reev wouldn't be overseeing my match. I wouldn't be able to concentrate with his eyes on me, pretending he had no idea who I was.

When my time arrived, the Watchman sent me through the doors leading out to the arena floor. This arena was different from Avan's, which had been plain, packed dirt. Trimmed grass and a circle of hedges made up our fighting field. At the opposite end of the green stood a tall, wiry boy. He smirked when he saw me.

I used to like being underestimated. It kept me and my secret safe. But now I wanted to wipe that smirk off his face.

In the viewing box behind me, Avan and the others appeared.

"Knock him off his feet, Nel!" Grene shouted. Maybe she wasn't that annoying after all.

"Match number thirty-nine: Nel versus Muree."

When the bell sounded, the boy didn't hesitate. He charged across the field.

He threw his entire weight into his attack. I dropped low and drove my knuckles into his stomach right beneath his ribs. He grunted, bending over, the breath leaving his mouth in a sharp gasp. I kicked out at him.

His hands caught my foot and jerked me forward. I wasn't as nimble as Grene; my other foot slid out from under me. I threw both arms up to protect my face, but his fist planted in my gut instead.

He released me, watching as I fell to my knees, panting.

"You're not so bad," he said, grinning. He circled me. "But now we're even."

I glared up at him, turning my head to keep him in sight. His leg drew back. I rolled away, shoving to my feet as another kick grazed my hip. His attacks came fast, each blow pushing me back. I staggered and then ducked left.

His heel kicked my shoulder, and I grunted as I hit the ground. The threads vibrated around me—tugging, tempting. I ignored them.

His foot came down again. I let it, gritting my teeth as his heel connected with my chest. Then I swung up and rammed my fist as hard as I could into the side of his knee. Muree cried out and toppled over with a loud *oomph*.

Show me you're better than this, Mason's voice echoed in my ear.

I may not have come here to win, but I didn't come to get my ass kicked, either. I scrambled to my feet. Before Muree could recover, my foot smashed into his face.

He slumped over, groaned, and didn't get up.

CHAPTER 30

GRENE AND TARIZA GAWKED AT ME AND THE BOY ON THE ground. Then they erupted into excited shouts. Avan gave me a soft smile that made me feel warm and giddy. I looked away and hurried through the doors that led to the prep room.

My teammates came and buzzed around me. Tariza slapped my shoulder, and Grene jabbed enthusiastically at my ribs.

Avan's quiet "Nice job" made the most impact, though, and I pushed my hair behind my ear, flustered.

I shared in their excitement for a little while, but with my match over, my thoughts turned to tomorrow. I had less than a day to find Reev. Now I wished I had waited to give the signal, but I had been so eager and so sure. *So stupid.*

We stuck around the prep room to watch Tariza's and Grene's matches. They both won, although Tariza had to be taken to the medical wing and checked for possible broken ribs. Avan and I promised to visit him later and begged out of running laps around the track with Grene. She gave us a knowing look. But Avan only waved and pulled me along after him.

On our way to the dorms, we passed through the common room. It had a lot of space but managed to look welcoming, with two fireplaces and a bunch of thick rugs and couches. Cadets gathered around the announcement board posted above the hearth, and Avan paused to take a look.

The Tournament schedule had been recently updated with the results of the day's matches and the next fight brackets. Tomorrow, Avan's match was scheduled for one in the afternoon. My name had moved on to the next bracket as well, but where the name of my opponent should have been was the number *22*.

"Hey," I said, pointing to it. "What do you think this means?" I scanned the rest of the schedule and couldn't find any other matches marked with a number.

"Maybe it's your rank," Avan said.

"Maybe." I moved aside so that another cadet could get a closer look.

Avan's hand touched my back, warm even through the tunic. "Or maybe it's just a placeholder till they find the right match. From the way the sentinel judges looked at you, I think you managed to impress them."

It wouldn't have been an issue if my match was after noon, but it was at eleven. I would have to try and end it as quickly as I could in order to get us some time before our rendezvous behind the dorms.

Speaking of which, my irritation with Avan was gone. Now, I just felt guilty for not talking to him first. After all, he had chosen to risk his life by coming here with me. But I didn't know how to tell him except to blurt it out.

Back in my room, Avan sat at my desk and began pulling out books stacked against the wall. The top one had the Ninurtan flag across the cover, and he flipped it open.

"What are you looking for?" I asked. I unbelted my tunic and placed the corded braid across the top of my dresser.

"Information about the Tournaments."

"We've read all the public info on them." The books at school were secondhand White Court texts, so they probably contained all the same information.

"We're cadets," he said. "There has to be some insider info here. Maybe something about how the sentinels get selected to be judges or where they stay between matches."

It was worth a shot, so I left him to it while I bathed.

I had washed myself countless times with other girls less than five feet away, both in the Labyrinth and then in Etu Gahl. Yet now, undressing with Avan in the next room felt somehow . . . indecent. And thrilling.

Nothing but a slab of wood and a few feet of space separated us. Every inch of me blushed at the thought of him seeing me naked. As the room filled with steam, I allowed myself to imagine him opening the door. He would pull me against him and slide us both into the hot water—

I told myself to stop being foolish and focus on running my bath. Now wasn't the time to indulge in fantasies.

The privacy of my own washroom was such a novelty that after I cleaned up, I soaked in the tub until my fingers wrinkled. Avan was gone when I emerged from the washroom an hour later.

I changed into another of the identical uniforms in my closet, and dropped the used one and the towel into the hatchway outside the washroom door.

We had a crude version of that in the Labyrinth, but I didn't use it. You were never quite sure you'd get your things back clean, or whether they'd be returned at all.

I picked up Avan, who apparently had left to wash up too. When he saw me waiting out in the hall, he blushed and stepped past me. I stared at his back as we made our way toward the stairs and wondered if he'd been thinking about me in the bath, too. And now I was blushing again.

Stop it. We are here to look for Reev, I reminded myself.

Avan's research hadn't turned up anything useful, but the matches had ended, so there was a chance we might find Reev alone. I had no idea what sentinels did in their free time, if they had any.

"By the way," I said, going down the stairs a couple of steps ahead of him so I wouldn't have to see his reaction, "I turned over the manhole cover."

"What?" His hand grabbed my arm, forcing me to stop. Pulling me off to the side, he lowered his voice. "What were you thinking? We don't even know where Reev is or if he'll cooperate—"

A tinge of that annoyance returned, and I thrust his hand away. "You might not believe in him, but *I* do. Reev will come around once I talk to him."

Avan raked his fingers through his hair, his jaw clenching and unclenching. He didn't look at me as he turned and started back up the stairs.

I watched him go, both angry and guilty at once. There was

no point fighting over what was done, so I pushed away from the wall and continued my search for Reev.

An hour later, with no luck, I was near the prep room when the cadets began filing downstairs for dinner. With a sigh of disappointment, I joined them.

Avan was already at the table with his tray, and aside from a brief glance, he didn't acknowledge me. My lips pinched.

Dinner consisted of the same portions and selections as this morning. Other than half a roll of bread, I'd had nothing for lunch, and my stomach was growling its displeasure. Grene and Tariza joined us a moment later.

"Nothing broken, then?" I asked as Tariza dropped his tray on the table with a clatter.

"Solid as a rock." He tapped his knuckles against his ribs.

"The scores went up in the common room," Grene said, taking a seat with the usual bounciness that made me think she wore springs on her feet. Weirdly enough, I was beginning to like her cheerfulness. "We're in the top ten!"

Great. Now I also felt bad that we were going to abandon them tomorrow. They had invested their futures in the Tournament, and they genuinely wanted to become sentinels. But if they were *mahjo*, then we would be doing them a favor. Winning would gain them nothing but a collar.

"My parents are going to be so happy," Tariza said. "Their request to visit was denied, so I'll have to send them a missive. I don't know how they would have gotten here anyway. They don't own a Gray."

Grene nodded sympathetically. "I've been to the North District once. It was *so* primitive. The Kahl says resources are limited, and essential renovations are done on a district-to-district basis; but when I become a sentinel, I'm going to change that." She flipped her hair and tilted her nose. Her challenging tone made me wonder if she was used to defending that particular goal.

Her good intentions surprised me. I had figured most people joined the Academy to improve their own status, not to help those around them. The Watchmen in the Alley had certainly proven that.

"That's admirable," Avan said, and Grene beamed, her shoulders relaxing. I was the only one who heard what he'd left unspoken: admirable but naive. And completely useless.

As we ate, I looked around the cafeteria and the rows of cadets. How many of these kids thought like Grene? How many joined with the hope of changing Ninurta, only to end up slaves to it? My eyes connected with a pair of green ones. I paused. They belonged to a boy with short brown hair and dark skin. He glanced at me and Avan surreptitiously to keep his teammates from noticing.

I realized I knew him. The last time I had seen him was a year ago, down by a bend in the river where he and his friends hung out. I didn't see many kids there anymore, not since he disappeared.

It seemed he recognized us as well.

Ninu must have kidnapped him for the Tournament. I wondered how much the boy knew about the sentinels and what he was—about the collar that awaited him.

His teammates chattered around him, but he remained silent, watching me and Avan.

He thought we'd been kidnapped, too.

What did they have over him to keep him here? Credits? I had talked to him a handful of times, but he didn't seem the sort to care about that. If anything, I'd guess they threatened his family. Would it be worth it to try and get him out?

Drek. I couldn't afford even to think it. I was here for Reev. There was nothing I could do for anyone else. I tried to ignore the boy's searching looks. I clenched my teeth and hoped the ache in my jaw would overpower the one in my stomach.

"I'm heading back to my room." I couldn't stand the weight of the boy's eyes on me. I waved off Avan's attempt to come with me, but he got up anyway. As we reached the cafeteria door, I froze.

Standing guard was the sentinel I'd met the morning Reev had disappeared, the one they had tried to chase off at the Labyrinth. I ducked my head, but it was too late. He'd seen me staring at him.

Then a curious thing happened. He looked away again, his expression unchanged. He hadn't recognized me.

No, that couldn't be right. It wasn't a lack of recognition but a lack of . . . anything.

Feeling bold now, I stopped in front of him, waving my fingers to get his attention. "Hey, remember me?"

Behind me, Avan whispered, "What are you doing?"

The sentinel spared me a dismissive glance. "Lights-out in thirty minutes. Keep moving, cadet."

"But don't you know me? We met outside the Labyrinth. I gave your mom a letter for you. I would have asked her for one in return, but I didn't know I'd see you again."

He said flatly, "You're mistaken. I have no family in the East Quarter, and I have never been assigned duties outside the White Court."

I searched his face but couldn't find any signs that he was lying. Or anything else hidden behind his blank expression.

"But you *do*," I insisted. I had to make him admit it. "Her name is Lila Sevins. You came to the Labyrinth looking for her."

"Move along," he said. "Or I'll report you for insubordination."

"Nel, come on," Avan said. I ground my teeth together as he led me away.

"He didn't know who I was," I said, yanking my arm out of Avan's grasp. "He had no idea. And his mom—he left her in the Labyrinth. He should have heard the way she cried when I gave her the note. How could he forget her?"

"Kai," Avan said, his voice so soft that it hurt to hear. "Remember what Mason said about burning their minds? He's not even the same person anymore."

"I know," I snapped.

I know, I know. Cleansing. But I didn't want to believe it.

"I don't know why anyone would want to be like that," I said, gesturing wildly at the cadets we passed. They gave me confused and condescending looks, making a wide berth around me, but I was too upset to care. "Can't they see there's something wrong? How are they all so *blind*?"

"Kai," Avan said. His hand found my arm again, and he tugged me up the stairs toward our dorms. "You need to calm down."

"No, what I need to do is find my brother. The longer he's

here, the more chance he has of ending up like *them*." I shoved open my door and slammed it behind me.

I closed my eyes. Avan was right. I had to get ahold of myself. I waited until I felt calmer, and then I opened my door and peered out. Avan was gone, and cadets had begun to trickle in from dinner.

A voice echoed down the hall from somewhere near the stairs announcing lights-out in ten minutes and for cadets to please return to their dorms immediately or suffer the consequences, blah blah blah. How many times did they have to remind us of imminent punishment for everything? No one had slapped my wrists for leaving the hall earlier.

Once I was sure the Watchman had moved on, I hurried toward the staircase. I wished I had a way to signal Irra's hollows and let them know I needed more time. Maybe if I went to the manhole and flipped it back over . . . But how could I be sure that it'd work?

I returned to the hallway that led toward the prep room. It was as good a place to check as any. The fire from the sconces had been dimmed for the night.

"Kai."

His voice, behind me. I turned.

Reev stood at the end of the hallway. He stretched out his hand.

CHAPTER 31

I DIDN'T WALK TO MEET HIM. I RAN, THROWING MYSELF against his chest. *This isn't a dream. Please don't be a dream.*

He didn't respond right away. But then his arms closed around me. I sank against him, squeezing my eyes shut. He wasn't wearing his leather tunic, and I pushed my face into his soft undershirt, letting the cloth absorb my tears.

Reev. Reev. He was here. He remembered me. I held on, my fingers digging into the familiar comfort of his arms.

"What are you doing here?" he asked quietly. I relished the sound of his voice, letting it wash over me.

"I came for you, of course." I drew back to get a look at him, but the hallway was too dim. "Are you okay? Have they done anything to you? Why didn't you find Avan after his match this morning? You recognized him, didn't you?"

"I was being watched," he said.

"You could have signaled me or—or done *something*, I don't know. Do you have any idea how it felt, wondering—"

"I'm sorry," he whispered, pulling me in and placing a kiss against my temple.

All that frustration and anger—none of it mattered anymore. There was no room for that now.

"It's complicated," he continued. "I can't stay long. How did you even get here?"

"We went to the Black Rider. He helped sneak us in, and he's going to help get you out. We have a plan." I gripped his shoulders and rose on my toes, bouncing like Grene. In less than a day, we would be gone from here. Everything would be okay. "Will you be at my match tomorrow morning?"

"I don't know. I haven't been told which matches I'm to oversee. But yours is at eleven."

I beamed. He had figured out my alias. I never should have doubted him.

"I need you to meet me at noon behind the dorms. There's a manhole where one of the Rider's hollows will lead us out."

Reev went still. I could only tell he was breathing because I was pressed to his chest.

"Reev?"

He nodded. "I know where that is."

His hands slid to my waist, and he nudged me back. I let him, joy engulfing all the uncertainty. I had more things to tell him, but they could wait until we were safely out of Ninurta.

He peered down at me as if waiting for something.

"What did they do to you?" I reached behind his neck. "Why didn't you tell me about—" Reev squeezed my wrist. I let out a small gasp.

254

Immediately, he loosened his grip. He brought my wrist to his lips to kiss away the hurt the way he used to when I was a kid. The action made me smile.

"Like I said. It's complicated." His voice was rough. "I'm sorry I kept it from you, but they've begun cleansing my memories. I can't—" He looked pained. "The Kahl means to put a new collar on me afterward. It's been . . . difficult."

All the better that we were leaving tomorrow. I wished we could go now. I couldn't stand letting them have my brother a moment longer.

"It's just one more night," I said, more to reassure myself than Reev.

He glanced over his shoulder, his hand tensing around my wrist. "I should go. They've probably noticed I'm missing."

"Reev—" He cut me off by hugging me again, and I touched my forehead to his shoulder.

I wanted to catch the threads to stretch out our time together. How was I supposed to let him go? At least the separation would be brief.

"Please be safe," I told him.

"Of course. Be careful in your match tomorrow. I'll see you soon."

"Are you sure you'll be able to—"

"Yes," Reev said, and gave me a nudge toward the stairs. He softened the action with a smile. "Now get back to your room before we both get in trouble."

I couldn't stop smiling. At my floor, I turned down the hallway and came up short. Avan stood outside his door with another boy. Neither of them noticed me.

It wasn't the fact Avan had broken the lights-out rule that gave me pause, it was the body language of the boy with him. He was shorter than Avan, around my height, with sleek, well-groomed White Court hair and large eyes that watched Avan with enough interest to make me seethe. He rested a fine-boned hand against Avan's arm. His body seemed to strain forward without actually moving.

I wouldn't have minded if this boy was my opponent tomorrow.

Avan moved to open his door. His smile was practiced but still warm enough not to be entirely false.

When he turned to face the boy again, his back to me, the boy leaned in. I sucked in my breath, unbalanced, as if my feet had been knocked out from under me.

Avan pressed a hand to the boy's shoulder. He must have said something, because the boy's face went red and he seemed to shrink in on himself, averting his eyes. Then he awkwardly rubbed at his neck as his mouth formed what looked like the words *good night*. He hurried away. Avan stepped into his room.

"Savorn."

His back stiffened. Then he relaxed and looked over his shoulder, a real smile on his face.

"What are you doing wandering around?" He opened his door wider and motioned for me to come in.

Once the door shut, I said, "I found Reev."

Avan's fingers paused in unbelting his tunic. "It occurred to me earlier that our rooms might be monitored."

I glanced around at the blank walls. "How? Peepholes in the ceiling?"

"If Kahl Ninu can enslave *mahjo*, then I wouldn't underestimate him."

Drek. I rubbed my temple. Well, it was too late now. We'd already said more than enough to condemn us.

"Tell me anyway," Avan said, probably thinking the same thing.

I grinned. "He's agreed to the plan."

Avan turned away and tugged off his tunic. I admired his back, the lean muscles and angular planes I now knew by heart. I did not, however, know about the fine scars scattered across his shoulder blades. They were pale against his skin. Had those been caused by his dad or maybe by a past lover? My happiness wilted.

Avan didn't notice as he tossed the tunic into the hatch in the wall. He disappeared into the washroom.

"That's great," he said over the sound of splashing water. "Wasn't expecting it to be that easy."

Something in his tone made me feel defensive. "Reev recognized us during your match. He couldn't say anything because he was being watched."

"Okay," he said, reappearing. He had dried his face with a towel, but wet strands of hair curled beneath his jaw. A bead of water splashed against his collarbone. "I trust you."

I smiled. With those three words, he had put me at ease.

He crossed his arms over his chest, stomach muscles flexing as he leaned against the door frame. Just as I had imagined, his tattoo crawled across the side of his chest in jagged black branches. What I hadn't imagined were the three brilliant-green leaves at the tip of the longest branch—the only leaves on the tree.

Before I lost my nerve, I pointed to his chest and asked, "What does that mean?"

He looked down, his fingers tracing one crooked branch. The corner of his mouth twitched up. "It's stupid."

"Tell me anyway," I said, repeating his earlier words.

His hand dropped to his side. "I got the trunk and the branches done when I moved out of the shop. The tree had one leaf. Kind of like . . . the start of something new." He rubbed his neck and shifted so that he was turned away from me. He actually seemed embarrassed. "Something good, I mean. I figured I would add more leaves as . . . well, as things changed."

I knew it had been important for him to get his own place and to get some distance from his dad, but I hadn't understood how much it meant to him to separate himself from the life he'd known beneath his dad's roof. Knowing this now made me wish I'd done more than kick that man's decrepit ass.

"That's not stupid," I said. Avan looked back at me.

Now *I* was embarrassed. I busied myself poking through a book at the top of a pile. I had to know, and since we were both already feeling awkward . . .

"What was that about just now?" I asked. "We're not supposed to mingle with other teams, remember?"

"I guess you haven't noticed everyone breaking that particular rule," Avan said, his words laced with amusement. I looked up, and, sure enough, he was flashing me his dimple. "I was asking around. We were on a tight deadline to find Reev."

"That was about Reev?" I remembered the way the boy leaned in, as if expecting Avan to reciprocate.

Avan pushed off the door frame and crossed the room. "He took my friendliness to mean something else. It tends to happen."

"I've noticed." I propped my hip against the table, watching him approach, his dark eyes searching. His lashes were longer than mine. I drew an unsteady breath. The weight of unspoken things settled into the space between us, space I wanted so badly to close that my body ached with it.

His throat moved as he swallowed. "Can I be honest with you, Kai?"

"Aren't you always?"

He opened his mouth but closed it again.

I searched for words to replace his silence. "Did . . . did you mind it? His misinterpretation."

I winced at my clumsiness. Avan's smile twisted into a smirk. I brushed my fingers against his lips, wanting to wipe away that look.

He caught my hand and held it. His breath warmed my fingertips. I shivered.

"No," he whispered against my skin.

Then he let go, and I pulled my hand to my chest, fingers curling into my palm as if I could carry with me the feel of his mouth and breath.

"Because he didn't mean anything by it," Avan continued. "It was sweet."

His eyes grew distant. I wondered if he was recalling people who hadn't been so sweet. I touched his cheek to bring him back.

And what about me?

"Do you . . . um . . . prefer . . ." I shouldn't ask. It was none of my business.

"I don't have a preference," he said. "It's not always about gender."

I nodded, focusing on a white scar along Avan's collarbone. There was a slight bump there, as if it had been broken once and hadn't healed quite right.

"Can I ask you something else? Since we're being honest with each other."

Avan's expression turned wary. "Okay."

"When were you going to tell me about what you are?"

"I'm a lot of things," he said. "You're going to have to be more specific."

"You're a descendant," I said, ignoring his teasing.

His eyes widened just a fraction. But then his lips curved—beautiful, charming, and completely fake.

"You're *mahjo*. I know you've realized it."

He looked down, his lashes casting shadows beneath his eyes. "I don't know," he said.

He stepped away and sat at the edge of his bed.

"Of course you do. But there's something I don't understand. Why—" The image of a young, bruised Avan formed in my mind. *Why didn't you heal then the way you do now?*

I couldn't ask it, even though he probably knew what I was thinking. I would have to wait until he shared it with me.

I nervously tucked a piece of hair behind my ear. "Never mind."

"I'm sorry," he said. "People like to ask questions. I'm usually better at deflecting them. It's just, with you . . . I feel like I have to be more guarded."

"Why?"

He spoke carefully, measuring each word. "Because I'm not used to anyone having the power to hurt me anymore."

"I don't want to hurt you."

He smiled that crooked smile. "It's not always a bad hurt."

Oh.

We'd been skirting the issue for a while now, but I didn't know how to deal with the feelings Avan stirred in me. I wasn't even sure if they were real or just my imagination twisting his words and gestures to mean what I wanted. All I knew was that I sure as drek couldn't do this while Reev was still a slave to Ninu.

But after—after Irra helped Reev, we'd be free of Ninurta forever. I could see the same conclusion in Avan's eyes. The promise of an end we both wanted.

"I've missed having you nearby at night. I wish you could stay here with me," he said softly. His mouth twitched. "And not like that. Although . . . maybe like that, too."

My whole body went hot. I straightened off the edge of the table, hyperaware of how easy it would be to cross the meager distance and step into his embrace.

I wanted him, and the strength of it was shocking. I wanted to put my lips against the scars on his back and claim them for my own. I wanted to whisper in his ear to teach me everything I didn't know, to let him pull me into his bed and make me forget all the fears weighing on my heart.

The way his eyes narrowed and his fingers curled into the mattress showed he knew exactly what I was thinking.

I licked my lips. "I should—"

Avan reached me in two steps. I sucked in a ragged breath, my body helplessly arching into his as he buried his hands in my hair. My fingers dug into his shoulders, hard muscles tensed at my touch. His mouth hovered above mine, excruciatingly close.

His dark lashes lowered, and he touched our lips together. His kiss was gentle at first, tentative. Then I made a quiet, needy sound, and something in him seemed to snap, because he pushed me back against the table. His mouth slanted hungrily over mine. My own self-control unraveled around me as I trembled, clutching him to keep from falling even as I kissed back just as fiercely.

How many times had I imagined this moment? I felt my longing answered in his urgency, in the way his hand moved down my back, the way his body pressed into me. His lips skimmed kisses down my jaw, my neck.

Then he stopped. His mouth was hot, but still, against my skin. He whispered, "Go."

I tried to catch my breath. "What?"

Slowly, his hands lifted from me, and he stepped back until we were no longer touching. I shivered from the sudden lack of heat.

"You were saying," he said, hunched over, his hand pressed to his eyes, shielding his expression from me, "that you should go."

My thoughts rushed back, along with all the reasons why this couldn't happen right now. Reev came first, my own selfish desires second. Without a word, I turned and let myself out.

The next morning, I was so anxious that—aside from an initial awkward greeting during which we both avoided eye contact—even Avan couldn't distract me for long. My stomach insisted I eat, and I knew I'd need whatever strength I could get, so I forced the food down and headed up to the prep room.

Reev wasn't among the sentinels, but I wasn't worried. He would meet us behind the dorms in just over an hour.

I paced in the corner.

"You've got this, Nel," Tariza said. "If we win all our matches today, we'll make the top five. Top five teams are guaranteed to continue to the next round."

I cast him a grateful look for the encouragement. Against all odds, I had begun to think of us as a real team. It would be hard to leave them.

A Watchman called my name. Hands patted my shoulders as I stepped forward. Which arena would I get today? Tariza's had been sand, the silted floor slowing down movement and testing balance. Grene's had been under a foot of water, enough to make her natural grace a little sluggish. Both would work against me considering speed was my main advantage.

When I pushed through the doors, I found myself standing in the same arena that Avan had fought in yesterday. Packed dirt.

Behind me, Grene and Tariza shouted my name excitedly as

they entered the box with Avan. The three sentinel judges sat in the stands across from me. The door at the other end of the arena opened.

Reev came through. My joy at seeing him was cut short when no one else followed him out. He stood opposite me.

"Match number sixty-one: Nel versus Twenty-two."

CHAPTER 32

I LOOKED BACK AT MY TEAMMATES. AVAN'S FACE WAS GRIM, his mouth set into a hard line. My throat closed.

Reev was 22.

"Hey!" Tariza shouted. "That guy's a sentinel. What's going on?"

No one answered. I had to stop this. My foot moved forward. A loud clang of the bell made me jump.

From the platform above, the announcer said, "Please remain where you are until the start of the match. Violation will result in forfeit of victory."

I didn't care about that. Reev looked right at me, but there was no sign of life in his face. His eyes were as empty as the sentinel's in the cafeteria.

The bell for the match sounded. I started forward again.

"Wait," I said, hands outstretched. Then I gasped and ducked. Reev's knuckles grazed my jaw.

He advanced, his expression cool and focused—but not on me. Only on the match, the attack. I was nothing but his opponent.

"Reev." I didn't care that my voice wavered and broke. I blocked another punch, but the blow vibrated down my arms. I fell back with a cry.

Reev didn't let up. I knew his moves. I knew how to dodge and to deflect his strength. Reev had taught me all this. But he didn't remember.

I had to make him remember.

I blocked a kick, grunting as the impact jarred my shoulders, and then I struck hard. My fist connected with his jaw. It felt like punching a wall. My knuckles throbbed. Reev slowed for barely an instant.

He was faster than when we used to spar. Either Ninu had made him faster or he had held back with me. But he wasn't holding back now. His foot kicked my chest. The air rushed from my lungs as I fell. Pain again as I hit the ground and skidded across the arena floor, no breath left even to cry out. The dirt scraped my cheek and hands. Everything ached. The ground swam in front of me. I rolled onto my back, gasping as yellow blobs floated overhead. I blinked, making out the clouds. Air finally filled my chest.

Dust burned my eyes and settled in a bitter film on my tongue. *This isn't happening.* I rose to my elbows, groaning.

Reev stalked toward the stands and reached into an empty seat. He withdrew a sword with a silvery blade.

"That's illegal!"

"Hey! Stop the match!"

I could hardly hear Tariza and Grene shouting behind me. My awareness had narrowed on Reev, moving closer, raising the blade at his side. Sentinels aimed for a clean strike. Mason had said so.

"Reev," I whispered. "Stop." This couldn't be right. I had *just* talked to him last night. *No. No no no."* We had a plan. Don't you remember?" *What should I do? I don't know what to do.*

"Get up! Kai, get the drek up!"

Avan's voice jolted through me. I scrambled backward, my palms sliding against the dirt. The scrapes stung. I glanced toward my boot where the knife was hidden, but every instinct I possessed repelled the very thought of reaching for it, of using it against Reev.

Reev didn't hesitate, though. He followed me and swung his blade.

I threw my mind against the threads. Time crawled nearly to a stop. This close, his eyes were clearly visible. They were hollow. Devoid of emotion or thought. He intended to kill me. No one rushed onto the arena floor to stop him—not the announcer or the other sentinels. This had been planned.

I blinked away tears. I only wanted to save him. Everything I had done had been for Reev.

And, if I was honest, maybe a little for myself, because I didn't know how to be without him. It was pathetic, a seventeen-year-old girl this scared to be alone. Even now, with his blade blurring the air in slowed time, I couldn't give up. I had to believe in Reev, I had to—

Time snapped forward. I flinched, watching Reev's face. With time speeded up, this would be quick.

Reev's blade flashed, followed by a streak of movement. A

ruffle of black tunic. A spray of red. A cloud of raised dust.

Time adjusted itself. I stared up at a broad back. Avan knelt in front of me, his head bowed. Blood spread out around him in a crimson fan. Then he slumped to the side and hit the dirt with a *thud* that echoed in my chest.

CHAPTER 33

"AVAN!" I SCRAMBLED TO MY KNEES AND GINGERLY ROLLED him onto his back. His body was limp. *"Avan."*

There was so much blood. He looked pale. Ashen. Why wasn't he healing?

"Wake up, Avan. Come on, please, please, *wake up."* *Heal, damn it! Why won't you heal?*

Because healing wouldn't work after he was already—

I searched frantically for the medic, but no one had stepped forward to help. What was *wrong* with everyone? Two sentinels led Reev out of the arena. I couldn't breathe.

Tariza and Grene were trapped halfway over the box's barrier. More sentinels had appeared to block their way and herd them out of the arena.

Avan drew a shuddering breath. I almost fell over. He wasn't dead. I brushed the hair from his temple. His skin was warm. A line had appeared between his brows, his lashes fluttering as he tried to open his eyes.

"Don't move," I said, my hands hovering over his chest. I

didn't know where to touch him without hurting him. "Don't—"

I realized his chest was no longer bloody. As I watched, bone, muscle, and skin knitted back together beneath the gaping hole left in his tunic. Nothing remained but smooth skin, marred only by the ragged black branches of his tattoo.

I gave him a bewildered look. Could all descendants heal like that? From a wound that would have killed anyone else? A wound that, for a moment there, *had* killed him?

He wouldn't meet my eyes. He rolled away from me and stood. I watched him, my mouth agape.

"What the drek?" I said, louder than I intended. Avan reached over and pulled me up. He smoothed dust off my cheeks. I shook away his touch. Pain flashed in his eyes at my rejection.

"There's something I need to tell you," he said.

"What just happened?" I couldn't stop staring at his chest. The tear in his bloodstained tunic and my pulse pounding in my ears were the only evidence he had been wounded.

"But I think an explanation will have to wait."

More sentinels had surrounded us. I whirled around, backing up against Avan's side. His hand clasped mine and squeezed.

"You're not dead," I whispered, focusing on that truth. I pressed against him.

"I'm not dead."

"Stay that way."

He swept his thumb along my knuckles. "You got it."

They flanked us through the halls. Cadets stared as we passed. Grene and Tariza were nowhere to be seen. I hoped they wouldn't be punished just because we were assigned as their teammates.

I clutched Avan's hand as tightly as I could as we descended a hidden flight of stairs. The sentinels moved with the same liquid grace as Mason's, passing over the polished stone steps with a whisper. At the bottom of the stairs, someone grabbed my arm and pulled me to the left. Avan was pulled to the right.

Our linked hands broke apart. Avan nodded at me reassuringly and then turned away.

A sentinel took me through a small room that connected to a cell. The cell was square, with white walls and a vent in the corner. A candle burned in a simple metal fixture on the wall, the flame trembling as the door shut behind me. The room was empty except for a cot that, while small, took up nearly an entire wall.

I sat, pulling my knees to my chest. I wasn't sure what to worry about first. Where had they taken Reev? And what about Avan? What would they do to him now that they'd seen his healing ability? Would they take him to the Kahl and brand him with a collar?

A tremor raced through me, and I curled up tighter.

The cot was clean. I had expected something less hospitable. Their prison was nicer than my room in the Labyrinth.

I thought I understood what had happened with Reev. Mason had said the collar connected the sentinels to Kahl Ninu. Disobedience was rare. Reev had been lying last night. Cleansing hadn't just begun; it was complete. Reev had played me.

I had lost him.

I dropped my forehead against my knees and squeezed my

eyes shut. I wouldn't cry. This room had to be monitored. I wouldn't let them hear me cry.

Behind my closed lids, I saw the moment in the arena again. The blur of movement as Avan threw himself in front of Reev's blade. His body, bloody and broken, slumped at my feet. My hands shook, and I curled them into fists. I dug my nails into my palms until the pain drove away the tremors.

Shame burned my throat. Avan had saved me, and here I was feeling sorry for myself.

Could *mahjo* really cheat death? Maybe that was how they survived the branding. Whatever the reason, I had to save Avan. I wasn't going to lose him, too.

For a while, I paced my cell. But then fatigue set in, and I laid down to stare at the perfect blankness of the wall. A dirty cell would have given me some stains or cracks to look at. This was a white nightmare, broken only by the shadows from the candle.

A knock jolted my eyes open. When did I fall asleep? On the door, a narrow strip at eye level slid to the side, and the white door went as clear as glass. I startled and rose from the cot. Beyond was the second room, larger than this one, which connected to my cell and the door that led into the hall.

Reev stood in the next room. Looking at him hurt, but looking away would hurt more. *Please*, I thought, even though I knew it was useless.

Next to him was a young woman. She slouched in a wooden chair, her stocking-covered legs crossed at the ankles.

She watched me with black eyes like drops of tar. I approached the space where the door should have been and reached out a tentative hand. My palm hit the door, solid but invisible, and I drew my hand back.

"Reev," I said, willing him to look at me. He didn't. His expression remained as blank as the walls of my cell. I resisted the urge to slam my knuckles against the door.

"Kai." The woman had a soft voice, almost childlike. With her frilly pink-and-white dress and lacy stockings, she looked like a doll.

She twirled a slim finger through one of her pretty curls. Her hair was garishly red. I thought of Avan's bloody chest in the arena. I shook my head to erase the image.

"Can I ask about your powers? They're pretty amazing," she said.

I didn't think they were nearly as interesting as Avan rising from the dead. "Where's Avan?"

"He's being taken care of." Her black eyes gleamed. Her age was difficult to place. She could've been a child or a hundred years old. "Please. Tell me about your powers. Where did you learn to do that?"

I ignored her. Instead, I watched Reev, cataloging the changes in him. His trimmed hair—he'd only grown it out to hide his collar. His eyes, vacant but still that shining gray as familiar to me as my name. He stood immobile, as if he waited for a command.

The woman-child glanced up at Reev and then to me again. "R-22 is your adopted brother, isn't that right? We sifted through his memories, but they were incomplete, spans of time missing.

Not just locked away but erased completely. It was a very precise job."

I sank onto the cot and folded my hands in my lap. I had nothing to say to her. Despite my curiosity, I had never pried into Reev's past. How dare they rummage through his memories as if he was nothing but a history text?

"Seeing as you got into the Tournament unnoticed, I imagine you've met *my* wayward brother," she continued. "He likes to call himself the Black Rider. For old time's sake, I guess. It's what the humans once called him, when they still worshipped us."

I looked at her more closely. "Are you Ninu?"

I thought the Kahl was a man. That was how it had been taught in school.

She laughed, as if she was talking to a friend. "No way. I'm Istar. The humans knew me as Strife, and they used to pray to me in times of war." She breathed the words like a sigh, or a fond memory. "Now they've all forgotten. Guess I miss the old days, too."

CHAPTER 34

ISTAR. IRRA HADN'T MENTIONED HER.

"How many of you are there?" I asked. Talking to her through the clear door felt odd, like talking through a closed window, even though I could hear her well enough through the slit. The way she talked, she sounded as if she could've been one of the girls from school. Was she doing that especially for my benefit?

"Too few, if you ask me." She studied her nails, which had been painted pink with little white hearts on them. "But if you see Peace around, ask him if he's bored enough yet to come and visit."

I sincerely hoped not to come across any more of them, even if he was named Peace. "Is he in Ninurta, too?"

"Not for ages, as far as I know." She sighed again wistfully. "But you never can be sure who might be lurking around." She flashed straight, white teeth.

I looked at Reev, who had yet to move. "What are you going to do to Reev?"

There had to be a reason she'd brought him with her. Intimidation or leverage or something else to force my cooperation with whatever they wanted from me.

"R-22 is insignificant. He was a missing puzzle piece, now recovered." She sounded annoyed. "His entire team was like a disobedient anim— Ah!"

Her face brightened. Her abrupt mood shifts were jarring, but after having spent time with Irra, I figured this was another quirk of the Infinite. She fingered the lace at the bottom of her dress, which was short and layered underneath with starched petticoats. The outfit looked like something the girls in the North District might wear: an odd mixture of allure and innocence.

"You don't know?" She clapped her hands excitedly. Red curls bounced around her puffed sleeves. "I love a good story. You should hear the ones they used to tell about me." She closed her eyes, smiling dreamily.

"What story?" I prompted.

She sat up straight. "Your brother's, of course. The leader of his team was the only sentinel in Ninurta's history to overcome his collar's enchantments and disobey commands. As you can imagine, it was *very* troublesome."

I hoped he had given them hell.

"The other two in his team began to disobey orders as well. But, of course, they couldn't sever the collar's connection to Ninu, so do you know what the leader did?" She thrust her lips into a pout. "He dared to break into Ninu's private chambers and attempt to kill him." Her pout stretched into a feral grin. "But he was caught. Do you know what Ninu did then?"

I could imagine. When I didn't answer, she continued.

"He created a new collar. One that purifies the mind of all thought and knowledge, leaving a perfect shell for Ninu to refill. R-22 and the third member of their team were also meant to be purified as soon as they returned from a mission. But R-22 never came back, and his link to Ninu was broken by someone on the outside. Very few have the ability to tamper with Ninu's collar and not kill its wearer."

"The Infinite," I said. In spite of everything, I wanted to know more. Reev had gone through so much so young. What happened to his real family when he was taken? And who helped Reev to escape?

Istar said spans of time had been erased from Reev's memory. Whoever had broken his leash for him had wanted to remain anonymous.

I dug my knuckles into my stomach. Too many questions.

"So Irra told you that. And here I was hoping to give you another story." She slumped dramatically and then jerked upright again, eyes widening. "Oops. Time's up. Ninu wants to meet with you later." She stood, smoothing down her dress over the petticoats. "And when you see him, you'll give him all the information you have about Irra and your powers."

She twirled away. Reev turned to follow her. Watching him leave, again, fractured something in my chest. I had to bite my lip to keep from calling out for him.

Because I knew she wanted me to ask, and because I had to know, I said, "Or what?"

She glanced back. She looked delighted. "You'll be happy to know that R-22 is still intact. Ninu put up a very specific wall in his mind. It allows only certain knowledge and thoughts through while blocking everything else." She thrust one slender finger up in the air. "But if you don't cooperate, then R-22 will be sent for immediate purification."

Istar hadn't said when Ninu wanted to meet with me, so I went back to staring at the wall. The door had gone opaque again, but the slit remained open. Unfortunately, there was nothing to look at or listen to other than the sound of my own breathing. Enough time had passed that I'd grown hungry again, but I didn't think a meal would be coming, so I ignored the ache. It wasn't all that hard. I had a lot of practice.

Despite Istar's threat, her words had put my mind and heart at ease. Reev was still in there. If I could only get him out of Ninurta, then Irra could help him.

If Irra even let us back in. My capture meant that the Kahl knew Irra had the means of sneaking people into the White Court. Kahl Ninu would probably do exactly what Irra had said: strengthen and restructure his security and weed out the spies. All the information Irra and his hollows had worked to gain would be meaningless.

I pushed aside the guilt. First, I had to figure out how to escape.

At some point, I fell asleep again. I hovered at the edge of a dream when a groan jarred me awake. I looked around, but I was still alone. My eyes fell on the slit in the door.

I heard a hiss of pain, a low groan, and then a hoarse laugh and a familiar voice. "Heh. Is that all you've got? Keep tr—*nng*."

"Avan," I breathed. I leaped off the cot and slammed my fists against the door. "Avan!"

Through the slit, I could see that the door to the hallway had been left ajar.

Avan made a strangled sound. "Kai? *Drek.* Don't listen. Don't—" His voice ended on a groan.

Oh God. "Stop!" My shout rang in my ears.

I kicked and pounded the door until every bone and muscle felt bruised. Avan had grown quieter, but I could still hear him. I felt his broken breaths snag in my own throat, his gasps like a knife in my ribs. I sank to my knees, forehead against the door, fingers digging into the unforgiving metal.

It went on for what felt like forever. He kept trying to tell me he was fine.

Please. Please stop. Tears scalded my cheeks. I covered my mouth before any sounds could escape. Hearing me cry would hurt him more.

"Stop," I whispered.

The sound of a door shutting made me flinch. Avan's ragged breaths fell silent. I scrambled to my feet, squinting through the slit. Someone had closed the entrance to the hallway. I collapsed against my door, sliding to the ground. I held my breath, straining to hear, but there was nothing.

The silence was almost worse. My imagination supplied me with endless horrific scenarios. I covered my face. This was my fault. They were hurting him to get to me.

A voice said, "Did you enjoy that? I think you're ready to see Ninu now."

Istar. A *click*, and my cell door swung open. Still pressed against it, I fell forward, sprawling across the floor in front of a pair of dainty white shoes. I wanted to spit on them.

Large hands pulled me up. A sentinel, thankfully not Reev, hauled me along behind her. Most of the doors we passed were closed, and those that weren't showed empty rooms. I didn't know which room Avan had been in or where he was now, but letting me listen to his torture was supposed to rattle my nerves and crush my defiance. I wouldn't give in. Once they had what they wanted, they'd probably kill us both.

I tested the sentinel's grip, but she held fast. I could use the threads, but what then? How was I supposed to help anyone else escape when I didn't know how to help myself?

We climbed a short set of stairs before passing through a stone arch. The next staircase spiraled up through a circular shaft, like the stairs that led to Irra's gargoyles. A tall window allowed natural light into the narrow stairway. As we passed the window, I realized we were high enough to see beyond the walls of the White Court to the dirty roofs and blackened chimneys of the North District.

I knew where we were. The highest point in the White Court: Death's tower.

The home of Ninu's executioner was the last place anyone wanted to be.

Wooden doors opened at the top of the stairs. Behind them was a broad space with dusky mosaic tiles and brocade furniture. Sheer curtains draped the high walls, which were a warm, ruddy color and climbed up and up to a glass ceiling that displayed a gradually darkening sky.

Istar entered the room ahead of us, her shoes clicking against the tiles. Windows framed the room, providing a magnificent view. Just as you could see the tower from anywhere in the city, from here you could see all the way to the stacked freight containers of the Labyrinth.

An unexpected pang of yearning hit me. I was a long way from what had once been home.

A torch in a stone sconce cast a halo over a woman standing by the windows. She wore a slim silver gown. It shimmered when she turned to face us, every angle of the dress catching the fading daylight. Her white hair was asymmetrical—jaw-length on one side and down to her collarbone on the other. The longer side had a black streak through it.

She looked familiar, but I would've known who she was no matter what. Ninu's right hand.

"Leave us, Sister," she said.

Istar pouted, but she did as she was told, taking the sentinel with her. The doors shut behind them, leaving me alone with Death.

CHAPTER 35

"HELLO, KAI."

I moved into the room. I didn't think Istar had brought me here to die. Not yet. And I doubted Death performed her job in this room.

"I am called Kalla," she said. Her gaze dropped to my feet. "You were supposed to be disarmed."

The knife. It was still in my boot.

Before she could order the knife removed, I said, "*You* were supposed to be Ninu."

A hiss of air indicated a door opening.

At the far end of the room, a man entered through an alcove hidden behind the fall of curtains. He stepped into the light. He was tall enough to be imposing, although not nearly Irra's height, and he had neatly cut graying hair. He wore a high-collared, midnight-blue tunic, trimmed in silver thread and glossy buttons. The blue matched his eyes, which took me in with only mild curiosity.

Ninu looked exactly the way I'd imagined. I straightened my shoulders, unwilling to let him intimidate me.

"I'm delighted to meet you, Kai." His voice was clear and melodic, almost ingratiatingly sweet.

On a glass table sat two crystal goblets and a decanter partially filled with a luminous purple liquid that looked like the alcoholic drinks the hollows had served. He poured himself a portion and held the goblet up to me in salute.

I glared. I wasn't going to engage in mock formalities.

He sipped his drink. When he turned to face me again, there was an edge to his smile. "Wonderful," he said.

He studied my face. It made me want to back away. Instead, I held his gaze.

"You're a coward," I said, surprised by how steady my voice was.

"I am Kahl. What would you have me do, Kai? Barter with you?" His shoulders moved with silent laughter. "Perhaps you think your information or your abilities provide enough weight for negotiation. But you'd be wrong. I have your brother, and I have your friend. Surely you see where you stand."

"Stop toying with me," I said. "What do you want to know about Irra?"

I knew playing dumb at this point would be a bad idea. If I didn't have the answers he wanted, he wouldn't hesitate to hurt Reev and Avan. Unfortunately, he might do the same even after I told him. I didn't know much beyond what he already did, and I didn't think lying would be very smart. There were no choices here.

He swished the purple liquid in his goblet. He didn't seem to be in any hurry.

"Your friend—Avan, is it? Interesting young man. No matter how many ways we cut him open, he just doesn't die."

The shaking started in my hands and spread to my arms.

He set his goblet on the table and clasped his hands behind his back. "And no, to answer your burning question, your friend is not of the Infinite. Isn't that right, Kalla?"

"A most curious human," she noted.

If Avan wasn't a descendant—and no one knew what he was—then that only made what had happened in the arena more baffling. He was a mystery, like me. I had to find him. I had to save him.

The exit was behind me, but it was likely guarded by sentinels. There was the door Ninu had come through, but that was a good thirty feet across the room. I'd never make it in time.

But I could *make* time. Irra had said that even the Infinite couldn't escape the River's flow. If I held the threads, I could probably at least get to Ninu before time caught up. And the knife in my boot would have found his heart.

"You seem impatient," he said. "I'm willing to indulge you. I should very much like it if you could now tell me how to find Irra's base."

"I'd love to," I said. "I hope Irra welcomes you by rotting out your eyes."

"I look forward to the hospitality." He looked at me expectantly. His forehead was unlined. Still, he clearly seemed old, unlike Istar.

I sent a silent apology to Irra, but I wasn't too worried. I had the feeling Etu Gahl wouldn't be found unless Irra wanted it to be.

"It's lost," I said. "Beyond the Void."

Ninu tilted his head as he glanced at Kalla. "Irra's errand boy said something similar. But it was difficult to make out with all the screaming."

Whoever had been sent to meet us behind Zora Hall at noon must've been met by Ninu's sentinels instead. Did that mean DJ or another hollow was dead?

I prayed it hadn't been Mason. It couldn't have been. Mason would have been rebranded, not killed. *Please. Please.*

"His death was quick," Ninu confirmed. "But Avan will not be shown the same mercy. In fact, it seems not to be an option at all. So he will continue to suffer until you agree to lead me to Irra."

I swallowed. "Lead you?"

Ninu approached me. Good. The closer he was, the better my aim. I tried not to look at Kalla, afraid to give anything away. Why hadn't she demanded I hand over the knife?

"Of course," he said. "I've sent my sentinels on enough pointless ventures into the Void. This time, you will return under the pretense of a successful extraction."

I didn't cringe when he touched my face, despite the primal urge to snap at his fingers.

His next words were spoken inches from my ear. "Irra will open his gates to you, and you will lead us into his fortress."

He turned away. Only someone as confident in his power as Ninu would present his back to his enemy. Lucky me.

I leaned over, fingers dipping into my boot. The knife handle felt warm against my palm, as if anticipating my intent.

Before Kalla could warn him, I threw my mind against the threads. Time slowed and grew slack around me. I could move freely against its current. Ninu was half turned, his expression frozen in astonishment.

Beneath the ribs—that was where Mason had said to strike with a weapon. The knife slid in with scarcely any resistance.

Time snapped forward. I pulled the knife free. Blood darkened Ninu's tunic as he crumpled. My stomach roiled, but I hardened myself with the memory of Avan's body in the arena and his moans filling the blank space of my cell.

I spun around and pointed the bloody knife at Kalla. "Where are my brother and Avan?"

Kalla adjusted the strap of her silver dress and pursed glossy, red lips. She didn't seem concerned by the fact that I'd just killed the Kahl. She wasn't even looking at me.

A second later, I understood why.

A voice came from the shadowy alcove across the room, sinking into my skin.

"I haven't seen that specific power for a long time."

CHAPTER 36

A SHADOW EMERGED FROM THE ALCOVE AND FOCUSED INTO the shape of a man. He wasn't as tall as the one I'd just stabbed, and he was slender, with thin lips, a beaky nose, and white-blond hair cut close to his scalp. He looked young, not much older than Avan. His eyes were a cool green that reflected the same emptiness I'd seen in Irra's.

He frowned at the body leaving a bloody puddle on the mosaic tiles.

"I liked him," he said. His voice crept through the room. It skittered across my skin in a way that made me want to rub my arms and shake it off. "Now what am I supposed to tell the public about their fearless leader?"

I looked from the man on the floor to the one standing over him.

"You're Ninurta," I said.

He gave me a brittle smile.

"And he's what?" I asked, gesturing to the body. "A puppet?"

Ninu touched his forehead, his lashes fluttering as he briefly shut his eyes. The door behind me opened. I shuffled back as a pair of sentinels entered. I didn't relax my grip on the knife even when they walked past me.

"Well," Ninu said, "it would be a little alarming to have a leader who never died. Human minds are fragile things. Supply them just enough magic and miracles to keep their reverence, but not enough to challenge what they think they know of the world. Can't have another self-inflicted cataclysm, can we?"

The sentinels gathered up the body, carrying it between them like a plank of wood.

Ninu grunted as he surveyed the mess left behind. "I do hope that won't stain."

I forced my eyes away from the blood on the floor, the same blood that ran in dark-red rivulets down the blade of my knife, gathering around my clenched fingers. The knowledge of what I'd just done swarmed inside me, threatening to make me sick all over the tiles. But I held myself in check. I couldn't think about it now. There would be time later for breaking down.

If I survived this.

I was a fool. I hadn't considered a puppet leader. I assumed Ninu could change faces. He was Infinite—I couldn't begin to fathom what he could do. But I had hoped, because the knife had scared off the gargoyles, that it might be able to hurt him. Maybe even kill him.

Well, it had done its job, just not on the right Ninu. And now I'd lost whatever minuscule advantage I'd had. Maybe I could slow time again and— But would the same tactic work twice? I'd have to get Ninu closer. I wouldn't be able to hold the threads long enough to cross the room.

I shifted sideways to keep both Kalla and Ninu in my line of sight. I wanted to drop the knife and wipe my hands on my tunic, to rid myself of that awful stickiness, but I couldn't let go of the last thing standing between us, no matter how useless it might be.

"If you want my help, then let Reev and Avan go. Safely," I added in case he tried to twist my words.

"Of course," he said. "In time." He smiled, a gradual stretch of his lips, as if whatever thought he found so funny was slow to form. "Time."

"Now," I said.

"You're a lot like your father. Both annoyingly stubborn."

Father? Was this some sort of trick?

"Your abilities are much rougher, though," he went on. "Lack of practice, I think. And your mortal body obviously holds you back."

Irra had said Ninu was the youngest of the Infinite. He couldn't possibly know more about their ways than Irra. Ninu must be trying to mislead me. "Let my brother and Avan go now, with the promise that they won't get hurt, and I'll take you to Irra."

Ninu cut his hand through the air. "Irra is nothing but a fly that needs to be swatted."

The anger in his voice vibrated in my bones.

"He can play hide-and-seek all he wants. I'll find him soon enough," Ninu said.

What? I gritted my teeth and lowered the knife. Kalla had draped herself across a plush white sofa, apparently ignoring the conversation.

"Then what the drek do you want from me?" I shouted.

"What do I want?" His question echoed across the room. "No one but Irra could have helped you infiltrate the Tournament. So when R-22 reported your presence, I saw an opportunity finally to catch him."

It had been Reev. Ninu's wall in his mind had allowed him to recognize me and still betray me.

"But you tried to have Reev kill me," I said.

"We needed only one of you," he said simply. "Your friend's information would have sufficed. And what better way to demonstrate our power than to let him watch his friend die by her brother's hand? But then I saw what you did in the arena." His eyes closed again, head tilting. "Irra must have suspected who you are, and yet he sent you anyway."

What if Ninu really did know something about my past? "Who am I?"

"Irra had no information to offer you?"

"He didn't know," I said. The flicker of uncertainty in Ninu's face gave me a brief moment of satisfaction. He might be just as confused by all this as I was.

"You are an answer to a question," he replied confidently. "A means to an end. A bridge to the other side. Take your pick."

I decided he had no idea what I was. "If you don't care about finding Irra, then what was the point of sending Istar to intimidate me? And your puppet's threats?"

"My human counterpart was told only about your significance to Irra. And his threats still stand."

"But what do you *want* from me?"

Someone tapped at the door behind me. "Perfect," Ninu said.

The door opened. Two sentinels guided Reev and Avan into the room. Reev entered by his own will, as distant and cold as his guards. Avan had to be supported. I struggled not to show the way my body went weak at the sight of them.

Avan was still in his cadet uniform, which now hung off his shoulders in bloody shreds. Physically, he looked okay, but the state of his clothes was evidence of what they'd done to him. And when I searched his face, the damage was clear. His eyes wouldn't meet mine, but I could see that they were weary and dark with pain. His gaze darted around the room. Alert but uncertain. Haunted.

I rushed forward, choking on his name. The sentinels stepped in front of him.

"Get out of my way!" I shouted, shoving the bloody blade up beneath one sentinel's jaw. She didn't move; she just looked to Ninu for orders.

"Please, Kai," Ninu said, his voice crawling beneath my skin. "You're not helping either of them."

"Stop it!" I pointed the knife at him. "Quit trying to get inside me."

His mouth curved in a predatory expression. "Good, you have enough of your father in you to be immune."

"And stop talking about my father! He's dead." What I really wanted to say was "What do you know?" But I couldn't care about a dad I couldn't remember. Reev was the only family I had, and he stood next to Avan, awaiting Ninu's orders like a dog.

"Oh, believe me, no one would prefer that truth more than I would," Ninu said. "You have his eyes, do you know that?"

I glared in response.

He laughed. "On you, they're kind of beautiful. Like the pale blue of the River." He stepped closer to me despite the knife pointed at him. "How much do you know about your powers, Kai?"

I didn't touch the threads. I wanted to hear more.

"Your father trapped you in a human body and abandoned you to a confused sentinel without even a note of explanation. He's always been so difficult."

"Tell me what you want," I said again.

"The River, of course. Access to it, to be precise."

Did he mean the threads?

"I thought the Infinite could already feel it." Or rather, they could feel when I manipulated it.

"That doesn't mean we have access," he said flatly.

"I don't know how to teach anyone—" I paused because Ninu was waving his hand at me.

"No, no, I need access to the actual river."

"A real river?" I assumed Irra had been speaking metaphorically.

"As I'm sure you're aware, it exists all around us. But it also has a physical location, hidden in a place only Time can grant access to."

Well, then I had no idea how to get to it. But I crossed my arms and pretended otherwise. "Why do you need it?"

"Time flows forward. Only ever forward." His lashes lowered, and he looked almost melancholy. "But you were born of the River. You have the power to manipulate its flow. To move it *backward*."

"I can't." Of everything he might have asked from me, he wanted me to perform the impossible. "I've tried, but I've never been able to do anything more than slow it down." Except that one Sunday, but Ninu didn't need to know that.

"In your current form, yes," he said. "But you can free yourself. You're his daughter. Time wouldn't bind you permanently to a mortal body."

"You're crazy," I said, because it was the only way to make sense of his words. I glanced at Avan and Reev. Reev remained unresponsive, but Avan was glaring blearily at Ninu. "I'm not one of you."

He gave me a pitying look. I couldn't tell if it was real or more mockery. "We'll see how long you can cling to that lie. It was cruel of him, allowing you to know a human's life."

"I *am* human." I was different. A freak. But I was still human. I wouldn't let him take that away from me.

"For now. It was cruel, but also clever. It hid you from me. I needed a favor that Time refused to grant," he said, his expression stony. "I almost trapped him; he escaped and hid you with the humans. But you were meant for more, because here you are. And now I will ask of you what I wanted from your father."

I didn't know why he pretended I had a choice. Not with Reev and Avan here.

"Throw away your mortal body, Kai. Claim your true powers, and give me back my past."

I could hear the longing in his voice. It was real, as wistful and desperate as what I felt when I thought about my brother and a freight container we had called home only because we had each other to fill it.

If I closed my eyes, I could see Ninu's longing take shape: Towers of shimmering stone and crystal, not like the buildings in the White Court but older, like the ones from the history texts. Trains that spat plumes of smoke, speeding across green fields that stretched for miles. The vermilion robes of the *mahjo*, magic heavy in the air and carried along the wind like spices. And the Sun. The Sun ever present in a blue sky more vivid than any poster. Beautiful and clear like a cherished memory.

Maybe he was still weaving magic. I shook my head. The last thing I wanted was to understand him.

"The world then—*my* world—wasn't paradise. But it was better than this," Ninu said quietly.

"But you're Infinite," I said. You'd think they would be used to changing times.

He laughed again. "Now, yes. But not always." He gestured to Reev and Avan. "So? What do you say, Daughter of Time?"

I still wasn't sure what he wanted from me. I had no idea where the River was or how he expected me to stop being human—which I had no intention of doing. Did he really think I could just drop him into the past? While I couldn't argue that it would benefit all of us to get rid of him, I didn't exactly have instructions for how to rewind time.

"Do you want to think it over?" Ninu asked. "I'm sure I could find something to entertain us in the meantime."

The sentinels released their hold on Avan's arms and retreated from the room. Avan wavered, but he remained standing. I started forward, but Ninu's voice stopped me.

"R-22," he said. Reev's vacant eyes focused on Ninu. "Are you armed?"

"Yes," Reev answered.

Ninu must have given him an unspoken order, because Reev withdrew the torch blade from his belt. The blade was a foot and a half in length and glowed as if the metal absorbed light instead of reflected it. He wielded the weapon in a flowing series of arcs. I wasn't sure what Ninu had ordered him to do until Avan cried out and dropped to his knees.

A red line appeared along the length of Avan's arm. Blood ran down his skin, outlining his knuckles in red. Then the bleeding stopped and retraced its path up his wrist and forearm, and the wound closed. Gasping, Avan bent over.

I lunged at Ninu. The torch blade cut into my path. I jerked back. I looked from Reev's blade, which he had thrust between me and Ninu, to Ninu's expressionless face.

I will kill you, I silently promised. *For Avan and for Reev, I will kill you.*

"Would you like to see another demonstration, or have you decided?" Ninu asked.

Reev lowered his sword. I looked down at my knife and the red streaks across the chipped blade. What was it Irra had said about the blood of *mahjo*? The price paid for stripping them of their magic: the sentinels and the hollows—their blood was poison to their Infinite ancestor.

What was the likelihood that Ninu's puppet had been one of his descendants?

Worth a shot.

"Fight me," I said. I made a point to tuck the knife into my belt.

Ninu's brows rose.

"If you win, I'll do whatever you ask. But if *I* win, then you let me, my brother, and Avan go free."

"I'm not a fan of bargaining. And I'm fairly sure I didn't leave room for it."

"Why not? Afraid you'll lose?"

He gave Kalla an amused look. I had almost forgotten she was there, still lounging on the sofa. To my surprise, she said, "What harm is there in indulging her? She can't possibly win."

"I think he's afraid of a human girl," I said, hoping Ninu's grudge with Time would make him too proud to back down. "Daughter of Time, right? Bet you never beat my dad, either."

Ninu began unbuttoning his tunic. A mix of triumph and anxiety shot through me. He shrugged off the sturdy black material, revealing a loose gray undershirt, and folded it neatly over the table. "I'm willing to play along. Feel free to use your powers if you think they'll help you."

The knife felt heavy against my side, but I didn't grab for it. Not yet.

I planted my feet and waited as he approached. I would probably lose. But I would make sure to kick his ass in the meanwhile.

CHAPTER 37

NINU KNEW HOW TO FIGHT ME. WHENEVER I SLOWED TIME, I felt a vibration through my body and my grip slipped too soon. While he couldn't affect the threads, he could still affect *me*, and I didn't know how he was doing it.

He also knew how to take advantage of my powers. Because he was aware of time slowing, even for the mere second I could hold it back, he could calculate how to counteract the rebound. As soon as the threads flung us forward, he attacked, striking at my openings. I was trapped in that sliver of increased time, and I had a split second to react. It wasn't enough.

My tailbone struck the floor, followed by my shoulder blades. I hissed in air, back arching. Biting down on a groan, I rolled onto my side and glared up at him. He was faster than his sentinels.

"I've fought your father," he said. "He was more of a challenge."

I stood, the knife jostling against my hip. I had to be patient. Wait for an opportunity. Movement to my right drew my eye, and I glanced at Avan. He was on his feet again. Reev had him by his upper arm. I wasn't sure if it was to restrain him or hold him up. Avan watched me, a line between his eyebrows. He mouthed a word: *Mason*.

End it quickly, Mason had said. My powers weren't the advantage I thought they'd be, so how could I use my speed instead?

I charged Ninu, pulling at the threads but releasing them an instant later, this time without Ninu's interference. I dived left, plucked at time again, and then cut right and aimed for his side.

Ninu caught my wrist and wrenched my arm up behind me. My shoulder screamed.

"Better," he said, his voice low against my ear. "But still clumsy. Try again." He laid his palm against the middle of my back and gave me a light shove, releasing my arm.

I stumbled for a moment but found my footing—and my knife. I spun, fist jabbing out. He stopped my punch again and then ducked. The knife in my other hand missed his throat. *Drek*.

I panted, forcing my thoughts to focus. Time slowed. I flipped the knife, blade side down. Again that vibration through my mind. The threads sprang free too soon. I swiped upward. His arm rose. The block jolted through my shoulder. His knuckles rammed into my gut.

All the air left my lungs. I hit the floor, curling around my stomach, gasping. Nothing else existed but the pain.

"Kai." Avan's voice. "Get up."

My nails clawed against the smooth tiles as I pushed up onto my hands and knees. I rose unsteadily to my feet.

Speed is my ally. Breathe. In and out. Focus. *Time is my power*.

Ninu spread his arms wide in invitation.

I rushed him. I didn't think about where to hit next; my body moved on instinct. Punch, duck, kick, block. *Don't stop. Don't stop.* Ninu's head snapped to the left. My knuckles throbbed, but grim satisfaction fueled my next strike.

His hands snatched my wrists. His grip was unforgiving. His eyes narrowed. Then he let go, and I darted back to avoid the hit that barely missed my chin. His attacks came fast, pushing me across the room. I tripped. Pain stabbed my face. My vision went dark at the corners. I found myself back on the floor, looking up at the glass ceiling. I blinked rapidly, letting the rising heat in my face burn away the daze.

I let the humiliation feed my anger. *Think, Kai.*

"You *are* your father's daughter," Ninu said. He tugged at the loose sleeves of his shirt and smoothed down the wrinkles. "But he was a better strategist. It'll come with experience."

I shut out the questions that rushed forward. I didn't know what to believe, but whether Ninu was telling the truth or not, I couldn't let him or anything else distract me.

It took me longer to regain my footing this time. As he waited for me, I trailed my mind along the threads, deliberating. Time flowed in a current that didn't ebb or swell but was constant. I could push against it, slow it down, slip free of its net. But what would happen if I tried to break it?

"Giving up already?"

I ignored the taunt. I imagined my hands skimming the current the way I once had at the river's bend in the North District. Then I slid my left foot back and sprang forward. Ninu blocked before my fist could land, dodged before the knife could find skin. He deliberately didn't retaliate, and whatever powers he possessed, he wasn't using them except to interfere with mine. His restraint was insulting.

I imagined pressing my hands against the threads, letting them tangle around my fingers. Around me, time slowed. I imagined digging my fingers in and pulling. Wrenching. Ripping. The threads were so tightly knit that they barely gave. But it was enough.

Time warped around us. Motion became a dizzying whirl. For one brief moment, the threads dragged me *backward*.

I immediately altered my attack. I dropped to my haunches and struck.

I think I was as shocked as Ninu when my knife sank into his stomach. Red bubbled up around the blade. His hand lifted to grab mine. I let go of the handle and twisted out of reach.

His fingers replaced mine around the handle. He regarded me with the same air of approval that Mason had after I'd managed to hit him.

So. Not his descendant then. *Drek!*

I had stabbed him, but was this enough to win? I shifted my weight, considering another attack.

"Good job," he said. "You're a fast learn—" He stopped. His eyes lowered to the knife.

With a quizzical tilt to his head, he pulled the knife free. Blood rushed from the open wound, blossoming across his shirt like one of Irra's roses.

In his hand, beneath the fresh coat of red, the blade glowed. He dropped it. Instead of falling, the knife hovered in the air. I watched, stupefied, as the blood on the blade thinned, then disappeared, as if the glowing metal had absorbed it. Light encased the weapon. I had to squint to look at it.

Avan called my name, but I couldn't look away. The shape of the knife changed, elongating into a staff and then flashing brightly as a curved blade materialized at one end, translucent and shimmery like starlight. When the light receded, I realized it was a scythe.

I reached out tentatively, then flinched when it flew away.

There was a muffled smack as the staff hit its owner's palm. Both Ninu and I looked at Kalla in confusion. Kalla rested her weapon against the floor and traced a glossy fingernail along her alabaster cheek. Her features shifted. Her eyes grew larger, chin sharper, red lips plumper. Her hair spilled down her shoulders in a tumble of white waves.

"You," I said, backing up. The memory of her reeled through me—a nervous and pale young woman, half dressed, her thin arms offering me a battered knife and a map. "You're from the Raging Bull."

Ninu sank to his knees, his bloodied hand pressed against his stomach. Then his gaze lifted to meet mine.

"I wanted my life back," he said. "It wasn't a great life. But it was mine." He closed his eyes.

Kalla twirled the scythe in her hand, and it vanished in a flare of light. She didn't look at her brother.

"The Infinite are incapable of killing one another directly," she told me, brushing her long hair over her pale shoulder.

"Your knife—"

"My scythe," she corrected me. "I am the second oldest of the Infinite. My weapon can kill anything."

"But why?" I asked, inching toward Avan and Reev. Avan looked as bewildered as I felt, but Reev hadn't reacted in any way to seeing his Kahl stabbed. "You're Ninu's right hand. Why would you help me?"

Death smiled. "Time has ever been my ally."

CHAPTER 38

I SKIRTED AROUND NINU'S BODY, NOW SPRAWLED ON THE floor, and rushed to Avan.

"Are you—?" I cut myself off. It was an idiotic question. Of course he wasn't okay. "I'm sorry."

He gave me a rueful smile. "Why are you apologizing?"

His hand came up, fingers grazing my sore jaw. You'd think I would be used to getting punched by now, but the pain felt new each time. I leaned into his touch. I didn't know what any of this meant, but I prayed Kalla was on our side.

Reev looked around, his eyes slow to focus. Then he hissed in his breath, reaching back to claw at his collar as if it pained him.

"Reev, stop," I said, tugging at his hand.

Kalla's heels clicked against the floor as she circled Ninu. He lay on his stomach, face angled away from me. No sentinels appeared to carry him away.

"Ninu held ultimate control over the collars," she said. "Without him, Reev will recover shortly, although Ninu's mark should be removed from the collar as a precaution."

Relief made my body sag. I squeezed Reev's hand.

Kalla cocked her head, a sudden awareness in her eyes. I searched the room. I felt it, too. The threads, the current, time itself—had stopped. The view from the window revealed the smoke from distant chimney pipes caught in still-frame, like a picture, and Grays fixed in place like figurines amid a miniature cityscape. The entire city, everything outside this room, had been frozen.

"Congratulations, Kai," someone said. "You've liberated Ninurta."

The voice was worse than Ninu's, not because it burrowed beneath my skin but because I knew, deep down, that it was familiar. I knew it the way I knew the threads that currently snared the city like a giant spider's web, inescapable even by me because, while I could manipulate them, *he* had woven the threads and designed their pattern.

The air in the room quivered, and then a man was standing next to Kalla. It wasn't his presence that surprised me. It was the fact that I had felt him coming. Avan clasped my shoulder. I reached up to rest my hand over his.

"This is Kronos," Kalla said. "Although I don't think an introduction is really necessary."

He didn't look like anyone I remembered. But then I saw his eyes: watery blue like the icicles that formed on the tree branches in winter. He smiled. I didn't smile back.

Any sense of relief I had before disappeared. I brushed away Avan's hand and released Reev's. My body tensed, waiting.

He extended his arm, the black folds of his cloak rustling in a current that only he and I could see. Kalla touched her fingers to his raised forearm, a simple but familiar gesture.

"You have questions," she said to me. "But the answers have always been there. Ninu assumed that when R-22 disappeared, Irra had taken him for his hollows. So how did Ninu find Reev again?"

"The energy drive," I said warily.

"And who do you think told Reev about the energy drive? Who decided to hold it there, practically on top of the Labyrinth?"

My mind ran through the possibilities. "But you couldn't have known. You couldn't have predicted that I would be attacked, that I would need to—"

I saw the face of the woman who'd attacked me that day in the alley. White skin, black-streaked Mohawk, and bright-red lips, the only splash of color against her pale features.

I felt as if the air had been knocked out of me again. "It was all you," I breathed.

"You're softhearted, Kai. I knew you wouldn't leave me to die in that alley. And I made sure that the tax notice was delivered directly to Reev."

I cupped my head in my hands. The attack; the energy drive; tricking Reev's boss in order to send me to the Rider, the only person with the means of sneaking me into the White Court. So I could—

"You did all this," I said, looking between Kalla and Kronos. "Why? To get me here to kill Ninu? How did you know who Reev was anyway? That he and I—"

"You know the answer to that," Kronos said.

When he moved, his hair—as long as my own—rippled like water, its color shifting, liquid strands in constant motion. As with the rest of the Infinite, I couldn't pinpoint his age. He was at once young and wizened. Looking at him was like trying to focus on stones resting in the riverbed beneath the swaying waves.

"Who am I?" he asked.

With absolute certainty, I said, "My father."

Someone grabbed my wrist. I started, backing away only to realize it was Reev.

When our eyes met, I could see it was really him. A brief rush of joy filled me. "Reev."

He opened his mouth, but Kronos cut him off.

"Welcome back, Reev." He looked at me. "His final mission before his purification had been against me—Ninu needed his full force of sentinels to invade my palace. But I'd known at once that Reev was different from the others. His connection to Ninu had already begun to fray. I read into his past, his desire for freedom, and I granted it. In exchange, I'd left him a most precious charge."

So he was the one who'd freed Reev. My dad. It felt strange just to think the words. *My dad.*

Reev's hand tightened around my wrist. He had been meant to find me, to take me in. For some reason, knowing we had been designed to meet didn't bother me. Reev was meant to be mine.

"To hide me," I said.

"Ninu was one of the few Infinite with the power to, in a way, counter my own. You probably realized that in your duel."

I nodded. It had been unbelievably frustrating.

"The blood of descendants who are not our own will not kill us, but it does weaken us. Ninu had managed to injure me in the battle before I could force him and his sentinels from my palace. But as long as I refused to reverse the River for him, I knew he would target you in my place. I couldn't protect you."

He had left me on a riverbank with no memory of who I was, no family, and no understanding of what I could do. The truth finally sank in. Ninu had been right. It was cruel. Letting me think I was human—the only thing I knew how to be because I sure as drek didn't remember being one of them—it was too cruel.

I stared at Kronos. I could tell he wasn't fully recovered. Irra wore the emaciated look like a perfectly fitted tunic, but Kronos looked ill. His cheeks were too wan, and his shoulders sagged beneath his cloak, as if all of time weighted them down. He might have been handsome if he'd been healthy.

"Why didn't you tell me who I am from the start?" I asked Kalla.

She glanced dispassionately at Ninu's body. "Ninu had few *mahjo* to begin with, but after Rebirth, he was especially careful not to leave any human descendants. Since we were incapable of killing him directly, we needed someone with the strength of a full-blooded Infinite—someone who could wield my scythe and not be drawn into death by it—but, at the same time, not bound by our laws. Kronos trapped you in a mortal body. You can age and sicken and die. It was a perfect disguise from Ninu, but we didn't realize until recently that it was also the perfect weapon. And since Ninu wanted you, it gave you access to him."

She hadn't answered my question. They could have just told me all this. Instead, they had manipulated my every move—and now, recalling my conversations with Irra, I had little doubt that he'd been in on this as well. I had been as much a puppet as Ninu's human decoy.

If they had told me what they wanted, would I have helped them? I didn't hate my life. It wasn't ideal, but I had Reev, a place to sleep, and enough food to keep me going. What did I care about their stupid immortal feud? I had always wanted to know where my powers came from, but that didn't mean I wanted to be like them.

I didn't want to be Infinite.

"Exactly," Kronos said, watching me closely. "You wouldn't have done as asked. Your humanity, your emotional attachments hinder you."

I scowled. "You can read minds, too?"

"Your eyes give away your thoughts."

"You wanted Reev dead," Avan cut in.

I turned to him. He looked steadier, and he'd been watching the conversation unfold with an increasingly dark expression.

Reev added, "They probably expected Ninu to have me re-branded already. And once you killed him, there would have been nothing left—no *emotional attachments*—holding you to your human life. They would have used that to persuade you to join them."

They thought Reev's death would convince me to let my humanity go. They obviously knew nothing about humans.

From the moment Kalla attacked me in that alley, I had performed according to their script. But, because of Ninu, it hadn't gone exactly as planned. Instead of just creating a mental block, Ninu could've begun Reev's rebranding at any time, and he hadn't. For that, I was grateful. They were out of their immortal minds if they thought I would want anything to do with them now.

"You screwed up," I told them. "I'll never be one of you."

"I never intended for you to remain human, Kai," Kronos said. "Ninu may be gone, but Reev's life remains tenuous."

I didn't care that he was my dad. Reev was my *family*. I moved to put myself in front of both Reev and Avan, and silenced their objections with a glare. "If you hurt him, I swear I'll never leave this body. I'll find a way to bind myself permanently."

"That's impossible," Kalla said.

"Then why do you look so nervous? I'd rather die human than be like you."

A weak laugh pierced the room. It resonated in my chest. On the floor, Ninu stirred. It was the slightest movement, the most he could manage.

"Yes," he whispered. "Yes. That's the right choice. Don't ever let them take that from you."

I felt nothing but hatred for Ninu, but I understood his words.

Kalla's perfect lips pursed. Even annoyed, she looked unnaturally beautiful. I should have realized it at the Raging Bull.

"Persistent, aren't you?" she said.

"Well, it is rather difficult to pass on with our dear friend Time weaving his interference," Ninu replied. "I stand now at the gates to your realm, Sister."

I could sense all the tones and tremors in his voice. It conjured images of glass shrines that reflected the sunlight and billows of greasy smoke that reminded me of the market outside Zora Hall. Then he dragged in a shallow, wet breath, and the images dispersed.

"There are no more restrictions holding you. Help me along, won't you, Sister?"

Kalla's scythe appeared in a flash of light. She approached Ninu, weapon raised. I looked away, focusing instead on the stubble on Avan's jaw. It was a good look on him.

Kalla's blade whined as it sliced the air. I flinched.

CHAPTER 39

A SHIVER OF POWER WENT THROUGH ME, AND I KNEW NINU was gone. I held my breath in the silence that followed.

Kronos sighed heavily. "I'm not unreasonable, Kai. I do not wish for you to hate me. You are, after all, my daughter."

I didn't tell him that, after all their scheming, our relationship didn't mean much. Especially since I couldn't remember any of it. I wanted to ask if I would get my memory back, but the answer scared me. If I remembered, if I knew where I'd come from, would it change who I was now?

For the first time, the answers were within my grasp, and I couldn't reach for them. Not without betraying Reev and Avan.

"I may not be fully recovered, but I don't have need of my heir yet," Kronos continued.

"You're immortal," I pointed out. "When will you ever have need of me?"

His eyes were cool. "I am the oldest of the Infinite, and immortality has grown weary. When I have decided it is time to rest, I will call on you. For now, you may remain with the humans. But the next time I come, you will be prepared to join me. And I will not be so charitable."

I didn't reply. He would just remind me of the control he had over the lives of anyone I cared about.

"For now," he said, apparently taking my silence for agreement, "make your peace with your human bonds."

I leaned back against Avan's chest and felt his fingers against my waist.

Kronos gave me a steady look. I had the impression I amused him, but I couldn't be sure.

"I have one final task before I leave," Kronos added.

I waited for him to elaborate. He looked over my shoulder. I twisted around to stare at Avan.

"Avan?"

His knuckles brushed my cheek. "I know what you think I am. But I'm not *mahjo*."

"Some humans," Kronos said, "possess the ability to sense the Infinite. As one of them, and due to his affection for you, Avan was in a convenient position to be your guardian."

I moved away from Avan, and he let me go. I looked between them, from Kronos's stoic face to Avan's guilty one.

"You knew? All along, you *knew* and you didn't tell me?"

"I didn't know all *this*," Avan said, gesturing around us. "I told you I already knew what you could do, Kai. I knew you were special; and when Kronos came to me, I finally discovered why. But I wasn't expecting any of this."

"With Reev gone, you were the only person I thought I could trust, and you've been *lying* to me from the start."

"I had to be able to protect you."

"I knew you would need help, so I offered him a proposition," Kronos said. "He made an adequate guardian."

As furious as I was with Avan, I had to defend him. "Adequate? He saved my life." Probably more than once.

Kronos looked down his nose at me. "Precisely." Then he said to Avan, "You recall what I told you about your time?"

Avan nodded.

"Okay," I said, lifting my hands. "Quit being cryptic and tell me what's going on."

"He asked me to keep you safe, and he gave me the power to do it," Avan said. He rubbed the back of his neck, as if the admission embarrassed him. "But if I told you the truth, the deal would be off. In Etu Gahl, when I thought that was the end of your search for Reev, I wanted to tell you then."

What if you could find out for sure? Avan had said that first night. *Would you want to know?*

Suddenly, I couldn't catch my breath. "Why didn't you?" I asked, overcome.

"Because Irra promised a way back into Ninurta, and I had to be there to protect you."

"I can take care of myself." I spat out the words. Not only had he lied to me, he hadn't trusted me to keep myself safe.

"I know," he said. "And I know what you're thinking, but you're wrong. You're a strong person, Kai. I've always admired that about you. But anything could happen, and I had to be prepared for both our sakes."

"How long have you known?"

"Since the day before Reev disappeared."

"Did you know Reev would be kidnapped?" Rage swelled inside me.

"No," he said, stepping close. His hand cupped my cheek. "I would have stopped it if I'd known."

I believed him. I knew that Avan wouldn't let anything happen to Reev if he could prevent it.

"As I said," Kronos interrupted, "his affection for you worked in my favor. In order to protect you from whatever the Outlands and Ninu might place in your path, I froze his time. Any injuries he sustained would be temporarily revers—"

"I understood the risks," Avan said softly.

I remembered Avan's broken arm after our crash. Irra deliberately cutting him. The complications with drawing blood.

Reev's blade laying open his chest.

I shook my head, staring at the base of his neck where his collarbones met. My anger ebbed as the memories came together. My hands found his shoulders, nails digging into his skin that was firm and alive. *They couldn't mean—*

Avan tilted my chin so I'd look up at him. "Kai, I—" He paused, appeared to search for the right words, and then sighed and leaned forward.

His kiss wasn't at all uncertain. I drew in a shuddering breath, taking the air from Avan's parted lips and holding it. Everyone and everything else faded away as I lifted on my toes and kissed him back. His fingers trailed down my neck, gentle enough to make my chest hurt. His other hand lingered at my waist, his restraint evident in the way he gripped my hip.

His mouth moved desperately over mine, his taste against my tongue. I pressed closer, curling my fingers against his chest. His heart beat a frantic rhythm against my palms. I couldn't remember how to breathe, but that was okay because Avan's breath filled me.

He whispered against my lips, "I love you. You have to know that."

All the words I wanted to say scattered. I could only hold on to him and nod. He pulled back so I could see his eyes, beautiful and sad and filled with emotions I wasn't used to seeing there.

"I thought I knew how I felt about you," he said, "when we were in the Alley. When I was convinced you saw me only as your friend. But now I know the truth." He touched his forehead to mine, his dark lashes closing. "I love you, Kai. Which is why I can't let you see this."

Confusion made me frown, but his kiss and his words still burned inside me.

"Reev," Avan said, drawing back farther. His hands fell away. "Can you take her?"

"What?" I reached out, but Reev took hold of me instead.

"Come on, Kai," Reev said, his voice too soft. Too careful. I tried to elbow him off.

"What are you doing?" I demanded.

Avan said, "Kronos is going to release my time."

"But that means—"

"You can't watch this," Reev said. My feet faltered. Reev's hands were like manacles around my arms.

"Let me go!" I struck out at Reev, abandoning all my training and letting my limbs fly. A raging frenzy consumed me. This couldn't be happening.

My strength was no match for Reev's. He hauled me against him, his arm wrapping around my waist and dragging me toward the exit. Avan watched me go.

I shouted at Kronos, "If you do this, I'll never join you!"

My fingers grappled against the threshold, but Reev peeled them loose with a quiet apology. He reached for the door.

I didn't realize I was crying until the sob tore free. Stupid, *stupid* Avan—I took in the beautiful curve of his mouth, that drekking dimple, the warmth in his eyes. I had to make sure this image of him would remain with me always, seared into my mind.

He whispered, "Stay safe."

Then Reev slammed the door shut, time hurtled forward again, and Avan was gone.

CHAPTER 40

NINU MUST HAVE LIKED HIS SOLITUDE, BECAUSE THERE were a surprising number of secluded places on the palace grounds. My favorite was the enormous oasis right next to a block of official buildings.

The gardens stretched over three acres, filled with all varieties of trees, dirt paths and meandering streams, lush flowers and wildly overgrown plants as densely tangled as the forest. Scattered throughout were tables and benches set in patches of grass that had been allowed to grow wild.

When I'd first found the oasis, I had tossed my bag over my shoulder and lost myself in its winding paths for a week. Eventually, I'd come upon a gazebo at the end of a path laid with cracked stones. The gazebo overlooked a pond with water so clear that I could see all the way down to the silt bottom. Glittering gold and silver fish darted through the water.

I spent most of my time here. Like today. I'd folded a blanket to soften the gazebo's stone bench and sat watching the branches rustle and shake the leaves loose.

Everyone else had spent the last couple of weeks running around me, briefing and reorganizing the sentinels—those who'd chosen to remain—while making room for the recent arrival of Irra and a contingent of his hollows. Kalla had decided to continue the Tournament to avoid alerting the public.

The first thing I demanded of Kalla was to remove my alias from the citizen registry and clear my fugitive status so I could move about freely.

After Reev found me on the riverbank, I had tried not to obsess about what I couldn't remember. Tried to be someone Reev would want to keep by his side, despite the questions that filled the space where my memory should've been.

I had returned the false ID to Irra and hadn't bothered asking for my original one. There was no going back to who I'd been.

But that was okay. I didn't need the ID to tell me who I should be. Now, I could be whoever I wanted.

I had also gone back to the arena and found Tariza and Grene. It felt nice to see them again, although a little tricky explaining what had happened. When they asked about Avan, I had smiled and told them he had returned to the North District after recovering from his wound.

Across the stone floor of the gazebo, Reev sat on a wooden bench, immersed in an old textbook. Irra had requested that Reev and I remain in the White Court until decisions had been made about what to do now that Ninu was dead. Considering how the Infinite had manipulated me, I was certain they had a plan for what to do after they succeeded in getting me to kill the Kahl, but no one would tell me anything.

I folded my arms on the gazebo's ledge and cradled my head in the crook of my elbow.

Seeing him, having him here with me—I was happy, of course. Reev was safe. It was all I had wanted. But I should have been happier.

Watching him study was relaxing. He joined me most days with his textbooks. He liked it here as much as I did.

Sometimes, he got this look on his face. It never lasted more than an instant, but it was enough for me to notice his eyes grow distant and his mouth tighten. Familiar as I was with the emotion, I recognized it as guilt. I didn't have the courage to address it yet.

I hadn't allowed myself to think too long about what had happened to Avan. A part of me blamed Reev. But even if Reev hadn't killed him in the arena, Ninu had done it numerous times afterward.

He has so much of you already, Avan had said in Etu Gahl. *Is there anything left for anyone else?*

I finally understood what he'd been asking me. Although I hadn't recognized it at the time, there had been jealousy in the way he'd spoken about Reev. Not the petty kind—a sad kind of jealousy.

But it was too late now to give him a proper answer, no matter how badly I wished otherwise.

I should have told Avan how I felt. I should have protected *him.* I shouldn't have let him come with me. I shouldn't have been such a coward.

I turned my face into my elbow. I'd have to tell his parents sometime. I owed him that.

Tucking my feet up under me, I twisted around to face the pond. Lights flashed beneath the water whenever a fish swam close to the surface.

Reev's footsteps were soft as he approached. He did that on purpose so he wouldn't startle me. I knew he could move without a sound.

"I'm done studying for now. Want to spar?"

He thought beating up on him made me feel better. It didn't. It made me feel worse.

"Not now."

He reached out, hesitated, and then clasped his hands awkwardly in front of him. I didn't have to force a smile as I patted the seat beside me.

Things between us had been awkward at first. Reev had been as much a pawn as I had, and he'd been through enough already without me flinging accusations at him. With him just as worried about hurting me, neither of us knew how to talk.

But I had missed him so much—his presence, his safety, his voice—that this time I shut away the fear and asked my questions. Once I learned that Reev hadn't known who I was when he took me in, my doubts about his love had faded. Kronos had erased that part of his memory to protect me, and Istar's mention of missing spans of time supported that truth.

Reev had known, instinctively, that he was meant to protect me, but it wasn't until I used my power to steal another Sunday that he realized why.

We had been designed to find each other, but Reev's love was genuine.

He took my hand now. "Did you want to go for a w—"

A shout interrupted him. We both looked to see Mason and Irra coming up the path. Mason waved, smiling brightly. The sight of him brought an echo of the relief I'd felt when I first discovered he was safe.

"Reev," Irra said, "I'm going to review the store of energy stones if you'd like to accompany me."

Reev wanted to learn about how the energy stones were created. More than that, he wanted to learn about traditional, non-magical methods of producing energy. Kalla had confessed that the energy stones were her creation and not Ninu's, so the city wasn't at risk of collapsing from an energy shortage. But it was still much too dependent on magic, and we needed to revive the technology that had been lost after Rebirth if we wanted to progress and survive. Reev had spent the last two weeks studying the old texts.

I went back to watching the trees and then glanced over my shoulder when something brushed against my leg. It was Irra's oversize tunic.

Looking up at him was a strain on my neck, so I didn't bother. I waited for him to speak first.

"You should be aware that Avan said he wouldn't regret his choice to join you in the Tournament regardless of what happened."

My fingers scraped over stone. Even though Irra had been here for a week, he'd been so busy with Kalla that, aside from the initial greeting, we hadn't spoken. Why was he telling me this now?

"I was unaware of what Kronos had done to him. But when I realized, I gave him a choice. I would have given him a choice regardless."

"But you didn't warn him." I dug my nails into the gazebo's ledge.

"He knew the risks. He made his decision."

"Irra," Reev said, a warning in his voice.

"This was meant to comfort her." Irra sounded genuinely baffled. Mason shot me an apologetic look as Irra stepped away to join Reev on the path.

Once they left, Mason took the spot beside me. "So," he said lightly, "nice day."

I rubbed my temple and attempted to regain the tentative calm I'd felt before Irra showed up. "It was."

"We missed you in the training center yesterday."

"I didn't feel like being Hina's punching bag."

"The only reason she doesn't go easy on you is because she knows you can do better," he said, his instructor tone creeping into his voice.

I knew he was only trying to steer my thoughts away from the conversation with Irra. "I'll come tomorrow," I said.

"Good. Because Hina's planning to drag you there if you don't show up."

My lips twitched. "Thanks for the warning."

He relaxed against the stone, his eyes softening at the glimpse of my smile. "Have you decided what you want to do now?"

Sucking on my bottom lip, I turned his question over in my mind.

"I want to tear down the wall around the White Court."

"And how exactly are you planning to accomplish that?"

I didn't know. Everything was different now. Going back to the Labyrinth was no longer an option. I wouldn't be able to go anywhere in the North District without the constant reminder that Avan wasn't waiting behind the counter at his dad's shop.

Honestly, thinking about the work it would take to clean up Ninurta overwhelmed me, but with Ninu gone, all those promises he'd made about improving the North District seemed possible. With the right leaders, of course.

Not that I wanted the job. Even if Kalla offered it to me, I would refuse. But I did want to help. Maybe I could even bring Grene and Tariza onboard. They had wanted to change things as well.

"I guess I'll figure it out," I said. "We've got time."

Mason pulled one leg up onto the bench and rested his arm on the stone ledge. We sat that way for a while as fish skittered beneath the water and birds darted between the trees.

His fingers found mine, and he squeezed them gently. He'd been a good friend since arriving, never asking for more than what we'd had in the Void.

But I missed Avan. I missed him more than I could put into words, and every day, the missing grew. I tried not to think about it, the *lack* of him, but my dreams made it difficult. Every night, I had to relive different moments with him: lingering conversations in the halls at school, him laughing from behind his dad's counter, his body wrapped around mine in the Void, his steady presence beside me every night in Etu Gahl. His smile, his tattoo, the way he'd looked that night in his room when we'd made an unspoken promise that couldn't last.

Mason said, "Kalla asked to see you. She's in her tower, but you don't have to go. You don't owe her anything."

I wasn't as angry with her as I was with Kronos, but I didn't like her, either. As far as I was concerned, once they sorted out Ninurta's leadership, they could go back to wherever the Infinite were *supposed* to spend eternity and stay there. I didn't know how much time I had before Kronos—it was still weird to call him "Dad," even in my head—came back, either, and it was an unnerving feeling, as if I was walking around with a ticking clock over my head.

Kalla hadn't spoken to me since she restored my citizenship. If she wanted to see me now, it was probably important.

I slid my hand away from Mason's and stood. "Thanks."

"I'll walk you up."

"It's okay. Stay here. I'll come back after."

"Tonight, I want to show you the observatory," he said. "If that's okay."

I smiled, genuinely pleased by the idea. "I'd love that."

From the oasis to Kalla's tower was a quick walk through the palace grounds and the government buildings, separated from the public by yet another wall, although not as tall or imposing as the others. The arena had been built just outside the grounds but was connected to many of the buildings via an underground tunnel.

On the long staircase leading up to Kalla's tower, I contemplated all the reasons she'd want to see me. Maybe Kronos had come back. Maybe carrying her scythe around for weeks had taken its toll on me after all. Maybe Ninu wasn't as dead as he was supposed to be. I didn't know how death worked with the Infinite. Immortality was supposed to be pretty straightforward, but I guess there were exceptions.

The doors at the top of the stairs were open. Kalla stood in front of the tall windows overlooking the city. She'd taken a different form. She'd shorn her hair, that one black streak a feathery patch above her temple. Her face looked more angular, her cheekbones more prominent, eyes thinner, and mouth wider. She wore a silver tunic over a simple white shirt and fitted white pants.

"Join me," she said. The torches had been doused. The only light came in through the windows, and it left the corners dressed in shadows.

I hadn't been here since that night, since Avan—

Straightening my shoulders, I stepped in to greet Death.

CHAPTER 41

"AREN'T YOU CURIOUS ABOUT WHAT YOU ARE?" SHE ASKED.

I stood next to her by a window. With my hands pressed to the glass, I could almost imagine myself floating above the city.

Of course I am. But you killed Avan, and you would have killed Reev. "I'm human," I said. And I still planned to stay that way.

"For now," she murmured. "Did you know that Ninu was once human?"

I glanced away from studying the crooked lines of the Labyrinth in the distance. Ninu had said something about not always being Infinite.

"How's that possible?"

"There are ways. He and Istar were both human. But Istar was from a much earlier time. She has been Infinite far longer. And she came to enjoy it."

"Where *is* Istar?" I asked. I wanted to know which parts of the city to avoid.

Kalla smiled. "She doesn't get along with Irra. She finds

him unsightly, and he finds her obscene. She's chosen to leave Ninurta for the time being."

Even though he'd been in on Kalla's plan, Irra had helped sentinels like Mason. Finding out he'd essentially chased away Istar only improved my opinion of him.

"Ninu, on the other hand"—Kalla touched her forehead to the windowpane, only the red spot of her lips visible in the reflection—"when he was human, the world had already shifted away from worshipping us, directing their prayers to our progeny. The *mahjo*. It was a century before Rebirth. His predecessor, the Conquest before him, came to an unexpected end at the hands of one of his descendants. An accident, from what I gathered."

How did you accidentally kill an immortal? There was obviously more to the story.

"Ninu—Jem, as he was called then—had been nearby. He tried to help my brother, but nothing could be done."

Condensation spread across the glass as she spoke, fogging her image. I didn't understand why she was telling me this. She had wanted Ninu dead. There was no point in sympathizing with him now.

"The number of Infinite is constant. Seventy immortals to shape the human world but never directly interfere."

"I'd say that rule was shot," I muttered. But I remembered that when Irra first told me about the Infinite, he had said something about maintaining a constant number of them. Seventy was a daunting amount. I hoped I'd never have to meet them all.

"This is not the first time the Infinite have interfered with the humans, you know."

Considering that their human descendants were still running around, this was hardly difficult to believe.

"Although Ninu was the first to insert himself publicly among them. I suppose it was wishful thinking." By the tone of her voice, she obviously didn't share Ninu's desire to be anything less than Infinite.

"What did you get out of all this?"

She looked at me imperiously. "Me? The Infinite are not always so self-serving. Ninu violated our laws and had to be stopped. But it left us with a difficult choice and a position to fill. There are laws among the Infinite that aren't so easily broken. Just as there are ways to eliminate the Infinite who have strayed from their purpose, there are ways to fill the void after such a loss. For coming to my brother's aid, we chose Jem as his replacement." Her eyes shut as if she was picturing a memory. "In the beginning, the wonders of being immortal awed him. He took joy in exploring his new world."

She frowned.

"But he grew discontent. Lonely, perhaps. He longed for the lost years of his human life and the people he'd left behind. So he appealed to Kronos and asked for access to the River. He wished to return to that day he found Conquest and change his fate, to alter his decision to help him so that another might have been chosen."

I think I understood where she was heading. "I don't want to be Infinite. I thought I made that clear. I'm never going to be like you or Ninu, not after—" Not after everything they'd done to me and the people I loved.

But I still had questions, the most demanding of which was, if Kronos was my father, then who was my mother? I was the daughter of an Infinite, but I wasn't *mahjo*. Ninu had said I was born of the River, but what did that *mean*? Why was I different? Were there others like me? I knew that a part of me would always yearn for the truth and wonder *What if . . . ?*

Kalla stepped away from the window, her head bowed. "Sometimes, I think it best you remain human. We have seen the chaos of one Infinite who longed for his human life. But you are of the River. The damage you could inflict on the balance between humans and Infinite far exceeds anything Ninu has done."

"Then tell Kronos to find another heir. And get yourself a different Ninu while you're at it."

"The world has grown so fragile," she said softly.

There was a bit of longing there as well. What did someone who had never known human emotions long for?

"The humans are resilient, but time weathers all things. Eventually, they too will leave us. What then, Kai?" She crossed the room, stopping in front of the table with the crystal decanter. It was empty.

I leaned against the window. "What do you want?"

She looked at me. "To introduce you to Conquest. Our newest brother—"

The door in the alcove opened. A man walked in. I felt suddenly weightless. It was as if the window behind me had given way and dropped me into free fall.

Avan approached Kalla. He wore a red tunic with flowing sleeves trimmed in gold and a braided belt at his waist. His matching pants and black, knee-high leather boots fit him perfectly. He looked as if he belonged here.

My eyes blurred with tears. I drew in a broken, desperate breath. I stepped forward but then paused. Was this even real?

Avan's expression was blank, his gaze cool. He regarded me the way he would a stranger—a weird, weepy stranger.

I tried to speak but couldn't. My hands clenched, afraid to reach out.

He nodded at me politely and addressed Kalla. "You called for me?"

His voice was low and rumbling, a beautiful sound I never expected to hear again. It vibrated around me and lingered in the room, draping my shoulders like a warm shawl. I dug my fingers into my chest in a vain attempt to contain the spreading ache.

My eyes met Kalla's. "What did you do?"

"I brought him back."

I had wanted to rip apart the River myself and change things. But not like this.

"Why?" I whispered. "Why would you do this to him?"

"I thought you'd be pleased," she said, red lips curving.

Yes, I realized. Even now, she was still trying to manipulate me. She had thought I would be happy enough to change my mind.

As Conquest's replacement, was Avan meant to replace the

Kahl as well? All Avan ever wanted was to live his life according to his own rules, but now he was tied to the Infinite in a way that he hadn't been even to his dad.

My anger strengthened me. I searched his face and prayed for something, anything, of the old Avan. But there was only a stranger's curiosity.

"Who are you?" Avan asked me. Some of that familiar wariness returned in the way his brows twitched together, and my heartbeat stumbled before picking up again.

I was at a loss for how to answer him. Even if there was a way to undo this—which I doubted—I wouldn't be able to let Avan die again. He couldn't remember me, but it was enough that he was here. He was alive.

I tried to control the torrent of emotions swirling inside me. I joined them by the table. Standing in front of him, I saw that his eyes were no longer brown, but a lucent shade of gold. They reminded me of the Sun right before it broke through the clouds.

I looked away. His eyes cut through me in a way no blade ever could. Staring at his chin, I thrust out my hand and offered a weak smile. His fingers closed around mine.

"I'm Kai," I choked out, and pulled away.

Except he didn't let go. His gaze moved over my face. He tugged on my hand. I followed, letting him pull me closer. He brushed his knuckles along my cheekbone.

I exhaled slowly, afraid to hope. "Avan?"

"I don't know you," he said quietly.

A tremor fluttered through my body.

"But I think I must have. Looking at you . . . It makes me want to remember." He gave a small, crooked smile. "Does that make any sense?"

I stopped fighting myself and leaned into him, resting my forehead against his chest. For a second, he did nothing. Then his arms closed around me. His hands rested against the curve of my back. He even smelled the same.

"Kai," he said into my hair, a note of wonder in his voice. "Kai," he repeated, as if to imprint my name on his memory.

Outside this tower, the city continued in ignorance of what had happened to its Kahl. But not for much longer. I didn't know what would happen now—if Kalla and the new Kahl, whoever that was, would allow the much-needed changes to take place. Every wall Ninu had erected was like a collar to control and divide the people. Would they embrace a city without divisions? Or would they build even stronger ones to replace them?

Avan and I had left Ninurta with only one purpose. None of this had ever been about changing anything. But whether by the Infinite's design or not, we had made our decisions, formed new friendships and enemies, new loves. We had changed too much. Our previous lives felt as distant and surreal as a dream.

I held Avan close. Now, in this moment, we could begin to shape a new kind of home.

Acknowledgments

INFINITE THANKS TO MY AGENT, SUZIE TOWNSEND, FOR BEING my champion and for believing wholeheartedly in this book. Thanks also to the team at New Leaf: Joanna, Kathleen, Pouya, Danielle, and Jaida. I'm so grateful for their tremendous support and expertise.

Immeasurable thanks to my brilliant editor, Robin Benjamin, the perfect advocate for this book with her invaluable insight and sharp-eyed editorial skills. I wonder every day how I got so lucky. Thanks also to the team at Skyscape for taking a chance and believing in a debut author: Courtney Miller, Miriam Juskowicz, Timoney Korbar, and Erick Pullen. Thanks to Tony Sahara for a stunning cover that I want to creepily caress and to Megan McNinch for visualizing Kai's world into a kick-butt map.

Enormous thanks to my amazing critique partners: Mindee Arnett, who is a marvel and inspires me daily; Lauren Teffeau, who practically oozes talent; and Anna Adao, who is as clever as she is awesome. I could not have done this without their constant support and spot-on input. Thanks also to my early beta readers: Chessie, Brent, Raven, and especially Kalen.

Super special thanks to the ladies of GfA: Natalie Parker, Amy Parker, Amy Tintera, Corinne Duyvis, Michelle Krys, Gemma Cooper, Deborah Hewitt, Ruth Steven, Kim Welchons, and Stephanie Winkelhake. I can't imagine how I could have gotten through the last few years without them. Thanks also to the dear friends I first met in fandom who have stayed with me through the crazy years and supported me in the pursuit of my writing dreams, especially Sofi, Patricia, Carolyn, and Emily. I adore you ladies.

Of course, none of this could have been possible without the support of my family. My mom, who had to deal with me reading all night until she caught me with my bedroom light on at 4 AM. My older brothers, La and Nai, who always believed I could do it. My brother Matt, who shares my love for all things geeky. My sisters May and Kay, who were among the first to kindle my love for reading and who've always supported me, even when I was just a snot-nosed kid jotting down stories about exploding heads. And to Kou, whom I miss with all my heart.

Last but not least, all my love and thanks to my husband, Cha, who tolerates my insanity when I'm freaking out about a deadline, and my children, Katalina and Oliver, who are the world to me.

About the Author

Lori M. Lee was born in the mountains of Laos. Her family relocated to a Thailand refugee camp for a few years and then moved permanently to the United States when she was three. She has a borderline obsessive fascination with unicorns, is fond of talking in capslock, and loves to write about magic, manipulation, and family. She currently lives in Wisconsin with her husband, kids, and a friendly pitbull. Visit her at: www.lorimlee.com.